I0606596

It had been one thing going wrong after another, but he wasn't expecting this…

Matt took a long swallow of his Coke and felt the sugary liquid coat his throat. He raised his eyes to Kurt. "What did you find at the apartment?"

"Funny you mentioned that. Lil says there was blood on the bathtub. Not a lot. More like smear."

"DNA," Matt said. "Did they test it?"

Kurt frowned. "Against whom?"

"Whoever abducted him," Matt said. "Duncan's blood is probably still in my living room. Check that." When Kurt didn't respond, he added, "You got another explanation why he would disappear two days before his hearing?"

"They'll probably test it against your DNA," Kurt said, then quickly added, "Only for elimination purposes. I assume they took a swab."

"That's not funny, Kurt."

"Not meant to be. Think about it. You don't want questions raised over your innocence. You have nothing to hide. Do you?"

"No." Matt wiped sweat from his forehead. His skin felt clammy. "But innocent people are railroaded every day."

"Stop worrying."

Matt looked away and took another long swallow of his Coke. His cell phone rang. The sound filled the room. He squinted at the caller ID. "It's Greg," he said aloud. "I'm a little busy right now, Greg," he said into the phone.

"You're going to get a lot busier, partner. We've had a blowout. Someone set the Dennis Number Two on fire. I'm at the site. I need you here. Now."

Matt Langdon has it all. A beloved son in college. An ex-wife who understands him. An exploration business in oil and gas which has shown a profit. Then, suddenly, his investors back out, and he faces bankruptcy. As Matt rushes to meet the one man he believes can help him, he finds an injured girl on the road. If he's late for his meeting, he could lose his funding. But he can't leave the unconscious girl. Being a Good Samaritan changes everything when he's arrested and charged with assaulting her.

Lillian Wallace is an investigator for Matt's attorney, and she's determined to discover the truth. A close look at the mystery girl reveals she holds the key to a past Matt never knew existed. Dark secrets are exposed as the girl recovers and points a finger at Matt's long-time nemesis—a murderer who has gone undetected for years, and who will now stop at nothing until he destroys both Matt and the girl…

KUDOS for *The Past Never Dies*

In *The Past Never Dies* by Laura Elvebak, Matt Langdon is on top of the world, with everything going right for him. That is until the morning he stops to help an injured girl on the road. Late for a meeting, he puts the girl in his car and rushes her to the hospital, pays for her care, and then hurries to his meeting. But things start to go downhill right away. His investors begin pulling out of his latest oil-drilling project, the cops accuse him of assaulting the girl he tried to help, and his son confesses that he hates college and wants to come home. Just when Matt almost convinces the cops he was only trying to help the girl, she claims she was on that road looking for him. Now Matt has to not only clear his name but figure out who the girl is, why she was looking for him, and how he can prove to the cops that he is innocent when the girl claims she can't remember who hurt her. Elvebak tells a chilling tale of greed corruption and murder, with an innocent man caught in the middle just trying to survive. A good solid read. ~ *Taylor Jones, The Review Team of Taylor Jones & Regan Murphy*

The Past Never Dies by Laura Elvebak is the story of a man caught up in forces from his past that he is not even aware of. Matt Langdon's troubles begin the morning he spots a strange injured young woman on the highway. He knows if he calls nine-one-one, he will be there forever and he is already late for a meeting. So he puts the woman in his car and ferries her to the hospital himself. Leaving her there, he heads for his meeting only to find that the financing he thought was a done deal is falling through. His problems are compounded when a cop with a chip on her shoulder decides she wants to charge with assault on the injured girl. He tries to explain that she was injured when he found her, but the cop isn't willing to listen. Then he discovers the girl is not what seems. She is a link to his past he has long buried, and when she came looking for him, trouble was sure to follow. As usual, Elvebak's character development is superb. You can't help feeling for Matt, and the other characters, as they struggle to make sense of clues in of a web of lies and deceit. A tense, fast-paced, and chilling mystery you won't be able to put down. *~ Regan Murphy, The Review Team of Taylor Jones & Regan Murphy*

ACKNOWLEDGMENTS

Thank you to my critique partners, the Wednesday group, Dean, Kay 1, Kay K 2, Amy, Julie, and Bob, and the Thursday group, Gene, Clif, Anita, Doug, Jennifer, and Dylan, whose insights and suggestions help to make this book what it is today. A big thanks, also, to Charlie, Susie, Isabella and Curry, for their continued support and for providing a cozy living room each Wednesday night.

THE PAST NEVER DIES

LAURA ELVEBAK

A Black Opal Books Publication

GENRE: MYSTERY/THRILLER

This is a work of fiction. Names, places, characters and incidents are either the product of the author's imagination or are used fictitiously, and any resemblance to any actual persons, living or dead, businesses, organizations, events or locales is entirely coincidental. All trademarks, service marks, registered trademarks, and registered service marks are the property of their respective owners and are used herein for identification purposes only. The publisher does not have any control over or assume any responsibility for author or third-party websites or their contents.

THE PAST NEVER DIES
Copyright © 2017 by Laura Elvebak
Cover Design by Jackson Cover Designs
All cover art copyright © 2017
All Rights Reserved
Print ISBN: 978-1-626947-41-2

First Publication: SEPTEMBER 2017

All rights reserved under the International and Pan-American Copyright Conventions. No part of this book may be reproduced or transmitted in any form or by any means, electronic or mechanical, including photocopying, recording, or by any information storage and retrieval system, without permission in writing from the publisher.

WARNING: The unauthorized reproduction or distribution of this copyrighted work is illegal. Criminal copyright infringement, including infringement without monetary gain, is investigated by the FBI and is punishable by up to 5 years in federal prison and a fine of $250,000. Anyone pirating our ebooks will be prosecuted to the fullest extent of the law and may be liable for each individual download resulting therefrom.

ABOUT THE PRINT VERSION: If you purchased a print version of this book without a cover, you should be aware that the book is stolen property. It was reported as "unsold and destroyed" to the publisher, and neither the author nor the publisher has received any payment for this "stripped book."

IF YOU FIND AN EBOOK OR PRINT VERSION OF THIS BOOK BEING SOLD OR SHARED ILLEGALLY, PLEASE REPORT IT TO: lpn@blackopalbooks.com

Published by Black Opal Books **http://www.blackopalbooks.com**

DEDICATION

Shawn, Brian and Tanya

CHAPTER 1

Dawn daubed the sky with shades of pink by the time Matt Langdon finished his morning run. Sweat pooled under his eyes and darkened his armpits. His mind raced, memorizing and highlighting all the selling points he would present to the broker at breakfast. All he needed was a simple "Yay" to secure the future of Black Gold Exploration. Ironic, he thought. A person poured his energy, his knowledge, and experience of a lifetime into a business, only to see success or failure balanced on the scales of an outsider. Didn't seem fair or right.

His phone signaled a text. He glanced at it.

Good luck. Call me later. Greg.

Greg Jertize was his landman and partner. Together, with two other geophysicists, they had built Black Gold Exploration from a dream they shared to a physical reality. They amassed small fortunes and watched their profits rise and dip on a rollercoaster ride alongside the economy. Now their existence depended on investors who would gamble on Black Gold's two most promising wells. The broker who held the critical scale, Sterling McAdams, spoke for those investors. He was the go-between Matt had to convince.

Matt reached his rambling, ranch-style house, nestled

in the curve of the cul-de-sac, and jogged along the wind-
ing driveway until he reached the back porch. His two
Australian Shepherds barked their greeting from their en-
closed pen behind the white gazebo.

Once inside, he heard nothing except the whirring of
the air conditioner. He took a moment to clear his head
and savor the solitude. He opened the refrigerator door,
let the cold air breathe into his skin, and took out a bottled water, which he drained. In his bedroom he shed his
clothes and stepped into a shower of fine hot spray.

He looked successful, he decided, pleased with the re-
flection that smiled back at him from the full-length mirror. He had chosen a pale blue shirt and a tan summer suit
for the meeting. His slim build made him look taller than
his five feet, nine inches. His daily regimen never varied.
He ate healthy, exercised daily at the gym in addition to
his morning runs, and the results showed. He couldn't be
more ready to face the morning.

As he started up his orange Jeep and backed out of the
driveway, his chest tightened. *No*, he told himself. *Don't
let negative thoughts in. They only poison your attitude.
This is yours. You've earned it. Breathe. In and out.*

His fingers played on the steering wheel while he
faced the street. The Jeep's engine rumbled like a hungry
tiger.

Let's do this.

He took his usual route on the back streets, past the
live oaks, tall and thick enough to hide the bright sunlight. Beyond the trees to his right, the bayou drifted
along in a lazy crawl. On the other side, an expanse of
overgrown weeds separated the road from a storage fa-
cility. Once he came to the freeway, everything would
change. Traffic would snarl the rest of the way, which
was why he always left early to give him plenty of time.

An opening in the overhead branches brought a glare

from the sun that made him pull down the visor. Even with his sunglasses on, he was momentarily blinded. The sun disappeared again in the next instant, and Matt blinked several times. His eyes stung. The Jeep swerved to the other side of the road. He braked hard.

Through the windshield he saw a bundle of white in front of the Jeep's front fender. His stomach twisted. He didn't recall feeling a bump or jolt. Surely he would have known if he had hit something. He looked again. Maybe trash thrown out of a car? That must be it. He could back up, circle around, and drive off.

But then movement stirred under the white material.

This was not happening to him. Not now. He glanced at his watch and the skin on his face burned. *Just go! Put the Jeep in gear and hightail it out of there.* Even as the thought crossed his mind, he opened the car door and eased out.

Sprawled in front of the Jeep was a slim figure in a white dress, streaked with dirt and blood. She lay face down, a mess of blond hair covering her head.

Shit. Matt knelt beside the figure. "Hello? Can you hear me?"

No sound.

He gingerly moved the hair away.

"Oh, Jesus," he gasped, taking in the sight of a young female. Maybe late teens or early twenties, he guessed. Hard to tell in her condition. Her skin was scratched and thin lines of dried blood ran along the edge of her hairline. One eye swollen shut. Multiple bruises on her face and neck looked red and puffy. *A runaway? A kidnap victim? A date gone terribly wrong?* His imagination ran in all directions. He was never good at guessing a girl's age.

He put two fingers against her neck. *Pulse weak. Alive. Thank God.*

The street looked empty. His hands shook when he

took out his cell phone. The hour and minutes stared back at him from the screen. If he called nine-one-one, they would make him stay until the paramedics arrived. He would be questioned. He would miss his meeting. Sterling McAdams would not wait for him. The man had made that clear. Be on time, or else.

He paced back and forth, holding tight to his phone. He could call McAdams. Take the chance he would understand. He wouldn't be pleased. He'd postpone the meeting indefinitely. Matt's company would lose the funding. The luckiest sonofabitch in the world wouldn't bet against odds like that.

But he couldn't just leave the girl on the road. She was alive, but for how long? He wasn't a doctor. He couldn't tell how critical her injuries were. There was a small boutique medical hospital a few miles down the road. His options ran through his mind like water through a sieve. Could he even lift her without causing more damage to her body? What if there were broken bones or internal bleeding?

He had no choice. Not really. He returned to his car and retrieved a blanket he kept in a storage bin and covered the back seat with it. He turned back to the girl.

Why did I have to be the one to find you?

Slowly and carefully he lifted her. She didn't stir, didn't moan, or react at all. Gently he lowered her on the blanket, closed the door and got in behind the wheel.

He met no traffic on the way, which was a good thing since the Jeep was traveling thirty miles over the speed limit. The girl slid toward the door when he made a sharp turn into the Emergency driveway. He cut the motor, jumped out, and opened the rear door. He lifted her with care.

She was heavier than she seemed when he first picked her up. Running with her toward the emergency doors felt awkward, and he felt a sharp twinge in his back as he carried her inside.

He yelled for a gurney and a medic, but was met with stares from the waiting room. A middle-aged woman cradled a crying baby. An old man in a wheelchair hunkered over his legs. A young man in a torn work shirt staunched his bleeding arm. A metallic smell greeted him along with a rush of cold air. The startled desk receptionist looked up and half rose in her chair.

Matt swore under his breath. He turned away from them and banged on the doors to the treatment room. After several moments, a male nurse came out looking harried and belligerent.

"I found her. I don't know her." Matt offered her up to him like she was the prize in a lottery. "She's unconscious. Might have been beaten up."

The nurse didn't hesitate. Muttering under his breath, he rolled a gurney up to the door. Matt eased the girl down. She uttered a moan and her eyes fluttered open.

"Thank God." Matt let out the breath he was holding and told her, "You'll be okay."

The nurse regarded him with narrowed, suspicious eyes. "Sir, you need to talk to the clerk in the waiting room."

Matt checked his watch. He was going to be late. He could only hope that Sterling McAdams would wait for him. He glanced back at the girl. She tried to focus her eyes on him.

"I'll check back on you, I promise." He wasn't sure if she understood.

The nurse wheeled the gurney into the treatment room. He poked his head out before he closed the door. "The doctor will talk to you when he's through examining her."

Matt nodded that he'd heard him, and hurried to the

clerk behind a semi-circular counter. He opened his wallet and took out his credit card. "I found her in the road. I don't know who she is or how she got there. You can bill her services to me on this card. I can't stay, but I will be back."

The clerk sputtered, "Sir, you can't just leave. There are forms and procedures—"

"Sorry, I don't have time right now." Matt scribbled down the number of his credit card along with his name, address, and cell phone number. "That should be all you need. Sorry I couldn't help more."

Before the clerk could protest further, Matt raced out the door. If he hurried, he might make his meeting. If he was lucky, Sterling McAdams wouldn't notice the blood on his wrinkled clothes. Matt could explain. He could convince people of anything if he tried hard enough.

CHAPTER 2

Thinking about the breakfast meeting with Sterling McAdams gave Matt hives. Ever since he left the hospital, Matt couldn't concentrate. What explanations could he give McAdams that would make him sound sane? His appetite disappeared. The twenty minute drive to Conroe felt like an hour.

The hotel dining room mirrored the small town flavor of its surroundings. Paintings and photographs depicting tourist attractions decorated the pastel-blue walls. Tables with soft white covers were topped with bouquets of bluebonnets. The window table McAdams had chosen overlooked the lake, and the morning sun reflected off sailboats skimming the water. Matt, however, was prone to seasickness. The sight of the boats drifting on the rippling surface did nothing to ease his churning stomach.

Sterling McAdams studied him with hooded lids. "You don't look well, Matt. Are you okay?"

Matt fought to clear his head. "Sure. Nothing to worry about." *I wish.* Why hadn't he called to say he would be late? Why didn't he tell him about the girl? Simply put, he didn't want McAdams thinking of anything other than the funding of Black Gold Exploration. Nothing ugly should smear the picture he was trying to paint of himself and his company. He wished he could erase the last couple of hours, pretend the girl never existed.

"If this is a bad time, we can reschedule." McAdams's tone was terse. "I get the feeling I don't have your full attention this morning."

"Not at all." Matt's breath caught. He couldn't get rid of the image of the girl's face, the way she'd opened her eyes. The way she stared at him before he left. He took a deep breath. His stomach lurched. He pushed away the plate laden with an untouched veggie omelet. "A mild case of indigestion, nothing serious. I'm fine now. Go on. Please."

McAdams scrutinized him some more before continuing. "We've studied the maps and geological findings. The slides clearly indicate what's under the shale. The leases seem to be in order, but Mark wants a closer look at the site. As do I." His lips curled in a smirk. "Do you think you'll be up to joining us tomorrow? Clearly you are distracted this morning."

Why is McAdams stalling? What else is going on?

"I've got the agreements right here." Matt indicated his briefcase. "Your landman has seen the site numerous times. He's gone over all the statistics. As far as going to the site again, whatever for?" His nerves pricked like hot needles on his skin.

Should have called nine-one-one then left after they arrived. No one could stop me. Now, because he arrived late, he had more to worry about. Unnecessary delays, looking incompetent in front of McAdams.

He opened the briefcase and brought out the participation agreement. His gaze landed on a blood smear on the front of his pants. He looked up at McAdams, who hadn't seemed to notice. "Show this to your partners. Have your attorney look it over again. What's the problem?"

"The problem is you," McAdams said, unsmiling. "First you're late, and now you're acting paranoid. I'm beginning to think something is wrong with the pro-spects."

Matt leaned forward and flipped the bottom of his jacket to cover the smear. "Nothing is wrong. I'm ready to get back to business. Have you even approached the investors yet?" His phone vibrated inside his shirt pocket. *The hospital?* He ignored the sound, and the pounding of his heart. "This is a major well that will produce even better than the prospectus reads. If your people aren't interested, there are others who will jump at it."

McAdams shook his head. "There are no other investors, Matt. I've checked, and I've gone over your due diligence and the specs. All looks promising at first glance. We're interested, but we don't commit with blinders on. We're talking about millions committed on the word of one man. Your word, Matt, and your reputation is on the line."

"My reputation has been fully vetted, and you know it. Your men have seen the prospects, and they are just how I described." Matt's phone vibrated again. Still he ignored it. "We're wasting time."

McAdams pointed. "Don't you think you should get that?"

"Whoever it is can wait." Matt forced his breathing to slow. "What is it you want?"

"Full disclosure."

"You've got it already. You have figures, statements, tax returns, corporate documents. What more do you want?"

"Not just from your company. My people want to know the person they're dealing with. You, Matt."

Me? Again? Matt stood. He gripped the table's edge, not caring about exposing the blood stains anymore. "You've had all you need to make a decision. My personal life is private. If you have a question about my character, check out the references I've given you. They'll all tell you the same thing. What you see is what you get."

McAdams gazed at him. His eyes skimmed over Matt's clothes. His expression revealed nothing. "I'm happy to hear that, Matt." He picked up his cloth napkin and wiped his mouth. "Let's plan to meet again in a week."

Matt wasn't going to play this man's game any longer. Yes, the meeting started all wrong. Yes, he'd been late. Distracted. For good reason, not that he planned to confide in this guy. No, there was more going on behind this meeting. Something McAdams was hiding from him, and he suspected it had nothing to do with Matt being late.

"I don't think that's necessary," Matt said. "Bring your investors to my office tomorrow morning. I'll talk to them and we can get these agreements signed."

"I'll talk with my people." McAdams stood. "We'll talk again."

"Tomorrow," Matt repeated.

"I hope you're feeling better soon," McAdams said. This time he did not smile. He stood and they shook hands. McAdams left Matt to pay the bill.

Their conversation bothered Matt, not what McAdams said but what he didn't say. He couldn't concentrate as he drove away. *The girl.* He should have stayed with her. Cancelled the meeting with a quick call to McAdams. He had probably screwed up the deal now anyway. He'd figure out a way to fix it. He always did. That's what he was good at. The girl was something else. He'd done what he could for her. In all probability, staying at the hospital wouldn't have mattered to her. They had no connection to each other. *Why the hell did I leave my credit card information?* Like it or not, he had to go back to the hospital and face the outcome.

He parked in the visitor's lot in front. As he approached, he saw the police cars. He stumbled at first, but continued on. Of course, they would be summoned by the hospital. The girl had been attacked, after all. He didn't do it, but since he had found her, they would want a statement from him. That shouldn't take long. He wanted to see if she was recovering. She might want to thank him for saving her. He wondered if she'd named her attacker. Hopefully, she gave them enough to arrest the bastard.

He stepped inside to find the waiting room with more injured and sick. He went straight to the desk clerk.

"Hi. Remember me? I brought in a girl earlier. Can I talk to the doctor who treated her?"

She peered at him. Her answer was to press a button on her phone.

Instead of a doctor, two uniformed police approached him. He focused on the female officer, whose dark eyes drilled into him. He felt the heat of compressed anger radiate from her. He barely glanced at her partner who stood a step behind her.

"Matt Langdon?" Her voice came out cold. "I'm Officer Deborah Wallace. I need you to come this way."

Matt's throat constricted with concern. *Oh, God, what if she's about to tell me the girl died?* "I'm here to check on the girl. Tell me, is she all right?"

Instead of getting an answer, he was hustled into a small office with a rectangular table and three chairs. He guessed this area was normally used to fill out financial forms. The male officer closed the door. No one sat in the chairs.

"Is the girl all right?" Matt asked again.

Officer Wallace gave him a cool stare. "We'll talk about that later. I understand you're the one who took her to the hospital. Are you a relative?"

"No. Never saw her before. Like I told the nurse, I

found her on the road. She was barely conscious. I brought her directly here."

"Did you notify the police?"

"I did not. I couldn't wait for the police to arrive, and I didn't want her bleeding to death. She needed medical attention right away. I'm not the one who injured her, officer. I found her that way. I have nothing to hide. I left my name, address, and credit card information."

"So you claim. Why did you rush off?"

"I was late for a business meeting. A very important meeting. I came back. That should mean something."

"It meant you left your credit card information. Anyone would rush back for that."

He stared at her, incredulous. "No, you got it wrong, officer. I was worried about her. I wanted to make sure she would be okay. I'm not a doctor. I didn't know the extent of her injuries. I wasn't concerned about the money. I came back because I told her I would."

"Anyone else would have called nine-one-one," she said. "At least waited around to make sure she survived."

"I came back as soon as I could. Am I being charged with a crime?"

"We are questioning you as a witness."

"I'm in a closed room. Does that mean I'm not free to go? Don't you have to give me the Miranda warning?"

Officer Wallace studied him for several seconds. Then she looked up at her partner and gave a brief nod. He opened the door. "You are free to leave at any time, Mr. Langdon. I take it you are refusing to cooperate with this investigation?"

Matt's first instinct told him to get up and walk out. His second and third thoughts made him change his mind. He knew that walking out right now would only make him look suspicious.

"I've broken no law, Officer Wallace. I stopped when I saw her lying on the road and I rendered aid. That was the extent of my responsibility according to the law."

"Are you a lawyer, Mr. Langdon?"

"I'm a business owner. Look, I've cooperated with you. I'll continue to answer any questions until you're satisfied."

"Good. I do have a few more questions. Did you see another car on the road before you saw her?

"Unfortunately, no."

"So you don't know how long she lay there bleeding."

"I don't. I assume it was a hit and run. Please, tell me if she'll recover."

Officer Wallace's expression softened. "She'll recover, Mr. Langdon." She glanced again at her partner before turning back to Matt. "I'm still amazed by your generosity. Paying for her medical expenses was way over the top, more than what duty or responsibility called for. Even close relatives don't do that. I've known guilty men who try to buy their way out of a situation, but you claim that's not the case with you."

This was not going well at all. "Is it a crime that I didn't want her turned away because of no insurance? I didn't know her financial status. I didn't know anything about her. The only guilt I felt was not being able to stay with her."

"Your meeting was more important."

His face tightened. "I thought so at the time. Can I see her?"

"Since you're not family, the hospital won't let you see her. Would you be willing to come downtown and make a formal statement for the record?"

"What?" The words lodged in his throat. "I've told you everything I know."

"Mr. Langdon, you are the only witness we have, and

we need a recorded statement for the file. You said you would cooperate."

"Is the girl awake?" His voice shook. "Ask her if she knows me. Ask her if I'm the one who hurt her."

"I'm doing my job, Mr. Langdon."

"Good." He tried to control his anger. "I want to have my attorney meet us at the station." He paused as a thought occurred to him. "Funny coincidence. My attorney's investigator's last name is also Wallace."

Her eyebrows raised. "Your attorney is Kurt Pasternack?"

"That's right."

She smiled. "Lillian is my cousin."

He sighed. Was that good news, or bad? "Guess you know her boss pretty well, too."

"He's my ex-husband."

Shit. Didn't she have to excuse herself from the case over an ethics violation? He wasn't sure. Probably not in this case.

Officer Deborah Wallace turned away. "While we're here, I want to take a DNA swab from you. If you have no objection."

His first reaction was to ask if the girl had been raped. He knew he wasn't guilty of that. A DNA test could prove he never harmed her. "Whatever you want. Let's get this over with. Prove once and for all that I've done nothing wrong. I never hurt the girl, never touched her." He remembered something and was quick to add, "Except I carried her into my car because she was unconscious. Then I carried her into the ER. Make sure you make a note of that when you compare DNA or prints. Believe me, I never saw her before today."

"Better hope she collaborates your story, Mr. Langdon."

CHAPTER 3

Lillian Wallace was shocked to hear that the Pasternack Law Firm's most upstanding corporate client was being held at the police station. As far as she could recall, Matt Langdon only needed a lawyer when he had concerns about his oil and gas company or got divorced. He'd never broken a law, not even gotten a parking violation.

When Matt called the office, Kurt Pasternack was in court representing a frequent offender who managed to get himself arrested for the fourth time that month. Kurt told Lillian, "Find out what's going on with Matt. Break him out of jail if you have to. And, by the way, Deborah picked him up. Can't imagine what for. See what you can do."

Lillian had gone to law school, but never graduated. She then attended the police academy with the recommendation of Cousin Deborah, but just as she was about to graduate, an automobile accident laid her up for months. By the time she recovered, Kurt needed an investigator and Lillian took the job. She never looked back. She enjoyed her independence and the job fit the bill. Although Deborah and Kurt were divorced, the firm seemed to Lillian like family.

She wondered now what Matt could have done to get

her cousin Deborah in an uproar. She liked the guy. Not romantically. He really wasn't her type. She met his ex-wife when Kurt represented him in their divorce. *What did he ever see in her?* Carrie was Matt's polar opposite. An artist, a free thinker, serious one minute, raging crazy the next. Their divorce came as no surprise to their friends. What did surprise Lillian was seeing how their divorce brought them closer together. She assumed their son had everything to do with their bonding. Aaron, now nineteen, was an eclectic mix of both parents. He was an artist like his mother, a rational thinker like his father. Adhering to his father's wishes, Aaron attended A&M in College Station, Matt's own alma mater. Lillian wondered how long he would last. She remembered how Aaron had fought against going, but Matt had been adamant. College for Matt's only son was not up for discussion.

Lillian thought about Matt's son on the way to police headquarters. He would probably never be told about his straight arrow father being questioned by the police. She laughed at the absurdity while she parked in the lot in front of the building and went inside. She signed in, passed through the weapons detectors, and was given a visitor's badge. An officer directed her an interrogation room on the second floor.

Matt appeared more angry than afraid. His cinnamon-brown hair looked as if someone had used a mixer on it. The top two buttons on his shirt were undone. His jacket lay on the chair next to him, wrinkled and stained dark red. Was that blood? The air smelled of sweat, testosterone, and burnt coffee. He barely acknowledged Lillian.

"Coffee?" Officer Deborah Wallace waltzed in the room carrying two brimming cups. She set one down in front of Matt and offered the second to Lillian, who sniffed, made a face, and waved the cup away.

Lillian moved the jacket off the chair and hung it on

the back. She sat in the vacated seat next to Matt. "How are you, and what did you do this time, naughty boy?"

He reddened. "No jokes, please, Lillian. Where's Kurt?"

"Tied up in court. Sent me instead. I thought you were meeting McAdams this morning."

Deborah sat opposite them. "Did you set up the meeting?"

"Kurt did. Sterling McAdams was supposed to sign agreements to bring investors on board and save Matt's ass." Lillian turned back to Matt. "So how did it go?"

Matt's expression turned grim. "It didn't. I arrived late. McAdams wasn't happy. I wasn't overjoyed. See, I had to make a detour to take an injured girl to the hospital. Being a Good Samaritan probably cost me investors and almost got me arrested."

Lillian stared at him then turned to Deborah. "Someone please explain to me what he just said."

Matt slammed his fist on the table. "I just told you. She was on the road, semi-unconscious and bloody. I dropped her off at the hospital, gave them my credit card information, then went to meet McAdams. When I got back to the hospital, the cops were waiting for me."

Lillian turned to Deborah. "Did you get a statement from the girl?"

"She's not talking."

"Is she underage?"

Deborah winced. "I don't think so. The doctor thinks maybe she's early twenties."

Lillian leaned toward her in mock amazement. "She won't tell you her age? Is she too injured to talk?"

Deborah sighed. "No. Other than the bruises and a concussion, there doesn't seem to be anything seriously wrong with her. The doctor wants to keep her overnight because of the concussion."

"Matt didn't hurt her."

Deborah stayed calm. "I haven't arrested him. I told him he's free to go whenever he wants. He agreed to make a formal statement for the record."

Lillian turned back to Matt. "Give the statement so we can get out of here."

"When can I see her?"

Deborah's jaw set and she crossed her arms. "I'll call you this evening if she's up to visitors."

"Set the recorder," Lillian said. "He'll give the statement now."

The statement took less than ten minutes.

Deborah stood and offered her hand to Matt. "If you remember anything further, such as a car you might have passed in either direction, give me a call." They shook hands.

Lillian watched her heavy boots go down the hall then tucked her arm in Matt's. "I'm dying for a real cup of coffee. There's an equivalent to Starbuck's down the street. Coffee's good at half the price."

He ran his fingers through his hair and picked up his jacket. "I'm sold. Let's go. This place stinks."

The diner wasn't busy. They brought their coffees to a booth near the back.

"You're not at all like your cousin," Matt said, stirring cream in his cup.

"Actually, you're wrong. We're more alike than we're different. We decided to go in different directions, that's all. Deb is more like a sister than a cousin. She's always watched my back. I try to do the same to her."

"Does she like being a beat cop?"

"She says that's where the action is. I remember my uncle warning her about the psychological warfare involved in being a cop. He said they see the worst in people. He tried several times to talk her out of joining the force. But Deb was determined to be just as good as he was." Lillian smiled ruefully. "He's retired now with a full pension, and he's given up trying to change her. Funny, though, he never voiced the same objections to her two brothers. Linc worked undercover for a long time. I'm not sure what unit he's in right now. Alex, he's the oldest, teaches at the Academy. Deb thinks she's responsible for me and can get too protective at times."

"You need protection?" Matt questioned.

Lillian laughed and sipped her coffee. "God, no. I can take care of myself."

"You never wanted to follow family tradition?"

"I thought I did, at one time. Too many rules." She took another sip while eying him over the rim of her cup. "I have a question for you."

"About?"

"The road where you found the girl. Do you take that route often?"

"Almost every day. The road is a short cut to the freeway. I can take the freeway to work or out to Conroe, like his morning."

"Do you think it's strange someone picked that road to dump her?"

He sat back and stared at her. "You think someone deliberately beat her up and left her on the road for me to find. Oh, right, happens all the time." His tone reeked with sarcasm.

"Someone leaves a body on your way to work all the time?" Lillian mocked him.

He laughed. "That's the most ridiculous idea I've ever heard."

"You're right," Lillian agreed. "So is what happened at the meeting between you and McAdams. You're late so he tells you the investors have refused to sign the agreements. How did he know you were going to be late?"

"He didn't." He shook his head. "He would have told me the same thing if I'd been on time."

"You sure?" Lillian teased. "I know. You're right. That was a crazy thought. Hey, I have another idea. Let me go with you to see this mysterious girl. I'm dying to hear her side."

CHAPTER 4

Matt left the diner and headed home. One look in the bathroom mirror made him groan. No wonder McAdams seemed put off. There were the rust-colored patches brushed on the hem of his rumpled suit jacket. More spots on the bottom of his sleeves. He was surprised there wasn't more blood on him from carrying the girl to his car and again into the ER. More surprising, McAdams hadn't mentioned the stains.

He yanked off his clothes and jammed them into the hamper. He took a long shower, scrubbing until the grime and smell of fear sluiced down the drain. When he emerged from his bedroom, he was dressed in pressed jeans and a light blue shirt. He put on his running shoes and grabbed his keys and the file that held the original participation agreements. Now he had to face the people who really mattered.

He reached his office building half an hour later, almost six o'clock. He was surprised to see Becky, his assistant, still at her desk. She had stayed to hear the good news.

"We're working on it." He tried to sound encouraging. "Go on home. There're a few things I need to finish up. I'll see you tomorrow."

He entered his office and closed the door behind him.

With the lights off and the vertical blinds closed on the wall window, the room felt cold and unwelcoming. He opened the blinds and looked out over the parking lot, his yellow jeep in its customary slot facing him. The setting sun painted the low clouds a shimmering gold and red. Matt stood there for a long moment, taking in the sight. Such beauty never lasted, he reflected, feeling uncharacteristically melancholy. Even the solitude he savored like a rare painting would soon be interrupted. By the time he closed the blinds and switched on the Tiffany-style lamp on his desk, the knock at his door came. He half expected to see Becky, but instead his partner and landman, Greg Jertize, strolled in chewing the end of an unlit cigar. The tall, heavy-set man was the only person Matt couldn't avoid.

"Is that it?" Greg pointed to the file on Matt's desk. "All ready to roll?"

Matt sat down and crossed his legs. "Not quite. Before you say anything, there's been a few minor setbacks."

"Setbacks? Are you fucking kidding me? This was a done deal. What happened?"

"A combination of things. To begin with, I got there late. Something happened on the way and I got hung up."

"So you were late. Traffic jam. Accidents. Shit happens. What's that got to do with the price of bananas? The guy's an asshole. We knew that from the beginning."

"It wasn't traffic. There was an unconscious girl in the middle of the road. I couldn't just leave her there. I took a detour to the hospital."

"Excuse me? You did what?" The cigar fell out of his mouth. "Fuck, now I've heard everything. Couldn't you just call nine-one-one? You knew how important this meeting was. Let me remind you, you're not the only one who's affected by this prospect. I've dumped a hell of a lot of cash into this company to help keep it afloat. All of us did the same. We expect a return. What's more important, this company or playing Good Samaritan?" He paced back and forth in front of Matt.

"Calm down, buddy. I know how you feel, but trust me, we'll get through this. I got there and the meeting took place as planned." Matt had already decided not to mention his return to the hospital or that he'd been questioned by the police. No sense in making Greg crazier than he already was.

"I still don't get why he didn't sign. Once you explained the situation and got that out of the way, you got down to business. Right?"

Matt leaned back in his chair, putting his thoughts together before he spoke. "I didn't tell him about the girl. Think how it sounds, Greg. Look how you reacted. Even if he believed me, I'd seem unreliable. Like you, he'd want to know why I didn't call nine-one-one. It didn't sound like the meeting was my top priority. It was at first. Until I came across the girl. So maybe my priorities aren't the same as his."

"Bullshit." But Greg's tone had lost its bluster. He lumbered to the chair opposite Matt and sat. "Let's back up. You said a combination of things went wrong."

Back on familiar ground, Matt grew more confident. "He told me his partners want more background on me."

Greg jumped on this. "On you? Why? They have it all, CVs, the lot. Something going on I don't know about?"

"McAdams got me to thinking," Matt said. "He said the partners, not him, wanted more background. What if it's just one, a silent partner who recently came aboard? Someone with deep pockets."

"Someone who's after your ass." Greg ran his hand over his chin. "So your being late doesn't have squat to do with his not signing. He never intended to sign. That's what you're saying? Shit, I need a drink."

Matt thought about what Lillian had suggested. Now he couldn't think of anything but. He fished out a bottle of Jack from his bottom right drawer and unwrapped two glasses from a cloth. He poured two fingers in each glass.

Greg downed his in one swallow. Matt poured him another. "You got an enemy I don't know about? Because this is sounding like an ambush."

Matt downed the whiskey and felt the fire shoot down his gullet. "I can't think of anyone who hates me bad enough to screw with my company."

"Okay, let's think this through. I'll call McAdams tonight and tell him we want another meeting here. I'll tell him to bring his partners. All of them. No more of this sneaking behind our backs."

Matt put down his glass. "That might work."

"Another thing we can do is have Lillian investigate him and his partners."

"She did that already."

"No, I mean, really dig deep. Find out who's got it in for you." Greg leaned back and drummed his fingers on his knees. "Maybe it's as simple as his partners can't come up with the money. Instead of sitting back with our thumbs up our ass, we should look for other sources."

"We did that, too," Matt reminded him. "The Canadians, Costa Ricans, Mexicans, all of them ran out of money."

"There's always China."

Matt winced.

Greg laughed and waved his hand. "Yeah, I know. We'd have to pretend we're communists. Okay, forget that. What I'm saying is, we haven't lost the company yet. We don't know what really sparked this setback. We'll get them here on our turf. We're not defeated yet."

Matt rallied a grin. "Hey, that's my line. I'm the one who never gives up."

Greg thrust his hand toward Matt and they shook amicably. "Let's get out of here and get some dinner. Bet you never had a chance to eat."

"No, thanks," Matt said. "I've still got some calls to make. You go ahead."

Greg narrowed his eyes. "You sure you're all right?"

"We've been through worse, partner. This deal with McAdams is chicken shit. We'll get him back, or find someone better. This is not over yet."

When the door closed behind Greg, Matt slumped in his chair. He had seen many deals go wrong in the past. It was a cutthroat business. But in this case he couldn't name an enemy, no one who had reason to go after him. But as the face of his company, whatever happened was his responsibility.

He turned his thoughts to the injured girl. There was nothing he could do at the moment about McAdams. The girl was a different story.

❧❦❧

Dusk had fallen with the sky shrouded in gray rain clouds when Matt met Lillian in front of the hospital. The frosty hospital air sent chills on his skin after leaving the warm, humid air. Matt had called ahead and told the operator his name and asked for the girl he had brought in. She gave him the room number. The girl still had not given her name.

"Deborah didn't call you?" Lillian asked.

"Nope. Guess she changed her mind. But the girl has been moved to the second floor. That means she's ambulatory. The nurse said she might be able to go home tomorrow."

"The nurse told you all that?" Lillian said.

"I'm the guy paying the bill. Guess she thinks I'm her next of kin."

Lillian rolled her eyes. "You lied to her?"

"No, I let her think whatever she wanted."

"You're going to get us both in trouble," she said as they walked to the elevator.

The nurse looked up as they approached her station. Matt gave his name. She nodded as if she'd been expecting him. She paid no attention to Lillian.

"She's awake and alert, if you want to see her," the nurse said. "Room two-fourteen."

As soon as he pushed open the door marked 214, he saw Deborah Wallace standing guard by the bed. When she saw Lillian, a look of disappointment came over her face.

Matt looked past her to the girl in the bed. He saw blond hair, a face with two black eyes, and a red mouth. She lifted her head and stared at him. He stared back. He didn't know her.

"I told you I would call," Deborah said.

"But you didn't," he said.

"I wanted to talk to you before you showed up." She stalked toward him, ignoring Lillian. "In the hall, Mr. Langdon." She finally turned to Lillian. "You, too."

Now what? he thought, hesitating at the door, trying to look back at the girl.

Deborah gave him a shove and he stumbled out. Before he could respond, she turned on him. "You lied to me."

Her accusation hit him like a sledge hammer. "What are you talking about? I never lied to you."

Lillian turned to her. "What's going on?"

Without acknowledging her cousin, Deborah jammed her forefinger into Matt's chest. "If you didn't lie about knowing her, why is she asking for you by name, Mr. Langdon?"

Matt felt the ground shrink under him. He looked at the door, but Deborah blocked him. "I don't understand. I never saw her before today."

"Then how does she know you?" Deborah said.

Lillian intervened. "Obviously, someone told her your name and said you brought her to the hospital and paid the bill."

"It's the way she talked about you," Deborah said to him. "She said she wanted to see Matt Langdon and asked me to find you. I asked her if she meant the man who picked her up and brought her to the hospital. She said that must be Matt Langdon, but she never saw you."

"There was no sign of recognition a minute ago. Let me talk to her. What her name?"

"That's another thing," Deborah said. "She refused to tell me who she was or how she ended up on that road or who hurt her. Maybe she'll tell you."

When they came back in, the girl had propped her back against four pillows and tucked a blanket under her chin. Despite the bruises and scratches on her face and the black eyes, she didn't appear to be in pain. Her blond hair had been brushed and covered her shoulders. Her eyes were open, revealing a shade of blue that made Matt's heart twinge unexpectedly. She reminded him of someone, but for the life of him he couldn't remember who that could be.

He sat in the chair next to the bed and leaned toward her. His heart slammed against his chest. "Hello," he said, with dry mouth. "You're looking better than the last time I saw you. Do you remember me finding you?"

"No," she said, a look of suspicion in her eyes. "Who are you?"

"Matt Langdon. The police sergeant said you were asking for me."

"You're Matt Langdon?" she said incredulously.

Questions swarmed in his head. "You were looking for me?"

She stared at him. "If that's your name, then yes."

He felt Deborah's eyes boring into his back. "And what is your name?"

"Rachel." The way she said her name, she seemed to expect a reaction from him.

"Rachel what?"

Instead of answering, Rachel turned away. Tears squeezed from eyes shut tight.

This wasn't the reaction Matt expected. At a loss, he stood, turned to Lillian, and then to Deborah, who pushed him aside and leaned toward the girl who called herself Rachel.

"Rachel, look at me." She sat and waited until Rachel faced her. "How do you know Matt Langdon?"

The girl gave her a sour look. "I didn't say I knew him. I said I was *looking* for him. There's a difference."

"I'm sorry. I misunderstood you. Why were you looking for him?"

Rachel's tone had a defiant edge as she stared back at Deborah. "That's for him to know. I want to talk to him alone."

"That can be arranged. But we have some matters to clear up first," Deborah told her. "Do you remember who assaulted you?"

Rachel pressed her lips together.

Deborah pointed to Matt. "Was it this man?"

"Goddammit," Matt said under his breath.

Rachel turned her face into her pillow and closed her eyes. "I don't remember what happened. Leave me alone. I'm tired. I want to go to sleep."

Deborah rose to block Matt as he pushed his way to the bed, but he ignored her. The shock had worn off and anger rose in its stead. "Rachel—if that's your real name—you do remember that I'm the one who found you. You know I didn't hurt you. If you were looking for me, I am right here. Tell me. What do you want?"

Deborah grabbed his arm to pull him away, but he stood his ground.

"Let me," Lillian said, stepping between them and the bed. "We only want to help you, Rachel," she said. "When you feel up to talking to Officer Wallace, she'll be here to listen. What we need right now is your full name and where you live. You can tell her or you can tell me. I work for Matt Langdon. We want whoever did this to you."

Rachel didn't move.

Matt stood next to Lillian and softened his tone. "You were going to my house, weren't you?" When she still didn't answer, he pressed harder. "Who stopped you, Rachel? Who did this to you?"

The door opened and a different nurse stepped in. She glared at the visitors. "You need to leave now. Can't you see the patient is exhausted?" She muscled her way to the bed, looked down at Rachel, and said in a sing-song voice, "You're in pain, honey?"

Rachel raised her head. Tears streaked her face. "Yes, please," she whispered. "Tell them I can't answer any more questions."

The nurse turned to them. "You heard her. Everyone out."

When they were in the hallway, Matt said to Deborah, "You know she called the nurse."

"I know," she said, her expression grim.

"We can come back tomorrow," Lillian said.

"I'll let you know," Deborah said. "First we need to find out who assaulted her."

"She asked to talk to me alone," Matt said. "I think she'll tell me what happened."

"Why is that?" Deborah positioned herself in front of him. "It seems to me to be a very strange request since she denies knowing you by sight. At least in front of witnesses. I haven't cleared you as a suspect, Mr. Langdon. You were the last person to see her, and now she only wants to talk to you."

"She never accused me. You believe I hurt her and then brought her to the hospital?"

"Maybe you were guilt-ridden after you saw what you did."

"This is insane." He turned, wild-eyed, to Lillian. "You can't believe that."

Lillian remained calm and spoke in a reasonable tone. "No, I don't, and Deborah doesn't either. She's just doing her job, and that means following all lines of questioning. Let's all give it a rest and see what happens tomorrow."

Matt wanted to shout and protest his innocence. But Lillian gave him a warning look. It took everything he had to keep silent.

Deborah straightened her jacket and squared her shoulders. "He's your client, Lillian. Keep him under control." She headed toward the elevators.

Her admonition made Matt even angrier, and he wanted to shout at her receding back, but Lillian took his arm and steered him toward the stairs.

"I'll find out who she is and let you know," she told him. "Until then, keep away from the hospital."

CHAPTER 5

Matt left the hospital and went home, determined to put the entire day out of his mind. Monday was gone. He had the rest of the week to concentrate on how to revive his company. He wanted to put his questions concerning the girl called Rachel behind him. Whatever reason she had for searching him out, the policewoman had closed that door for now. He'd done what he could for her, and now he wished he could undo the whole experience. Should have called nine-one-one and left before they arrived.

No, he knew himself better than that. But he wished he'd never seen her, never traveled down that road.

Too bad his mind couldn't control his body. He got one of his rare migraines and had to escape to his darkened bedroom. After a while, with medication, yoga, and meditation, he finally slept.

He awoke at five the next morning with a clear head and put on sweats and running shoes. He made an extra effort not to think about Rachel-last-name-unknown. After a two-mile run and a cool shower, he arrived at his office at seven.

He worked with Greg throughout the day, going over leases and contracts. By late afternoon, neither of them had been able to schedule another meeting with McAdams, whose assistant proclaimed her boss unreachable.

Time for Plan B. Matt spent the remainder of the week contacting the investors listed in the original participation agreement. By Friday afternoon most sounded amenable to a different arrangement. Greg wrote up individual participation agreements after each investor agreed to an amount. Altogether, the upfront money almost equaled what was in the original agreement.

"Whatever's left is McAdams's share," Matt said. "Or his silent partner's."

"McAdams won't be happy," Greg said, with a gleeful smile. "I want to see his face when the bottom falls out of his deal and he realizes his partners have screwed him."

"He deserves it. Dennis Well No. 1 will be the big one. That baby is going to blow and flow big. I feel it in my little finger, and my pinky's always right."

"Except when it isn't." Greg wagged his own finger at Matt in a not too subtle reminder of past failures. "I'm just saying, don't get cocky. We've sent birth announcements out too soon before. Maybe you shouldn't have named the well after your ex-wife." Without waiting for a response, he laid a stack of legal-sized papers on Matt's desk. "You heard any more about that girl in the hospital? The creature who put a hex on our deal?"

"She's the least of my concerns," Matt said. "We have enough to deal with right here."

"Good. You're better off forgetting about her. Let's hope the policewoman forgets you, too, and finds the real criminal."

Matt's cell phone rang. He frowned when he saw the caller's name. His son. "It's Aaron. I need to take this."

"Tell him I said hey," Greg said. "I'm meeting Julie at Skaggs's. You're welcome to join us."

Matt gave him a distracted nod and put the phone to his ear. He listened quietly to his son's desperate words.

They were a repeat of the last week and the week before that. Aaron hated Texas A&M, the dorms, his roommate, and his studies. He wanted to come home.

When the other end went quiet, Matt sighed. "I'll come up tonight. We'll have dinner, just the two of us. We'll talk."

"You mean, you'll talk." Aaron's voice rose. "It's no good, Dad. I'd rather die than stay here. I don't belong. Don't tell me I'll get used to it, because I won't."

Not this again. "All right, calm down." As he sought to reassure his son, Matt felt the acid burn his throat. The dreams he had for Aaron's future dimmed with each call from school. He could feel the distance between them widening. He searched for the right words. "I can be there in a couple of hours. You talk, I'll listen."

"Yeah, right."

Matt heard the familiar echo of depression in Aaron's voice, along with a sense of hopelessness that hadn't been there before. Before he could offer more words of encouragement, the dial tone droned. He kept the phone pressed to his ear long after the sound stopped. Aaron was a good kid but he was too much like his mother. Carrie Dennis's erratic mood swings verged on violent behavior when she was off her meds, which was most of the time.

As if the call and his thoughts made her materialize, his ex-wife stood in the doorway to his office with hands on her hips. She was short and thin, with the tips of her raven hair painted red. A silky red and orange blouse flowed over black leggings. A black beret tilted sideways on her head, part of her artist's persona.

"Was that our son on the phone?" she demanded. "What are you going to do about him?"

"You know it was Aaron. I suppose you told him to call me."

Carrie acted like they were still married when it suited her, and would pop in whenever she felt the need to talk. When it involved their son, he couldn't deny her.

She peered into the empty conference room. "Where's Becky and Greg?"

"They left for the day."

"Pity. I wanted to say hi." She turned and faced him. "Your son doesn't belong at A&M. You enrolled him there because you're an Aggie. He only agreed to please you. He isn't you. He's an artist, not a jock."

Now Aaron was *his* son. "Painting and photography are hobbies. Once he's got his education, he can pursue his hobbies all he wants. He has to have a business foundation to support him first. We've gone over all this before. I thought we agreed."

"He's miserable. You have to pull him out of there. I'm worried to death about him." Her hands punctuated her words.

"I'm worried, too," Matt said, feeling the onset of another migraine.

"Well, what are you going to do about it? Talk to him again? Talk, talk, talk. That's all you do. But you don't listen."

"I'm going up there now. I promise to listen."

Carrie fumbled with her handbag, digging out tissues. "You'd better. Got to go. I'm meeting with Dr. Andrews."

"Your new psychiatrist?"

She pressed a tissue to her nose. "I'm going to talk to him about Aaron." She blew her nose and shoved the tissue back into her purse.

"Maybe you should make an appointment for Aaron."

"I will, if you bring him home with you." She fingered dangling crystal earrings that caught the late afternoon light from the window and sprayed the wall with stars.

"He'll have to stay with you. I don't have any room."

He pictured the half-finished canvases and empty frames stacked in every room of her townhome. As far as he knew, she hadn't let anyone inside for over a year.

"Of course," Matt said, "if I bring him home. But think about this. Who's going to support him if he drops out?"

"Give him a year. He's an artist, and a talented one. Send him to a liberal arts college away from Texas." Her stiletto heels clicked across the floor as she closed the distance between them. She wrapped her arms around his neck and kissed him on the cheek. "You'll figure it out. Give him my love and tell him to call me."

"I will," he promised, and walked her to the front door of the building. He watched until she reached her red Mazda convertible. She turned back to him and called out, "Don't forget."

He returned to his inner office when his phone rang again. *What now?* "Aaron?"

"No, Mr. Langdon. This is Officer Wallace. I need to talk to you."

Irritation at hearing her voice instead of Aaron's tempted him to slam the phone down. "Fine, but it has to wait until tomorrow."

"This is important," she said.

"Sorry, but so is a personal matter that needs my immediate attention. You can reach me tomorrow." Without waiting for a response, he hung up.

ഏഩ

Matt arrived at College Station three hours later. He called Aaron's cell but there was no answer. All throughout the drive, he thought about how to approach his son. He alternately defended the positives of college life and tried to understand Aaron's perspective. Neither side won. With deep foreboding, he climbed the stairs to the dorm room Aaron shared with a football player. The room was empty. He tried Aaron's cell again. Still no answer.

Outside the dormitory, he caught sight of Aaron's roommate on the lawn talking with several other jocks. He could barely tell them apart and struggled to recall the roommate's name.

Matt was almost upon them when the roommate turned his way.

"Hey, Mr. Langdon. Looking for Aaron?"

"Do you know where he is?" Matt's chest felt tight.

"Waiting on you over at Smithy's. Said you'd know where it is."

"Thanks." Relief washed over Matt. Smithy's was an icehouse. He remembered how Aaron had raved about their hamburgers. It was within walking distance, but Matt drove the Jeep.

He found Aaron in the back corner sitting alone in a booth. He slid in opposite him, eyeing the four empty beer bottles on the table, not counting the one in Aaron's hand.

Aaron looked across the table at him with bleary reddened eyes. "I know what you're thinking," he said, slurring his words. "I could get suspended for this."

Matt gazed steadily at him. "Is that what you want?"

Aaron shrugged.

"Won't look good on your academic record," Matt heard himself saying.

"Who the fuck cares?" Aaron said.

"Have you eaten?"

Aaron shook his head. "Not hungry."

Matt took the bottle out of Aaron's hand. "I'm going to pay your tab, and we're getting out of here." He waved to the young waitress and signaled for the check before turning back to Aaron. "She could get into trouble, you know. Serving an underage student."

"All the kids come here," he said. "They don't look at IDs."

"Do you come here a lot?"

"Some," Aaron admitted.

The waitress arrived with the check. Matt handed her a twenty. "Keep the change." He stood and helped Aaron to his feet.

"Where are we going?" Aaron mumbled.

"Home," Matt said.

When they reached the Jeep, Aaron swayed and slumped against the door. "I think I'm going to be sick." With those words, he bent over and vomited on the street. Some splashed on his pants and shoes.

When he was finished, Matt took out his handkerchief and handed it to Aaron. After a few swipes to clean himself off, Aaron eased into the passenger's seat. His face was white, but his breathing returned to normal. Matt switched on the engine, but didn't put the car into gear. Aaron wasn't a drinker, unless he had changed at college, but Matt wondered how much and how often he self-medicated.

Aaron's eyes opened and he turned to look at his dad. He gave a sheepish smile. "Sorry, Dad."

Matt put the car into gear and accelerated into the street. He said nothing until he heard a sob coming from Aaron. He glanced over to see tears running down his son's face.

"It's going to be all right," Matt said, not sure if he was reassuring Aaron or himself.

"I know I've disappointed you." Aaron hiccupped. "I couldn't cut it. I tried, honestly I did."

"You are not a disappointment," Matt said. "I

shouldn't have forced you to go to A&M. Your mom was right."

"Mom? Does she know you're bringing me home?"

"Let's say, she encouraged me. She's worried about you."

More sobs came from Aaron and he turned his face away.

Matt reached over and touched his son's shoulder.

They drove in silence. Aaron fell asleep an hour from Houston. Matt pondered his son's unlined face. Maybe he should ask Carrie to make an appointment with her doctor to see Aaron. The future looked bleak. Between his family and his business, he wondered why *he* didn't have a drinking problem. Because, he thought bitterly, nobody would look after *him*.

It was dark by the time Matt pulled up to his house. He parked in the driveway. Aaron stirred long enough to stagger inside. He refused Matt's offer of food and went straight into his bedroom and plopped on the twin bed. Matt covered him with a blanket and stood for a long time in the doorway until he heard Aaron snoring.

The next morning the insistent ringing of his door bell woke Matt from a deep sleep. *Damn! On a Saturday?* He lurched to the front door and checked the peep hole. Irritation turned to anger.

Officer Deborah Wallace stood in uniform. "Is Rachel here?"

"Of course not. When was she released?" He pictured the girl as he'd last seen her four days ago. He tried not to think of the medical expenses he had so recklessly volunteered to pay.

"Do I have your permission to search the premises?"

Her attitude stirred his anger. She had no reason to think Rachel would come here. "You got a warrant?"

"I can get one," she replied. "Is that what you want?"

"I want you to leave me alone. The girl is not here. I've been out of town, just got back."

"Your neighbor said someone was with you."

"My nosy neighbor is right. I brought my son home from college."

"May I see him?"

"No. He's been sick, and he's asleep. Get your fucking warrant if you don't believe me. I've had enough of accusations and invasion of privacy."

Officer Wallace looked past him. Matt turned to see what caught her attention.

Aaron stood behind him. He wore only his boxers. His hair was tousled, and his eyes streaked with red. "Dad? What's wrong?"

"Nothing." Matt's cheeks burned. "Go back to bed, son."

"Who is she?" Aaron said.

"Nobody important," Matt said with a meaningful look at Wallace.

Wallace didn't react. "I'd appreciate a call later today," she said. "Rachel is missing."

Matt tamped down his anger long enough to answer. "I have my own concerns, Officer Wallace. I don't need a runaway to complicate my life any more than it is already. If she shows, I'll call you to pick her up. Are we done here?"

Wallace glanced at Aaron then nodded to Matt. "For the time being. See that you keep your word."

Matt slammed the door. *Bitch.*

"What was that about, Dad?" Aaron joined him at the door.

"Nothing to worry about." He softened his tone. "How are you feeling?"

Aaron rubbed his head. "Lousy."

"I bet. I'm going to put on a pot of coffee. Why don't you get dressed and join me?"

"Yeah, okay. Only—" He hesitated, hanging his head. "No lectures. Okay? I don't think I can handle that right now."

"No lectures," Matt agreed. "Just coffee. Maybe breakfast."

Aaron nodded, and trudged back into his bedroom. Matt watched him go and then went into the kitchen to fill the coffeepot and set it to brew. After checking the refrigerator to make sure he had plenty of eggs and bacon for breakfast, he went into his bedroom to dress.

He still carried the dregs of annoyance from the detective's visit. Who was Rachel and what did she want from him?

He washed his face and ran a comb through his hair. He missed his morning run. He did his most productive thinking while running. Aaron was like him in that way. They used to run together. Maybe they would start doing that again if Aaron was willing.

He changed his shirt, and returned to the hall. He hesitated, listening for sounds coming from Aaron's bedroom. Nothing. Had he gone back to sleep? He knocked softly. When there was no answer, he pushed open the door. Rumpled bed sheets and a blanket lay atop the bed, but there was no sign of Aaron. He wasn't in the shower either. Panic set Matt's heart pounding.

"Aaron?" he called. "Aaron!"

He hurried to the kitchen. Two full cups of coffee sat on the counter. Sunlight streamed into the kitchen from the bay window that overlooked the backyard. Matt saw movement and he took a relieved breath. He should have known Aaron was out there. The gazebo had always been Aaron's favorite place to sit and relax. The dogs were with him, joyfully bounding around their favorite human.

He opened the door to the patio. He took two steps before he realized Aaron had a human companion.

What the hell was Rachel doing here?

CHAPTER 6

Deborah's call caught Lillian as she was leaving her Krav Maga class on Saturday morning. She listened while she tossed her gym bag on the passenger's seat of her blue Honda Accord and took the wheel.

"You can't file charges on someone for being a Good Samaritan," Lillian said when Deborah ran out of breath. "What have you got against Matt? Rachel isn't claiming he assaulted her. Is she?"

"No, but I bet she knows the person who did. She left the hospital and I think she's at Matt's house. I talked to his neighbor who claims he arrived home late last night with someone. When I knocked on his door, he wouldn't let me in or answer any of my questions."

"Okay, calm down. If she is there, so what? He doesn't have to let you in without a warrant, and you have no cause. Rachel told us she'd been looking for him. So she found him. Good for her. What else do you have to know?"

"The person who attacked her. What's so hard to understand?"

"Okay, start at the beginning." Lillian reached in her bag and brought out the notepad she always carried. She dug for a pen. "Does she have a last name?"

"She signed papers as Rachel Rosendekker." A pause. "Before you ask, there's no Missing Persons report on record."

"Then no one seems to be looking for her." Lillian was running out of patience with her cousin, but she had Deborah spell out the name and wrote it down. "How old is she?"

"Unless she lied on the hospital form, she just turned twenty-one."

Lillian wanted to throw her phone out the window. "Deborah, what's wrong with you? The girl's an adult. She hasn't filed a complaint, and she isn't missing. Let it go."

"I can't. Someone assaulted Rachel, and she's obviously afraid to name him. I want to catch the guy who's responsible. If it wasn't Matt Langdon, then how did she land on the road all beaten up and possibly raped?"

"You said there was no evidence of rape." Lillian could hear heavy breathing on the other end. "What does your supervisor say?"

"As far as the department is concerned, unless Rachel wants to charge her attacker, the case will stay open but cold."

"There's your answer." Lillian waited, but Deborah said nothing. "What do you want me to do?"

"Check on her. See if she's at Matt's. Find out who she really is and where she comes from. Why was she looking for Matt? He's your client, isn't he?"

"A business client, yes. Listen, Deb, you have the same resources as I do. Can't you do the research?"

"Holland will say I'm harassing Langdon. He's afraid of a lawsuit if I pursue this case."

Lillian bit her lower lip. "Honey, I know what you're doing. You're making this case personal. She's not me, Deb. You can't save every girl who's been assaulted.

You can't put my face on her. Stop blaming yourself for what happened to me. You did everything you could back then, but this is the present. The past is over."

"How can you say that? Those men are living their lives like nothing happened."

Lillian knew it was useless to argue with her. They had been over this too many times without a resolution. Fifteen years earlier, while Lillian was in law school, she was drugged and raped by two students at a party. Deborah was a rookie cop at the time and the arresting officer. The two young men were from wealthy families. On the evidence presented in court by both Deborah and Lillian, they were convicted and sentenced to eighteen months in prison. Deborah raged at their sentences. Eighteen months? Not enough.

After fifteen years of being a beat cop, Deborah should have been promoted to detective long ago, but she told Lillian she wanted to be on the street to search out and stop the bad guys. Lillian often wondered if her passion and narrow focus was the reason her superiors kept her from moving up a grade.

Lillian spoke in a calm voice. "I'll visit Matt at his house and see what I can find out. I'll let you know what I come up with. Don't get into any more trouble. Promise me."

Silence on the other end. A click and the connection went dead.

Lillian drove home. After a quick shower and a change of clothes, she went to the spare bedroom she used as her home office and opened her computer. She logged on to LexisNexis and entered Rosendekker and Texas in the search engine. She reached for a pack of cigarettes in her lower right drawer where she also kept a bottle of single malt scotch. She was an ex-smoker and she didn't light the slim cigarette she pulled out of the pack. But she held it between her forefinger and middle finger. Her search produced a company's name. Rosendekker Oil and Gas Exploration, a Delaware Corporation doing business in Dallas, Texas. Among the list of executives named was one Duncan Rosendekker.

She conducted a deeper search. She discovered Duncan Rosendekker was the president and chief executive officer of Rosendekker Exploration, a company that was originally Kittering Exploration before being bought out by said Duncan Rosendekker. Duncan was presently a widower. His deceased wife's maiden name was Victoria Kittering. They had one living daughter whose name was Rachel.

Lillian leaned back in her chair and reviewed the facts. Matt Langdon owned Black Gold Exploration and served as its president. Rachel's father owned Rosendekker Exploration. What else did they have in common? Investors? She considered Matt's recent and ongoing struggle to find funding. Was Rachel's appearance and attack a coincidence?

Rachel said she was looking for Matt when she was injured. The question that should have been asked was what happened to the car she rode in. Was she the driver? Or was someone else? Was anyone looking for it? She picked up the phone again and called Deborah back. In answer to her question, Deborah said Rachel had given them a description of the car. A red Camaro. She would let Lillian know when the car was found.

Lillian chewed on the unlit cigarette dangling from her mouth. Yes, she would definitely plan a visit to Matt's home. Not only because of her promise to Deborah, but she wanted answers from Rachel. Who drove the car? What was her motive for finding Matt?

CHAPTER 7

Matt recognized Rachel as soon as she rose to stand next to Aaron. He wasn't sure if he should be angry or glad that she had found her way to his home. What would Deborah Wallace do if she found the girl there? She could do nothing, he reasoned. He hadn't committed a crime. If anything, he should be rewarded for saving her.

He crossed the lawn. When he got closer, he noticed she was wearing hospital scrubs.

"Hey, Dad," Aaron said with a wry grin. "Look who I found in our yard. She says she knows you. What's going on?"

Before Matt could respond, Rachel spoke up. "Sorry, Mr. Langdon. I didn't know you had a son." She glanced down at her clothes and bit her lower lip. "I had to borrow these. I didn't have any of my clothes with me at the hospital. You saw what happened to the dress I was wearing. Total disaster."

Aaron stepped back and examined her appearance as though taking inventory. "I have a pair of jeans and a shirt that might fit her. We're about the same size and age."

"Let's hold off for now." Matt turned to Rachel. "I guess you didn't wait to be released by the doctor. You took quite a punch. Are you sure you're all right?"

She shrugged. "I've had worse things happen to me."

Aaron's eyes drilled into Matt demanding an explanation. Matt acknowledged him with a nod, but he didn't want to say anything until he could talk to Rachel alone.

"Aaron, I saw two cups of coffee in the kitchen that you'd poured for us. Would you mind getting them? Maybe Rachel would like a cup, too."

"Sure," Aaron said in a curt tone. "What do you take in your coffee, Rachel?"

"Just milk." She glanced at Matt. "I don't mean to be a bother."

"You're not," Aaron said before Matt could respond. "You're our guest. I'll be right back." As he passed Matt, he spoke under his breath. "She's a little young, isn't she?"

Matt looked up abruptly, but Aaron was already halfway to the house. He turned to Rachel. "Why did you come here?"

"I told you, I needed to talk to you alone." She returned to the bench and clasped her hands around her knees. "I heard you paid the bill. You didn't have to do that."

"Yes, I did."

"I'll pay you back."

"Let's skip all that. Answer my question. Why did you want to see me?"

She fingered a chain with a locket around her neck. "You didn't recognize my name?"

He glanced back at the house and saw Aaron staring out the window. "Don't play games. The policewoman knocked on my door earlier, looking for you."

"Officer Wallace?" A flash of fear shone in her eyes. "You can't tell her I'm here."

"Why not?"

"You just can't."

"That's not an answer. No more cat and mouse games. Tell me why you're here, or I'll call her right now. I don't like being accused of assault and attempted rape."

Her eyes widened. "Why would she accuse *you*? You saved me. And no one tried to rape me."

"Tell you what, I'll call her, and you tell *her* that." Matt pulled his phone from his shirt pocket.

"No, wait," she cried. "My name is Rachel Rosendekker."

Matt's hand froze on the phone. "Rosendekker. As in Rosendekker Exploration?"

She nodded.

His throat tightened. "Any relation to Duncan Rosendekker?"

"My father." Her lips twisted as if tasting a bitter fruit.

Duncan. Memories surfaced and with them a surge of revulsion and anger that went back as far as college. Another realization hit him. He stared at her, now seeing the resemblance he hadn't fully noticed before. "You're Victoria's daughter."

She fingered the heart-shaped locket that hung around her neck. She opened the locket and showed him the picture inside. "You do remember her."

He reached out his hand and almost touched the picture but withdrew in time. His throat tightened and prevented him from speaking at first. The beautiful Victoria stared out at him.

His Victoria. He was stunned that a picture could stir up such a whirlwind of emotions. The bitterness that poisoned their relationship still hurt after all these years, but his love for her had never dimmed. He turned away, and Rachel closed the locket.

"Of course I do." His answer came out harsher than he intended. In a softer tone, he added, "It was a long time ago, but she was a special person. Did she send you here?"

"In a way." Her lips thinned into a straight line, her chin trembled slightly.

He looked closer at Rachel and fought to tamp down his feelings. Rachel's blue eyes were the same shade as her mother's. That's what he'd noticed at the hospital.

"Tell me what you came here to say. Is she in trouble?"

"She's dead." Rachel waited, watching his reaction.

He sucked in his breath and his throat constricted. "When?"

Rachel's eyes glistened but she didn't look away. "Two years ago."

He sat back with a heavy feeling in his chest. He closed his eyes. Two years? The last time he'd heard from Victoria was over twenty years ago. Ancient history. Even so, now to hear Victoria was dead numbed him. His eyes opened to find Rachel staring at him with wet eyes. A stab of remorse struck him. She had lost her mother. "I'm so sorry. Sorry for your loss." His eyes filmed and he blinked rapidly. "Please forgive me. I knew her. This is a shock."

"You met in college." She paused and waited.

"We were good friends." He stopped himself before he gave too much away. The slope back into the past was slippery, and this was not the time or place to let himself go there. "You lost your mother. That's so hard. She was, what? Only forty?" He stopped, confused. "You said she died two years ago. Why come to me now?"

She watched him intently. "Before she died, she said that if I ever needed someone and she wasn't around, that I should find you. You were the only one she trusted."

He swallowed the lump in his throat. "I don't understand. I'm the only one she trusted? We haven't seen each other in twenty years. Why are you coming to me now?" He narrowed his eyes at her. "You're in trouble, that's why. Who stopped you? Who beat you up?"

"That doesn't matter. What I came to tell you does."

"It matters to me," he said. "I want a name."

Her eyes flashed in anger. "Are you going to listen, or not? What I have to tell you is more important."

With an effort, he eased up. "I'm listening," he said, bracing himself for what more could crash down on him.

"Duncan murdered Victoria. I can't prove it. I believe he wants me dead, too."

Matt felt he'd been given a one-two punch in the stomach and throat. He had never liked Duncan. He was many things. An ex-football linebacker who enjoyed giving an opponent pain, a ruthless businessman, a bully, a thief, a degenerate. But a killer?

He drew back putting space between them. "That's a strong accusation. Especially if you have no proof."

"It's true."

"Is he the one who attacked you and left you on the road?"

"No." She scoffed. "He would never dirty his own hands on me."

"He sent someone to hurt you?"

She thought for a moment, then shook her head.

Matt sat on the bench next to her. "Did you go the sheriff after she died?"

"No," she said.

"Why not?"

Her lower lip trembled. It was several moments before she answered. "Because he was a party to the killing."

Matt scratched his head. Her story was sounding more and more ludicrous. "Start from the beginning. How did Victoria die?"

She looked somewhere beyond him as seeing the past

play out in front of her. "They were deer hunting, just Duncan and Mom, the two of them. He came back and told everyone a story about a terrible accident. Said they got separated and he saw movement in the bushes and thought it was a deer. Said he didn't realize he'd shot her instead. Lies, all lies."

"Accident?" Matt repeated. "Was there an autopsy? There always is after a sudden death."

"No autopsy. No arrest. No evidence. He had her cremated the following day."

Matt was dumbfounded. "But the sheriff—"

"Got a new red truck, thank you very much."

"He—what? Do you mean—"

"I told you the sheriff was in on it. Sheriff Tandy and Duncan are drinking and hunting buddies."

Matt felt dizzy. Victoria murdered? He couldn't wrap his head around the words. He knew Duncan had a vicious streak, but this was too much, even for him. He could accept the story of an accidental shooting. Such things happened. It was the quick cremation part that didn't make sense. "You're saying the sheriff looked the other way and did nothing to stop the cremation?"

Rachel's back straightened and she faced away from him. "We live in the country outside a small town with no police force. Duncan is powerful there. His company employs most of the residents. Nobody would dare accuse him of murder, especially the sheriff. Duncan got him that job. If he says Victoria's death was an accident, that's how the death certificate would read."

"Maybe you're wrong. Maybe it was an accident," Matt said.

"It wasn't," Rachel said, her voice rising. She twisted to face him. "Sheriff Tandy took a bribe. What does that tell you?"

"Nothing, unless you can prove it."

"You want facts?" Rachel spoke without emotion. "Under the terms of her family's trust, my mother was to inherit millions on her fortieth birthday. She turned forty two months before she died. The trust fund was in her name, her personal and separate property. The way the trust was set up was to forbid Duncan access to any part of that money. Duncan believed that if she died, he would automatically inherit her property."

She paused to let the facts sink in Matt's head. He had always gotten along well with Victoria's family while they were dating. Her family owned Kittering Exploration, a medium-sized company. Farley Kittering believed in protecting his family in the event anything happened to him. This protection would have continued after Duncan married his daughter and took over Kittering Exploration. Farley might have foreseen the buyout of his company and the eventual change to Rosendekker Exploration, but he didn't have to worry about his daughter's wealth being taken by her husband. Matt didn't doubt for a minute that Farley Kittering would have set up a separate property trust for his daughter with a provision disallowing Duncan any part of Victoria's money.

Matt didn't voice these thoughts to Rachel. Instead, he said, "You believe Duncan killed your mother for her inheritance." He heard the skepticism in his voice. He still found it hard to believe Rachel's words.

"It doesn't matter what I believe. If I were to accuse Duncan of murder, no one in that town would listen to me, or they'd be too scared to do anything to him. He's a rotten sonofabitch, and I hate him."

Matt started to protest, but she stopped him.

"Mom knew what he was capable of. I think she suspected he planned to kill her. That's why she made out a new will. She got her revenge, and protected me."

Matt started to ask, but in a flash saw the answer.

"Victoria named you in her will. You inherited the trust fund." After the shock wore off, he realized he should have expected Victoria would know how to protect her daughter. She had learned what to do from her father. Now Rachel was a millionaire.

Rachel laughed, a bitter sound that speared through Matt. "Right. She put the trust in my name and stipulated that I should have access to the money on my twenty-first birthday. I celebrated Sunday. So, the joke's on me. Don't you get it? He'd rather kill me than see me inherit the money he had killed to get. That's why I left and why I can't go back. If you tell Officer Wallace, she'll tell Duncan where to find me."

Matt stared at her. The enormity of Duncan's crime against Victoria and his threat against their daughter made him reel. He stepped away from the bench, staggered and almost fell.

Rachel jumped up and grasped his arm. "I'm sorry. Are you all right?" Her voice cracked and he saw tears pooling her eyes. "I took a chance telling you all that. But I think Mom would have wanted me to."

Her story was outrageous. She must be crazy to think her own father capable of murdering his wife and then going after her. These were vile acts. Nothing like what she had told him ever touched Matt's own life. Yet, despite the insanity, he believed her.

One question nagged at him. "Why did she tell you to find me? Other than she trusted me for some unknown reason rooted in the distant past."

Rachel shrugged and gave him a helpless smile. "I was hoping you'd tell me."

"Uh, coffee's ready," a voice interrupted.

Both Matt and Rachel turned to Aaron.

"Sorry I took so long. I made a fresh pot." He looked at them, judging them with his eyes. "What did I miss?"

CHAPTER 8

Lillian waited until Sunday afternoon to visit Matt Langdon. She pulled up in front of his house and killed the engine, ready to open the door. She stopped when she saw movement near the front window. Looking closer, she saw a slim figure dressed in jeans, boots and a gray hoodie move stealthily through the bushes. A prowler? A very stupid prowler in the light of day. Especially on a Sunday when most neighbors would be at home.

Lillian opened her glove compartment where she kept her Glock. She felt the comfortable weight in her hand as she continued to watch the house. She turned off the inside light, opened the driver's door slowly and quietly, and climbed out. It could be a neighbor's kid, or someone who worked for Matt, but she dismissed both ideas.

She moved onto the sidewalk, but as quiet as she tried to be, the prowler whirled around, saw her and took off.

"Stop!" she ordered. "Stop!"

She couldn't make out whether the intruder was young or old, but she suspected he was young from the way he moved. The hoodie shadowed his face. He kept his head down as he zigzagged through the bushes and rounded the side of the house.

Lillian took off after him, turned the corner, and saw

him sail over the neighbor's fence, shirt tails flapping.

"Stop!" she yelled, but the figure disappeared.

A male voice called out, "Who's there?"

She returned to the front and saw Matt Langdon standing on the lawn between her and the house.

"Lillian?" he said in surprise. He stared at the gun she held.

She walked briskly toward him, gun held down at her side. "Someone was at your window, trying to sneak a look inside. Any idea who?"

He looked beyond her at the empty yard then shook his head. "Probably a neighborhood kid. Not dangerous, I hope." He gave her a questioning look. "What are you doing here?"

"Deborah said Rachel checked out of the hospital. I wanted to see if she'd found you."

"Come in and see for yourself," he said. "After you put away your gun."

She returned to her car and retrieved her purse, sliding her gun inside. Matt led her to a spacious, classically arranged living room. Cream-colored sofas and chairs surrounded a large coffee table that looked like the stump of a redwood tree, its surface glossy with polish. What looked like original art work and sculptures decorated the room. She was no art expert, but a few modern pieces caught her attention.

Lillian spotted Rachel in the corner of the room, curled up in a comfortable-looking lounge chair with a throw over her legs. When she drew closer, the bruises on the girl's face looked even worse.

"Do you remember Lillian?" Matt said, "She came with me to the hospital."

Rachel studied her. "Not really. I was kind of out of it."

"You were hurting. How are you feeling now?" Lillian asked.

"Better than I look." Rachel sat up straighter. "Was someone outside?"

"Some prowler trying to see into the window. Maybe he was looking for you."

Rachel's face tightened and she pulled the blanket around her. "I doubt it. Is he gone?"

"I didn't see him," Matt said.

"He climbed over the neighbor's fence," Lillian said, watching Rachel. "Does that happen often here, Matt?"

"No," Matt said. He, too, turned to Rachel.

At that moment, a young man walked in. He carried a tray holding a pitcher of iced tea and four glasses. He placed the tray on the coffee table and straightened. "Did you say we had a prowler? I'll go look."

"Don't bother. He's long gone," Matt said. "Lillian, this is my son, Aaron. I don't think you two have met. Lillian's my lawyer's investigator."

Aaron shook Lillian's hand. "Cool. Good to meet you."

"I picked him up from college yesterday for a short vacation." Matt explained to her.

Lillian smiled. "I've heard a lot about you. Matt brags about you all the time."

"Who are you investigating?" Aaron turned to Rachel. "Her?"

"No, this is a friendly call," Lillian said.

Matt offered her a glass of tea and she accepted and took a long swallow.

"I have an excellent security system set up," Matt said. "If I had a prowler, an alarm should have gone off. Let's go check the computer."

Lillian put down her glass and followed him down the hall to a fully equipped home office that made her jealous. Rachel lagged behind them and seemed curiously reticent as Matt booted up his desk computer. After a few minutes, the screen showed the front of the house. He rewound it to the time just before Lillian arrived. Sure enough, a figure lurked near the windows. Lillian watched as her car pulled up and parked in front. When she got out, the hooded figure moved along the bottom of the screen and darted out of sight.

Matt said, "Too bad we can't see his face."

Lillian turned to Rachel. "Any ideas?"

"Why are you asking me?" she demanded. "If the sneaky little bastard wanted something, why didn't he knock on the door?"

Rachel turned and walked out of the room. The others followed her back to the living room. She plunked down on the lounge and laid back.

Lillian couldn't help but notice the way Aaron took a protective stance next to the girl. "You and Aaron look about the same age. Did you know each other before today?"

Aaron burst out laughing. "Hey, we never met. She said she was here to talk with my dad."

Rachel folded her arms across her chest. She didn't look at Aaron. "I was surprised Matt even had a son. By the way, he's two years younger than me."

Aaron didn't seem to take offense to her words. "So you can imagine my shock to wake up and find this *older* woman in our back yard." His teasing tone didn't raise a response from Rachel.

Lillian said, "I'm curious, Rachel, why all the mystery in the hospital? You could have given your name and talked to Matt there."

Rachel pushed a blond curl from her forehead and swung her legs around to perch on the edge. "What I wanted to tell Matt was private. It had nothing to do with what happened on the road."

"Are you sure? Maybe the attack was meant to stop you from finding him," Lillian suggested. "Is that why you were too scared to talk in front of the policewoman?"

Rachel spoke matter-of-factly. "I wasn't scared. No one was trying to hurt me. My business with Matt was personal and nobody else's business."

"Okay," Lillian said. "If no one was to blame for your injuries, tell us what did happen?"

Rachel's lower lip trembled. "I don't remember."

"That's enough, Lillian," Matt interrupted. "She's here now, and I've invited her to stay as long as she wants. All these questions can wait."

Really? Why? This from a man who claimed he had never heard of Rachel before. "I'm curious. What's changed?"

Rachel jumped to her feet. "What's changed is none of your business." She moved in close to Matt. "I'm really tired."

She's using him, Lillian concluded. The idea made her angry. "Look at her, Matt. I doubt she gave herself those injuries, and I'd be damn curious about who she's protecting. Aren't you? She might be putting you and your son in danger from this creep."

"Don't listen to her," Rachel begged. She came within kissing distance of Matt.

His eyes softened, but he discreetly moved a few steps away from her. "Nobody can force you to talk, Rachel, but maybe you should reconsider. Lillian has a valid point."

"I say, do it," Aaron said. "Get that sick asshole."

Lillian tuned in to his words and the way he said them. There was much more going on here than they'd led her to believe.

"Aaron," Matt said sharply. "This is not your business."

"Bullshit. I'm part of this family. Your business is mine, too. You always said we were a team. Rachel came to us."

Rachel lowered her head in her hands. "I should never have involved you."

"After what you've told me?" Matt said gently. "We *are* involved, Rachel."

Lillian had heard enough. "You'd better involve me in whatever you're hiding. It sounds like you need my help, Rachel. Matt's my client and also my friend. You can talk to me." When Rachel didn't respond, she added, "If that guy I saw at the window is who you're running from, then he knows you're here. He knows Matt and Aaron are protecting you."

Rachel turned away from her and faced Matt. "I don't want that monster coming after you."

Matt shook his head. "He's not going to do anything to us."

"You know what that man is capable of. He'll go to any lengths to keep control over me."

Lillian felt the change in the tension. "Are we talking about the same person who attacked you?"

She might as well be talking to the wall behind them.

Matt lowered his voice and fixed his gaze on Rachel. "You have no proof."

"I know what he did—" Rachel said, her voice cracking.

Lillian interrupted. "Are you talking about the man who attacked you?"

Rachel finally looked at her. "No, I'm talking about the man who sent the boy I was with."

Thoroughly frustrated with both of them, Lillian raised her voice. "What man? No, wait. Let's start with the boy who may or may not have attacked you. Enough double talk. I need a name, and I won't leave here until you tell me. These are my friends and, if you're putting them at risk, I will stop you now."

"No, Lillian, stop," Matt said. "You got it wrong."

"No, she's right." Rachel raised her hands as if in surrender. "There's been too much unsaid. Lillian, the boy is Luke Jamison. His father works for my father. You've probably already looked him up, Duncan Rosendekker, president of the Rosendekker Exploration."

"You're right, I did the research," Lillian said. "You think your father sent Luke Jamison after you. Why?"

Rachel sank back on the lounge chair. "My father and I are estranged and have been for the last two years even when I was living at home. I don't know if my father sent Luke after me or if it was his own idea. I needed a ride and Luke offered to drive me."

"Why?"

"He likes me, I guess. He's nineteen. Same age as Aaron." Rachel looked away. "His father is the company's landman. Luke runs errands for my father and does other small jobs for too little money. Except last year for his eighteenth birthday, my father gave him the Camaro."

"That's very generous of your father."

"He can be generous when he wants to impress someone, or buy someone off."

"Which do you think he was doing when he gave Luke the Camaro?"

Rachel shrugged. Lines furrowed between her eyes as if trying to work something out in her head.

Lillian changed the subject. "Do you live in Dallas?"

"We have an apartment there, but mostly we live on a ranch west of the city in Riverton County." Rachel narrowed her eyes. "Duncan thinks he's above the law. He always gets what he wants, whether he pays someone off or does whatever."

Lillian reviewed what she'd heard so far. The only broken law she determined was the assault on Rachel. "Did your father pay Luke to hurt you?"

Rachel's eyes widened. "Luke tried to talk me out of my plans. Duncan made him promise to stop me from seeing Matt. We argued."

"Argued how? Words or did the argument get physical?"

"We just argued," Rachel said.

"Okay." Lillian took a breath. "Why didn't he want you to visit Matt?"

Rachel shook her head. "I don't know."

Sure you do. "You're old enough to do what you want."

Matt spoke up. "She's twenty-one, as of last Sunday."

Rachel and Matt exchanged glances. Lillian sensed a message passed between them.

"Is turning twenty-one a reason for not seeing Matt?" Lillian couldn't imagine an answer that made sense.

Rachel didn't respond. Instead she gazed intently at Matt. "You don't know him like I do. Nobody crosses him. He got away with murder once and he'll do it again."

Lillian was lost. "Who are we talking about now? Who got away with murder? Luke or your father?"

Rachel flushed. "Luke wouldn't hurt anyone. My father is the murderer."

"I'm sure you don't mean that literally," Lillian said, still attempting to keep up with Rachel's irrational statements that seemed to be thrown out there for shock value. She was about to dismiss the girl entirely and let Matt handle her.

Matt seemed to read her thoughts, "Tell her, Rachel.

Go ahead. Tell her like you told me. You can trust her."

Rachel looked uncertain. Tears swam in her eyes. She blinked them away.

The ground beneath Lillian shifted. She hated family secrets. Did Rachel really believe her father was a murderer? Her research about Duncan Rosendekker and his company never hinted at scandal.

"Families fight all the time," Lillian said, looking for a reason for Rachel's accusation. "Misunderstandings can be blown out of proportion." She stopped, seeing the look on Rachel's face. Too late she remembered Rachel's mother had died. The research she read hadn't mentioned how she died. She had to ask the question, but not sure if she wanted to hear the answer. "Rachel, who did your father allegedly murder?"

Rachel's face turned a violent shade of red. Matt and Aaron stepped forward as if to shield her.

"My mother," Rachel screeched. "He killed my mother and got away with it. That bastard convinced the sheriff her death was an accident. But he lied. Duncan shot her in the head and got rid of the evidence. Now he wants to get rid of me." Tears streamed down her cheeks and she collapsed in the lounge chair. "I hate him. He's a monster."

Lillian stared at her, shocked beyond words. *Her mother?*

Rachel's shoulders shook, her hands covered her face. Matt stood by looking helpless.

Aaron made the first move. He helped Rachel onto her feet and led her out of the family room, his arm around her shoulders.

Matt watched them leave, his face slack.

Lillian turned to him. "You can't believe that."

He rubbed his chin. "She believes it."

"How long have you known Rachel?" Lillian said,

feeling betrayed by lies. "She came to you looking for a friend."

He sighed. "I didn't know Rachel before I saw her lying on the road. You have to believe me. She came to me because her mother told her I could be trusted if she ever needed a friend. I have a history with both Duncan and Victoria that goes back to when we were in college. I dated Victoria. We were engaged for a short time until Duncan came along. Years later I almost did business with the guy until I found out how ruthlessly he treated his competitors. But if you're asking me if he's a killer? I can't answer that."

"What was the official cause of her death?"

"Accident." He paused for her reaction, but Lillian had none. "Rachel told me they were hunting deer when Duncan's gun went off hitting her in the head and killing her instantly. Duncan was cleared and Victoria's death was officially ruled an accident."

Lillian took a moment to process his explanation. She glanced toward the kitchen where Aaron was tending to the young woman. "Does Rachel know your history with her mother?"

He shrugged. "I don't know how much Victoria told her."

Rachel emerged from the kitchen. Dried tears smeared the girl's bruised eyes. She appeared recovered after her outburst. "If you want to know why I came here, it's to prevent another murder. You have to convince the next rich sucker not to marry him. Duncan feels pretty confident that no one will listen to me. But I'm telling you now, once he gets his hands on his new bride's fortune, she'll be dead meat."

CHAPTER 9

Duncan plans to marry again?" Lillian asked Rachel. "Who is this woman?"

"Elaine Westerfelt. She's got money, owns a small oil and gas company, one that Duncan would like to get his mitts on. Someone needs to talk to her besides me. Duncan won't let me near her."

They had moved to the dining room where a long, polished wooden table and matching chairs took up much of the space. Aaron put away the tea and then fixed sandwiches, though no one seemed hungry. At Matt's suggestion, he brewed a pot of coffee and brought cups and a decanter to the table, along with a sugar bowl and creamer.

Lillian leaned forward, forcing the young woman to meet her eyes. "Rachel, what evidence do you have? Whoever did the autopsy would know how she died."

A choked laugh was Rachel's immediate answer. "Autopsy? There was no autopsy. Didn't I tell you? Duncan had her cremated as soon as he could. Forget the autopsy. How do you like them apples?"

Lillian looked at Matt who just shook his head.

"Isn't that against the law?" Rachel asked.

Lillian desperately wished she could satisfy Rachel. "Unfortunately, once the sheriff released your mother's body to your father, he had every right to her remains. I'm sorry."

Tears shimmered in Rachel's eyes. "It's not fair. Why did the sheriff have to release her body?"

"I can't answer that. You have to accept the facts. Two years have passed since her death. Unless your father confesses, we have to assume his innocence. You're not going to convince Elaine Westerfelt, or anyone else, otherwise."

Rachel turned to Matt. "Can't you talk to her?"

Matt poured himself a cup of coffee as he thought this over. "I've met Elaine at parties and conferences. From what I've heard, she's smart, stubborn and doesn't get sidetracked easily. Once she's of a mind to do something, she does it. I haven't seen her in a while. I'm not sure she'd even remember me."

"You two can work that out later," Lillian said. "Right now, we need to address the question of Luke and what he did to you."

Rachel started to shake her head, but Lillian didn't let her speak.

"You were beaten up and left lying on that road. A good thing Matt found you when he did. Officer Wallace is looking for Luke and when she finds him, she'll file charges and he'll go to jail, end of story. Unless you can convince her of his innocence."

"He didn't hurt me," Rachel said.

Rachel's whiny tone was straining Lillian's patience. "And he didn't run away and leave you there? When Matt found you, you were in pretty bad shape," she said, recalling the police photographs Deborah had shown her. Although there was no actual evidence of rape, Luke could have attempted to force himself on her. If she fought back, that would explain much of her injuries. Lillian needed answers and she wouldn't get them with

Matt and his son hanging on every word. She turned to them. "I need a moment alone with her."

Matt nodded and motioned Aaron to follow him.

When they were alone, Lillian faced Rachel. "I have to ask you this, and I need you to be honest with me. Your clothes were torn and there was blood. Tell me the truth. Did Luke try to rape you?"

Rachel rolled her eyes as if she'd been asked the same question too many times over. "Luke would never rape me."

"What do you remember?"

At first Rachel kept her stare fixed on Lillian and her lips clamped shut. But as the silence dragged on, she began to squirm and tug at the ends of her hair. She looked down and to the sides. Finally she pushed her chair back. "You got to understand. Luke thinks he's in love with me. My fault. I let him kiss me once. I've told him I don't feel the same way. He's just a friend, but he wants more. He got mad when I told him I was looking for Matt. He misunderstood. He wouldn't listen when I tried to explain. We argued. I slapped him. He slapped me back. But that's it. I don't remember what happened after that, except I know he didn't try to rape me."

The dogs alerted them first with their barking and howling from their kennel. Glass shattered. The sound came from the rear of the house.

Matt sped through the room toward the kitchen. "The back door," he shouted. Aaron sprinted after him, but turned on Matt's orders and blocked Rachel.

Lillian pulled her gun from her purse and ordered both Rachel and Aaron to stay put while she slipped into the kitchen after Matt.

Matt had reached the curly-haired intruder and struggled to hold him. Youthful muscles fought against mature strength, fury and purpose on one side and adrenaline-fueled outrage on the other. Lillian held her gun down at her side while Matt brought the kid under control. She checked the back door.

The pine door stood open, its latch in splinters where it had been forced open. What used to be a curtained window on the top half of the door was now a jagged hole. The curtain pooled on the floor next to a rock and shattered slivers of glass.

Lillian confronted the intruder who slumped in defeat next to Matt.

"Luke Jamison?" Lillian said.

The sound of his name brought Rachel rushing into the room accompanied by Aaron. Outside, the dogs were barking at fever pitch.

"What are you doing here?" Rachel screamed.

"Getting you, you dumb bitch," Luke countered.

"You stupid idiot," Rachel returned with an air of disgust.

The back door swung open and Lillian's cousin Deborah, in full uniform, stepped inside with handcuffs ready. In a smooth movement, she cuffed Luke. "Good call, Lil. He fits the description you gave. It's jail for you, young man."

"What?" Luke squealed. "You're arresting me? She's the one you should arrest." He pointed at Rachel.

"You're full of shit, Luke," Rachel retorted. "I didn't break any laws."

Deborah stepped between them and turned to face Rachel. "So I was right. You did come here after leaving the hospital."

"I said I would," Rachel said.

"You can't stay here," Deborah said.

"I stayed here last night. Matt said I could. Why are you arresting Luke?"

"Breaking and entering is against the law. So is assault

and battery. I would think you'd want him arrested."

"I don't, and I'm not pressing charges."

"I will," Matt said, pointing to his damaged door.

Rachel whirled around. "Matt, you can't."

"I will. I don't care who Luke is, he'd better learn right now he can't bust through people's doors and get away with it."

Rachel looked stricken. She turned to Lillian. "Can't you do anything?"

Lillian shrugged. "I'm not a lawyer. But Matt's right."

Deborah stepped forward. "Luke, if that's his name, will be charged on both counts." She let her gaze sweep over Rachel. "And if you've lied to me, miss, I will arrest you, too. You can both have a taste of what a jail cell is like."

"I'll get you out of this," Rachel promised Luke. "What the hell were you thinking, breaking in here?"

Luke sputtered some more and tried to fight off the cuffs, but finally gave up. "I was trying to save you."

"That's a good one," Deborah said. "After beating her up and leaving her hurt and bloodied on the road."

Luke blanched. "That's not true. Tell her, Rachel."

Rachel backed away and did a complete turnabout. The warmth that shown in her eyes a second ago turned cold. "You left me there."

Fear flittered across his face. "You know why. Don't you remember?"

"That's enough." Deborah grasped Luke's arm. "You're coming with me downtown."

Now the fear was more evident in his eyes. "No, you can't. I know my rights. I get a phone call. Wait 'til my dad hears about this. He'll sue you. He'll get me out before you can lock the doors. You'll see what trouble you'll be in."

What an idiot. Lillian almost felt sorry for him.

"Daddy will come all the way from Dallas, young man?" Deborah's tone fell just short of mocking him.

"Holy shit," Aaron said behind her. "Can't believe I came home to this."

Luke seemed to notice him for the first time. He stared at Aaron, then at Rachel, and back at Aaron. Without warning he lunged, but Deborah caught him before his fingers caught Aaron's shirt.

"Who are you?" Luke demanded.

"I live here," Aaron said. "Asshole."

Lillian pushed him out of the kitchen. "Stay out of this, Aaron."

Luke called after him. "Fuck you, college boy. You better not touch her."

Aaron held up his hands as he walked backward through the dining room guided by Lillian, but he couldn't seem to resist a quiet laugh.

Luke spat on the floor.

"Hey!" Matt planted himself in front of the kid. "Did Duncan teach you your manners?"

"Don't say nothing about him." Luke's belligerence made him forget he was handcuffed and he almost wrenched his shoulder trying to swing his arm out.

Deborah gripped Luke's arm and pushed him outside through the broken kitchen door. Lillian followed them around the house to the front where the cruiser waited. Deborah opened the back door and pushed Luke in head-first.

Deborah turned back to Lillian.

"Thanks for calling me. You find out anything?"

"I'll call you later and fill you in."

Deborah nodded. "That girl worries me. She shouldn't be staying with a man she doesn't know, and who could be responsible for her condition."

"Matt's innocent. Trust me. I know," Lillian said.

Deborah gave her a curious look. "I'll expect an explanation later."

Lillian nodded. "You'll get it."

Deborah motioned to the boy. "What do you know about him?"

"Nothing, except his father works for Duncan Rosendekker. Kurt will call him."

Deborah nodded. "Tell my ex I'll see him when I see him."

Lillian cracked a smile. "I'll tell him you send your love."

Deborah scowled. "Better not, you bitch." Her tone was friendlier than her words.

CHAPTER 10

Matt slept fitfully that night. He worried about Rachel, who slept in the spare bedroom. He worried about his son, whether he should leave him home alone with Rachel. It wasn't that he didn't trust his son, but he didn't know Rachel. Earlier, he had planned to bring Aaron to work with him. He nixed that idea. Whether or not he trusted her, he couldn't leave Rachel alone in the house. She was too raw, too vulnerable.

The clock on his bedside table read five-thirty-two. Time for his morning run. He moved his legs but they felt like two logs. His eyes stung and his head throbbed. He shouldn't have opened the bottle of Jack after Rachel had retreated to the guest room and Aaron turned in for the night. How much did he drink? Enough to create a drum roll in his head and a blender in his stomach. He wasn't a habitual drinker. The Jack was for company or special occasions, or like now when his life had turned upside down. He stumbled into the bathroom and took a few aspirin. He returned to his bed, lay back down, and closed his eyes.

When he awoke two hours later, his head felt better, but his stomach growled. He listened for sounds of movement in the house. Nothing. He checked the bedrooms. Both occupants were asleep. He took a quick

shower, got dressed and made coffee in the empty kitch-
en. With toast and coffee in front of him, he sat at the table and pondered his present circumstances.

If he were honest with himself, Matt had to admit he
really didn't trust Rachel. Simple as that. He knew nothing about her. Last night she could have told him anything and he would have believed her. In the cold light of
morning, her story about Duncan murdering Victoria
struck him as odd. His longtime foe was devious and cutthroat in business. He would stoop to underhanded tricks
to screw his partners out of a deal he wanted for himself.
But was he capable of murder? Under the right conditions, Matt could convince himself of Duncan's guilt.

He pictured Victoria as he remembered her from college, like the photo he saw in Rachel's locket. She was
his first love. He had proposed, and she had accepted.
Then that asshole stole her from him. Then he kills her?
Matt wouldn't be able to live with himself if he didn't
avenge Victoria. If those were the facts.

Rachel's claim shook him down to his toes. She said
Victoria sent her to him. Not a death bed promise. Had
she suspected Duncan would try to kill her? She must
have been desperate. But how did the woman he'd once
known and loved know where to find him after twenty
years? Had she kept tabs on him? Did she hire someone
who reported back to her every six months or so? Didn't
make sense.

Now, after all this time, Victoria expect him to do
what, prove she had been murdered? Rachel said she'd
been cremated. In that case, there was no proof. No body
to exhume and examine.

Rachel was Victoria daughter. She was also Duncan's
daughter. The ties were broken twenty years ago when
Victoria chose Duncan over him.

Not his concern. He had his own problems to deal

with. He should be concentrating on saving his business. Not chasing ghosts.

His cell phone beeped, a text from Greg.

Where the hell are you? I need you here.

Now what?

Matt heard footsteps behind him. He turned to see Aaron, wearing boxers and a T-shirt, pouring himself a cup of coffee. His sleepy eyes and tousled hair brought Matt back to the time before Aaron left for college. Now his son was back home and he hadn't changed a lick.

"Is Rachel still here?" Aaron asked.

"Far as I know. Put on some clothes before she comes in and sees you in your underwear."

"She staying long?"

"No. I'm sure she has other plans."

"It's cool if she stays."

Matt flashed a glance at him. "There's nothing here for her. Remember that. Look, I have to go into work. Just let her sleep. There's plenty of food. You need me, I'm a phone call away. I'll check in with you later." He hesitated before adding, "Watch your step around her."

Aaron chuckled. "Don't worry, Dad. We're adults."

Matt shot him a hard look. "*She's* an adult."

"Jeez, what do you think we're going to do?"

"What I hope *you're* going to do is think about your own future, and your plans for the rest of the school year."

"Yeah, right. Aren't you going to be late for work, Dad?"

For a moment, Matt was tempted to forget about work and instead stay home to supervise. Then Greg texted again.

Matt stood and emptied his cup into the sink. He brushed his hand across Aaron's shoulder. "See you tonight."

The drive to work took him down the road where he had found Rachel. He slowed to a crawl, seeing the scene again in his head. He tried to be objective, even critical. He concluded he had done nothing wrong. He couldn't have changed the outcome.

There was no sign of what had happened. No blood stains. No debris on the ground. That seemed strange. Shouldn't there have been something left behind? He sped up, wanting to get the whole business behind him. He checked the rearview mirror only twice before the road turned.

Ten minutes later he parked in his usual slot behind the two-story office building. He strode down the corridor and opened the door marked Black Gold Exploration. Greg rushed into the hallway to intercept him.

"We got trouble," Greg announced.

Matt stopped in mid-stride. "The Dennis Number One?"

"No. McAdams. Got to be. He must've talked to the potential investors. An hour after I got here, they all had backed out of the participation agreements."

Matt felt his jaw drop. "All?"

"I'm going to ruin that sonofabitch," Greg said. "He got to them somehow."

"Have you talked to him?"

"He won't pick up. I think he's waiting on you."

Matt pushed past him and went straight to his desk. He sat there, stared at the phone, then peered up at Greg. "Tell me what happened," he said.

Greg opened his fist and plunked down a handful of pink message slips. "I tried emailing and calling them and got no response. We're screwed."

Matt flipped through the scrawled notes. "Nothing from McAdams?"

"Nada."

Matt couldn't sit still any longer. He got to his feet and paced. His head whirled. *Aaron…McAdams…Rachel …Duncan.* He stopped at the window but saw nothing. He continued to pace. Back and forth. *Dallas…the power was in Dallas. The rest of us schmucks are stuck in Houston.*

"Well?" Impatience cracked Greg's voice.

Matt turned slowly and walked to his desk. "How long can we stall the creditors?"

Greg threw up his hands. "Shit, I don't know. A few weeks? A month?"

"We can put them off longer than that, can't we?"

Greg's eyes narrowed. "Can we? I guess. You got a plan? Fuck! Tell me you got a plan."

"Give me a minute." Matt returned to his desk and placed both hands flat on top of the papers covering the surface. The print swam out of focus. When he looked up, he had the beginnings of a smile on his face. "Now I got a plan."

Greg wiped sweat off his forehead.

Matt's smile widened. "Relax, buddy. I'm going to fix this."

"How?"

"I'll let you know."

"What do you mean?"

"You need to cool it, partner. Take care of the office while I'm gone. I'm going to take a trip up Dallas way. Shake a few trees."

"Dallas," Greg repeated. "Wait. You're going to see McAdams?"

Matt grinned.

Greg shook his head and jabbed a finger at Matt. "You got that shit-eatin' look on your face. You're up to something bad, aren't you?"

"Stop worrying. Everyone's got to stop worrying,"

Matt said. "You and Becky take care of the office. I'll see you in a couple of days if this works."

"And if it doesn't?"

Matt didn't have an answer. He wasn't even sure his plan would work, but it was better than doing nothing.

He arrived back at the house thirty minutes later and followed the sound of laughter to the kitchen. Aaron stirred a pan full of scrambled eggs and sausage and didn't see him at first. Matt noticed he'd put on sweat pants.

Aaron looked up and colored at the sight of Matt. He dropped the spatula on the counter. "Dad? What are you doing home?"

Matt didn't answer him. He was staring at Rachel, who sat at the table in one of Matt's white shirts and what looked like a pair of Aaron's boxers. Her legs were bare and she propped one bare foot on the table. That didn't bother Matt as much as the cigarette in her hand and his bottle of Jack on the table in front of her. He felt his blood pressure shoot to the ceiling.

Rachel leaned her head back. "Hi, Mr. Langdon," she murmured.

Matt's head pulsed. He saw red dots blinking. *What the fuck was this?* He grabbed the bottle off the table and snatched the cigarette out of Rachel's hand. With a swing of his hand, he swept her leg off the table. She screamed and cowered.

"Get up," he said. "I'm taking you home."

Her eyes darkened and she curled a leg under her. "I'm not going back."

"You're not staying here." He put out the cigarette in the sink and put the bottle on the counter.

"Dad, you can't do this," Aaron said.

Matt glared at them both. "I'm gone less than an hour and I come home *to this*?"

Rachel unfurled and leaned toward him. "I know it looks bad, but I was hurting. I just wanted to escape. Aaron was so understanding and made me feel at home. He's been so nice." When she saw that her words had no effect on Matt, she lost the pleading tone. "I'm not a child anymore, and you can't force me to go anywhere. Besides, Lillian said Kurt was bonding Luke out of jail this morning."

"I don't care. You will not stay here and smoke in my house and drink my booze. I won't have a stranger in here I can't trust."

She lowered her eyes and put a sincere note in her tone. "I'm sorry. I won't do it again, I promise."

He watched her, his mind spinning. He was right not to trust this girl. He was still breathing hard. He had to calm down. Think what to do. He thought of his plan, and how he might be able to use Rachel.

"I'm going out of town for a few days, and you're coming with me."

"Going where?" Aaron asked.

Matt wrinkled his nose and turned toward the stove. Smoke rose from the skillet. "Turn that off before you set the place on fire."

Aaron took a brief, unhappy look at the burnt food, and did as he was told.

Matt turned back to Rachel. "We're going to Dallas to talk to your dad."

Rachel vigorously shook her head. "No fucking way. I'll run." She jumped to her feet, poised for flight. She waited for his next move.

Matt watched her, and a tempered calm settled over him. "Or," he said, "I take you to Elaine Westerfelt, so you can tell her what you told me."

Her voice rose. "I'm going to do what?"

"Last night you said her life would be in danger if she

married Duncan. This is your chance to warn her. Tell her what you believe happened to your mom, and why the same could happen to her. While you do that, I'll be in Dallas talking to your father. Don't get all uptight. This isn't all about you. He and I have business to discuss."

Aaron looked bewildered and scared at the same time. "Dad?"

Matt turned. He had momentarily forgotten Aaron was in the room. "It will be all right, son. I'm going to call Carrie. You can stay with her until I get back. In the meantime, I'll have her bring Rachel a change of clothes."

"What about Luke?" she wailed. "Where will he go when he gets out?"

"None of my concern. And he better not come here. He breaks in again, and I'll have him put away for good."

Rachel started to argue, but thought better of it. She resorted back to pleading and whining. "Why can't I stay here?"

"Because I don't trust you," Matt said bluntly. "Look at it this way, this is your best chance to redeem yourself. Call Elaine right now and let her know you're coming."

"I can't. I lost my cell phone in the accident. Besides, you don't just tell Elaine anything. You have to be invited."

"Look up her number and give it to me. I'll call her. Once I explain, I'm sure she won't have any trouble letting you stay."

And you'll be out of my hair, hopefully for good.

CHAPTER 11

Rachel ignored Matt and brooded through the first half hour of the drive to Dallas. He savored the silence and didn't attempt to engage her. He had enough concerns over losing his company without worrying about her.

Yet, she bothered him in so many ways. He couldn't blame her for acting out after everything she had been through. The sudden death of her mother. Her suspicions concerning her father, for which there was no way to prove or disprove. Not after two years and a cremation. How frustrating it must be for her to have no one who'd listen and take her seriously.

Victoria. Why did Victoria tell her daughter to find *him*? Why did it take two years for Rachel to act? He had no idea how he was supposed to help her. He hadn't seen or even thought about Victoria since she married Duncan. He had forced her out of his mind with a bitter vengeance. He grew a tough skin over that place in his heart where she'd once lived, so tough never to be penetrated in the same way again. He moved on. Got married to a woman he loved, not the same way he loved Victoria, but still he was reasonably happy until they divorced. Aaron came out of that union, and Aaron was the center of his life.

Now Victoria was truly dead and gone, and her daughter sat next to him. He felt that tough skin crack under the force of flooding memories he'd held in check until now. Why hadn't *she* sought him out while she was alive?

Rachel interrupted his thoughts. "Where will Luke stay after he's bailed out if he can't return to Dallas?"

"What?" It took a moment for Matt to snap out of the past. She repeated her question. "I don't understand, Rachel. You're worried about him? After what he did to you?"

She flung her head against the headrest and rolled her eyes. "Jesus Christ, men are so freaking dense. Yes, I'm worried. He's a good friend, that's all, and he didn't hurt me. Do you have an answer or just more stupid questions?"

Her attitude caused him to sharpen his own voice. "If you're that concerned, I'll call Lillian and ask her. Kurt is going to pay his bond this morning. So he's not your boyfriend?"

"No, he's not my boyfriend," she said, mimicking his tone.

"Oh yes, I forgot. He's two years younger than you. But that doesn't matter. He's smitten with you."

"Smitten." She laughed, a hollow sound. "What kind of word is that?"

"Old, like the way I feel. Don't act dumb, Rachel. He's in love with you. We could all see it last night."

She shrugged. "He'll get over it."

"Don't underestimate the power of a young man's first love. It can be the most exciting, wonderful, and excruciating experience he'll ever have. If you've dismissed his feelings for you, it might explain why he assaulted you."

With an impatient slap of her hand on the dash, she retorted, "He didn't do anything to me. I keep telling you that. Why don't you listen?"

Anger filled him and his hands shook. He jerked the wheel to the right and stopped on the side of the road. "You were beaten to unconsciousness. How do you explain that?"

"I can't."

"Well, whoever did that to you should get jail time." He glared at her. "What the hell really happened?"

Rachel shrank down into her seat. "I don't remember."

"Don't bullshit me," Matt said. "You said you argued."

She straightened. "Yes, but that's all I remember."

"What did you argue about?

"Finding you. He said we should go back home. I said I'd walk first."

"Did you get out and walk?"

"No," she cried. "Stop acting like a policeman. You're scaring me."

He stared at her, feeling his heart hammer against his chest. Finally he turned the car back on the road. "I doubt that. I don't think anything scares you, Rachel."

She folded her arms and stared straight ahead. "You don't know me at all."

"No, I don't." He was already regretting his outburst. Dealing with his son had taught him such tactics never worked. But Rachel pushed too many buttons and his hair-trigger response resulted. He leveled out his words, hoping they would register. "What I do know is this. Any man who beats up a female deserves prison or worse. I don't know what you're used to seeing or getting at home, but under no circumstances should you accept that kind of behavior from anyone."

Her jaw quivered but her tone was defiant. "I don't need a lecture."

She was right. When did a lecture ever win an argument? He pressed on the gas and shot over to the left lane. A driver honked his horn behind him. He turned up the air conditioner. Another hot, humid August day settled around them and caused tempers to flare. The other car swerved around him and the driver shot him a finger salute. Rachel returned the gesture.

Matt didn't spout a rebuke as he usually did when Aaron would flip off another driver. Time passed. He felt her staring at him. "What?" he said.

"Nothing." She stared out the window. But after a few moments, she gave him a second glance. "The way you talked about first love, is that how you felt toward my mother?"

The mention of Victoria felt like a hook tearing into scar tissue. He hadn't expected her question. "Change the subject, Rachel." He regretted the harshness of his tone, but hoped she would get the message and leave him alone.

But she didn't get the message. In a voice filled with anger and tears, she retorted, "She's my mother. You're sensitive about hearing her name? What the fuck? You haven't seen or talk to her in twenty years. You've had a wife and a son since then. *I'm* the one hurting. My mother's been gone only two years, and she didn't leave on her own. She was taken from me in the most horrible way there is. So fuck you, Matt Langdon."

He felt a stab of guilt drive deep inside him. "You're right, Rachel. I'm sorry, so very sorry. Of course you're hurting, and it's raw and painful. You had a double whammy. The loss of your mother, and the loss of your father."

She shot him as venomous look.

"Bear with me here," he said. "Someone doesn't have to die to be lost. You crossed your father out of your life when you believed he caused your mother's death. I understand why you can't forgive him."

"Forgive him?" The words stormed inside the car. "I want him to pay with everything he's got. The bastard intended to murder her and he succeeded. I'm not going to let him get away with it. I wish these were medieval times. I'd have him boiled in oil or torn apart on a rack."

The furious words punched his gut. He heard the raw hate and viciousness that came out of her. How long had they been festering inside her, waiting for a safe release?

He waited for her breathing to return to normal, and the red rash to disappear from her face. When he started to wonder if she'd fallen asleep, he said, "We were talking about first love and Luke."

She shifted and sat up straighter. "Yeah, about Luke's supposed feelings toward me," she said without emotion.

"That, yes, and you also asked if that's how I felt about Victoria. I never loved another woman like I loved her. We've both suffered a tremendous loss. Yours so much more intense and close to the bone. I shouldn't have overreacted."

Rachel glanced over at him, but said nothing. Her eyes were shiny and wet. She turned away again. Another fifteen minutes passed. She took a cigarette from her purse.

"Not in the car," he said.

She put the cigarette away and unwrapped a piece of gum from a pack. She offered one to him, but he shook his head.

"Lillian's pretty," Rachel said. "No really, she's beautiful. You and her ever—"

"No," he said before she could finish.

"Why? I could tell she likes you."

Uh, oh. Well, at least we aren't discussing Victoria. "Lillian's relationship to me is purely professional. She's the same with every client. Lillian works for my lawyer. We have a business arrangement and we don't mix business with pleasure."

"That's such a cliché. You're divorced. Haven't mentioned a girlfriend. You're not gay. Wait, are you? No,
and you're not that old. You're telling me you never
asked her out on a date?"

"No, and my love life is none of your business." His
lips trembled in his effort not to smile.

She turned her head toward him. "So you do have a
love life. What's her name?"

"Rachel, stop teasing. I know what you're doing, and
it won't work."

She gave him her impression of innocence. "What am
I doing, changing the subject?"

"Asking personal questions."

"I didn't realize you were off limits. You can ask me
questions, but I can't do the same to you? I like Lillian.
She'd be a good match for you. Is she seeing anyone?"

Matt wanted to laugh but didn't want to encourage
her. "I don't ask about her private life. That's why it's
called *private*." He tried to concentrate on the road. Cars
were slowing down ahead. A traffic jam already? An accident? "Why do you ask?"

"It's the way she looks at you," Rachel said. "Makes
me think she wants you to ask her out."

"You're letting your imagination run wild."

"What kind of men does she usually date?"

In spite of his internal warning, her question made him
think. He'd never known Lillian to date anyone. But
again, like he told Rachel, he wasn't concerned with
Lillian's private life. Aloud he said, "If she dates anyone,
he'd probably be someone in law enforcement. She
comes from a law enforcement family. You're acquainted
with her cousin, Officer Wallace."

Rachel laughed. "She's the one who practically arrested you for beating me up. Bet you don't have any fuzzy
feelings toward her."

He grinned. "You're right."

She unfolded another stick of gum and popped it in her mouth. They were slowing down again. Without looking at him, she said, "Did you really leave me at the hospital for a business meeting?"

Matt kept his eyes on the road. He heard sirens in the distance. The traffic was clogged. He glanced at the clock on the dash. Already after two in the afternoon. He pulled his thoughts back to her question.

"I was meeting a broker about lining up investors to save my company. I shouldn't have bothered. He probably noticed the blood on my shirt from carrying you. He couldn't pedal backward fast enough."

"You're having trouble getting investors?" She looked interested.

"Not initially. There were promises, but something changed their minds. That's why I'm going to Dallas after dropping you off at Elaine's."

"Will you be seeing Duncan?"

He frowned and turned to her. "Why would I?"

She shrugged. "If you're going to see McAdams, he's my father's broker, too."

He stared at her. "You know about the broker?"

"Of course. I worked part time in the office so I can learn the business. One day I'll be able to take over."

"You're full of surprises, aren't you?" His mouth felt dry.

"Fathers tend to overlook their daughters as business partners. I think it's the same with you and Aaron. He's smart. A good artist, too. He showed me some of his work."

"Takes after his mother," Matt said.

"Figured. But he takes after you, too. You're his idol. Did you know that?"

Matt didn't answer. Did Aaron look up to him that way?

An ambulance flew passed them on the service road. The crawl down the street lasted another half hour before the lanes started to clear.

An hour later they turned off the freeway in Bucknow, a small town in ranch country, two hours away from Dallas. Matt's GPS routed them down Main Street, dotted with quaint shops and restaurants. They passed City Hall, an imposing brick building. Another turn brought them to a residential area with modest homes. Rachel directed him to a back road that didn't appear on the GPS map. The lots were larger. Trees and tall fences hid the homes from the street. Matt spotted the gated estate entrance. Rachel had grown quiet since they had turned off the highway.

When he had called Elaine and explained about the accident, she was more than agreeable to have Rachel come and stay with her. Matt was still under the impression that Rachel had never talked to her because she had told him Duncan wouldn't let her. Now it looked evident that Rachel knew her way to Elaine's. He must learn not to underestimate her.

He turned his attention to the guard emerging from the gate house.

Matt gave the guard Elaine's name and his own.

Rachel was watching the guard as he spoke into the receiver. When he shook his head for a third time, she leaned across Matt and yelled, "Tell Elaine that it's Rachel."

Matt put his hand on her shoulder as she straightened. "Never met her, huh?"

"I never said that." Rachel's eyes squinted in the afternoon sun.

He wondered if she was laughing at him.

She went on. "I said Duncan wouldn't let me talk to her. He doesn't know I went behind his back. How do you think I knew where she lived? Asshole." The last was said under her breath, but audible enough for Matt to hear.

The guard peered into the car and acknowledged Rachel with a nod. He spoke again into the phone as the gate swung open to let them in. Rachel pointed down a narrow road. After two left turns, they came to an immense ranch-style house surrounded by towering oaks.

He followed a curved driveway to a wide maroon door. Rachel grabbed the door handle and hopped out of the car. She bent to look at him. "You can leave now. Go to Dallas. I hope you find your answers. Be careful though. Don't believe everything you hear."

"Not so fast." Matt turned off the engine and got out. He walked quickly around the front of the car until he was standing next to her. "We're going in together."

She got defensive. "I didn't mention talking to her because the last time I spoke to her, she threatened to call Duncan. She doesn't believe Duncan's a rat and a murderer. That's why she's still set on marrying him."

"Because you have no proof. When have you ever been absolutely straight with me, Rachel?"

"I've always been straight with you. Next time clean your ears." She broke away from him and strode to the door.

He reached her side at the same time the door opened. The woman standing there was not what he expected. Elaine Westerfelt was about as far from Victoria as Duncan could find. A tall, imposing woman with the curvaceous body of a stripper, an angular face, and the shrewd eyes of a hawk stood in front of him. White blond curls perched on top of her head like giant rollers and made her look even taller than she was. She wore riding pants and boots. Matt wondered if she was on her way to the stables or just getting back. He guessed the former from the lack of horse scent on her and the way her curls hadn't flattened from the helmet.

Elaine stepped toward them with both hands outstretched. One hand took Rachel's. With the other, she pulled Matt into the house. "So glad to meet you, Matt. I've heard good things about you. Black Gold is held up as a model for small businesses."

"Thank you," Matt said, feeling uncomfortable. "I didn't know that."

She turned to Rachel. "You look better than expected. How are you feeling?"

Rachel kissed her cheek. "I'm fine, Elaine. You look great, as ever."

"Thank you, dear." Elaine led them into a living room that actually looked lived-in. Two large sofas clustered around a maple coffee table. Throw pillows were scattered in no particular design. A white Persian cat, sitting on one of the pillows, looked up when they entered and leaped off with the grace of a ballet dancer.

"Do you like sun tea?" Elaine said. "I brought in a fresh pitcher this morning. You must be thirsty after such a drive. I can make some sandwiches if you're hungry."

"No, please don't bother," Matt said. "Not for me. I'm not staying."

"You will have some tea, though, won't you?" Elaine didn't wait for his answer but motioned to Rachel. "Come with me, dear. I could use another hand in the kitchen."

Rachel shrugged with indifference and ignored Matt as she followed Elaine.

Matt used the time to study the room, hoping to get a sense of the woman. He was drawn first to the gun cabinet in the corner of the room. Behind the glass doors were both old and new rifles, pistols and automatics. Several hunting rifles were displayed. The woman was a hunter. He wondered if Duncan ever had second thoughts about hunting with this woman.

He could see why Duncan was attracted to Elaine. The woman was CEO of an oil and gas exploration company, which meant she was a competitor. A marriage could merge their two companies, if both agreed. Also, she had the necessary wealth and property. She wasn't what men usually considered beautiful, like Victoria, but Elaine was striking. As a bonus, she fit into his world of guns and horses.

Elaine and Rachel returned to the living room. Elaine balanced a tray of glasses and a pitcher filled with sun tea and placed them on a mat on top of the coffee table. Rachel followed with a large plate of sandwiches, cut in fourths, with the crust cut off, and set it down next to the drinks. She fixed Matt a glass and poured one for herself. After that, she withdrew to a corner of the sofa. Matt sat on the opposite corner and faced a large picture window that framed a peach tree heavy with fruit. The air was fragrant with the scent of lemon and cinnamon.

Elaine eased into an upholstered chair opposite them. "Rachel has told me many times I shouldn't marry her father. What do you think of her allegations?"

"I don't know what to think," Matt admitted. "From what I know, there's no proof to establish guilt. The last time I dealt with Duncan, he tried to get me to invest in one of his prospects. The whole proposal sounded good until I went through the due diligence. I had too many questions and not enough answers. I backed out. I don't think he's ever forgiven me."

Elaine nodded. "I know which one you're talking about. You were smart. The prospect was dead on arrival. And you're right. He hasn't forgiven you. When did you first meet Rachel?"

"A few days ago. At the scene of her accident. I assume you know what happened."

Elaine directed her words to Rachel. "All I know is what you told me over the phone. I would have asked Duncan but you begged me not to bother him about it. You said you were hospitalized, dear. How serious was your injuries?"

When Rachel didn't answer, Matt said, "Not as serious as we initially thought. I'm sure she'll tell you everything in her own good time. That's one reason why she's here."

Elaine picked up her glass and stared into it as if pondering the contents. "And the other reason is to convince me not to marry her father. I know she believes he killed Victoria. She's told me this before."

Rachel said with solemn certainty. "And you'll be next if you marry him,"

Elaine shot her a warning look "News for you, honey, I'm not that easy to kill. Didn't the sheriff rule your mother's death an accident?"

"The sheriff let him get away with cremating her the next day," Rachel said. "Saved him an investigation."

Matt felt the growing tension in the room, He turned to Elaine. "How long have you known Duncan?"

She looked almost relieved at the chance to answer this question. "Almost five years, but we were not romantically involved all that time. Our companies worked a few projects together. We didn't start seeing each other outside of business until after Victoria died. I don't sleep with married men."

Matt was surprised at her candor. He didn't look at Rachel during this exchange, but sensed her discomfort.

Elaine set down her glass and crossed her legs. "I have a few questions for you, Matt. What is your interest in all this? Did you know Victoria?"

"They used to be lovers in college." Rachel piped up. "I'm not kidding. Ask him."

Matt didn't rise to the bait. He kept his irritation from showing. "I knew Victoria in college before she met Duncan. I also proposed to her before Duncan did. I never saw her after their marriage."

"That's more than twenty years," Elaine said. "Did you meet Rachel before she went to find you?"

"Never met her before. In fact, until she showed me her locket with Victoria's picture inside, I had no idea Victoria had a child."

Rachel scooted closer to him. "But Mom kept up with you all those years. Like I said, she told me where to find you if I was ever in trouble."

"Are you in trouble?" Elaine said to her.

"I don't remember getting hurt. Luke was in the car with me. We were arguing. When he realized where I was taking him, he wanted to turn back. That all I remember."

Elaine shook her head. "No, let's go back. You said you were looking for Matt because you were in trouble. The accident happened after you got to Houston. So what made you leave Dallas and your father?"

Rachel took her time answering. "I was turning twenty-one. I thought my father was going to kill me for my inheritance."

Matt exchanges glances with Elaine.

Elaine spoke first. "Why would you think that?"

"He killed my mother for the same reason."

"That doesn't make a lot of sense." Elaine rose to her feet. "He's a millionaire."

"He's a greedy bastard," Rachel said.

Elaine turned to Matt. "Do you buy this?"

Matt slowly shook his head. "I know Rachel is convinced in her heart, but there's no evidence to substantiate her claims."

"Exactly my point," Elaine said. "So why should I believe he'll try to kill me after we're married? What would be his motive? My company? No, he'll have full access."

Rachel's cheeks flushed. "You better have a pre-nup so he won't steal everything from you. Ask my grandfather if you don't believe me. Duncan took his company from him after he married Mom."

"Farley Kittering was paid," Elaine said.

"He was cheated," Rachel said.

Elaine turned from her.

Matt stood, seeing Elaine was getting frustrated with Rachel. "I should be getting on the road."

Elaine nodded. Her smile seemed forced. "Are you going to Dallas to confront Duncan?"

"Of course not," Matt said. "I have no business with him. I'm going to Dallas to get answers from a broker who was arranging financing for Black Gold. That has nothing to do with Duncan."

"Who's the broker?"

"Sterling McAdams. You know him?"

She hesitated. "I've dealt with him on a couple of occasions. Does he know you're coming?"

"Not yet. You see, I'm the one who found Rachel lying on the road. I was on my way to a breakfast meeting with him to firm up the agreements. I was late because I took Rachel to the hospital first."

"Good Samaritan." Elaine looked at him with renewed interest. "What did that do to your meeting? I assume he wasn't pleased. He's a man who insists his business comes before all else. A delay is like a slap in the face to him."

"That's about the size of it," he agreed. "Since then he hasn't answered my calls. So I decided to confront him head on."

"Your timing might be advantageous," she said. "The

Petroleum Club is giving a reception for a member to-night at the Omni Hotel. You can try McAdams at his office, but if you miss him, you might think about crashing the party. He'll likely be there. Potential investors usually show up at these functions as well, so be prepared to give a mini presentation."

"Thanks for the information. I'll do that." He glanced at Rachel. "You don't mind if she stays here?"

Rachel's head jerked up.

"As I told you over the phone," Elaine said, "she can stay as long as she wants. I have plenty of room." She winked at Rachel. "Maybe she'll tell me why Luke accompanied her to Houston. His daddy must be furious at him. Is he back home yet?"

At Luke's name, Rachel stood. "No, he's in jail." She glared at Matt as if the fault was all his.

"For what?" Elaine said, eyes widening.

"They accused him of assaulting me—which he didn't—and of breaking into Matt's house to look for me," Rachel said.

"Why did they charge him for assault?"

"They thought he beat me up and left me. I don't remember what happened, but I know Luke would never hurt me."

"You said he broke into Matt's house to get to you," Elaine said.

Matt said, "He broke the window in the back door to reach the lock. Once the police saw the evidence, they had to arrest him."

"That poor, misguided kid," Elaine said. "Someone has to bond him out."

Matt said, "My lawyer took care of it this morning. He called Luke's father who hired him over the phone and wired the money to pay his bail and a motel room. Luke has to stay in Houston until his hearing. Kurt will likely plead him out."

Elaine gave him a shrewd look. "Can't you have the charges dropped? Have him work off the price of a window."

"It's not my call," Matt said. "It's up to the D.A. and the judge."

"This lawyer, he's good?"

"The best. I'll give you his card. Call him if you ever need a criminal lawyer." He said this as a joke.

Elaine laughed. "I'll take it. You never know these days."

"That's the devil's truth. Life's unpredictable." He smiled. "I'd better get on the road, face what's ahead of me." Matt paused in front of Rachel. "This isn't good-bye."

"I know," she said. "I'll be at Luke's hearing. Don't worry about me. Have fun at the party. Hope you get what you want."

Her tone was flippant, but Matt discerned an underlying sadness in her words. "Thanks, Rachel. I hope you find what you're looking for, too. Be careful out there."

Elaine walked him to the door. "Have a safe trip, Matt. It's been really nice to meet you."

"The same to you." He looked over to Rachel, who watched him with narrowed eyes. He felt an unexpected tug at his heart and felt an urge to go back and give her a goodbye hug.

Instead, he shook Elaine's hand. "Thank you for your generous offer. Rachel has a good heart. She wants justice for her mother. Whether her suspicions are right or wrong, pursuit of the truth as she sees it could cripple her. Unless Duncan confesses, I don't see a resolution."

Elaine nodded in agreement. She gazed into his eyes. "You know, I met Victoria on a few occasions. I liked her very much. She loved her daughter more than anyone in the world. I hope Rachel is wrong about Duncan. If she's right, I don't know what I'll do."

As they reached the door, he ventured another question, thinking he must be crazy for asking. "It's none of my business, and you don't have to answer, but are you marrying him for love or for business?"

She drew back in a show of mock horror. "Why, Matt, are you accusing me of being a gold digger?"

"Not at all," he protested, feeling awkward and embarrassed. "You probably have more money than he has. What do I know about relationships? I couldn't stay married myself."

"Matt, at our age, the question should be, 'What's love got to do with it?'"

They both laughed, and he felt the tension between them slip away. He waved and got into his car. As he drove past the living room window, he caught a glimpse of Rachel with her face pressed against the glass.

CHAPTER 12

Lillian responded to Deborah's urgent call that came shortly after she picked up Luke from the jail and settled him in at the Residence Suites, a motel used for long-term occupants. Earlier that morning Hank Jamison had responded to Kurt's call by retaining his services with a wire that arrived in the firm's account shortly afterward.

Kurt proceeded to get a judge to set bail and then bonded out Luke. Under the conditions ordered by the court, Luke was required to stay in Houston until his case either settled or went to trial.

A dirty, disheveled Luke was shaky and scared. He'd never before been charged with a crime and jail was an experience, he told Lillian, he would never survive again. Kurt had to get him off because he was innocent. He only busted into Matt's house because he thought Rachel was in danger.

"Why would you think that?" Lillian had asked him. "Rachel told you she was coming to see Matt."

"I didn't know Matt. She didn't either. Just because something her mother told her years ago made her feel safe? I don't think so. She doesn't know the world like I do."

Outside of his last claim, his explanation made sense,

sort of. "There's also the matter of how Rachel got her injuries."

Surprisingly, Luke didn't provide an answer. He seemed wary and changed the subject. "I don't get why I have to stay here instead of going home."

Lillian tried to explain, but Luke wasn't listening. When they entered the motel room, he looked at the sterile surroundings with disappointment. He didn't lighten up when she showed him the small kitchenette and separate bedroom with a shower and tub. Instead of complaining, he seemed resigned.

Before she left him, she warned, "If you leave this room without Kurt or me for longer than a half an hour, you'll be back in jail so fast you won't know what happened. I think you'll look more favorably on these surroundings than the place you just left. I'll be back this evening to take you to dinner."

She hadn't got as far as her office when Deborah called her on her cell.

"Meet me at the police impound. You have to see this for yourself," Deborah said. "I don't know what this means to Luke's case, but I need answers, and so do you."

Lillian turned her car around and headed downtown. Deborah's cruiser waited with the engine running outside the entrance of the impound lot until Lillian pulled up behind her. Deborah signaled and rolled through the gate. Lillian followed her in. She tried to ignore the smell of gas fumes mixed with rotting carpet and hot metal that not even her air conditioner covered.

Lillian passed all kinds of cars from Mercedes and BMWs to faded trucks and paint-scratched or dented sedans. They came to a stop behind a row of cars toward the back of the lot. Next to Deborah's cruiser was a red Camaro.

Was this the Camaro that Duncan had bought for Luke?

Lillian grabbed her camera and joined Deborah who stood outside the cruiser. She started clicking away, moving around the car to catch every inch. Even though it was still morning, the heated air was heavy. Humidity seeped into her skin and left a sheen of moisture. She didn't envy her cousin, with all the layers she had to wear with her uniform, in addition to the Velcro, the bullet proof vest, and the heavy belt that held survival equipment, including her Glock 17. Especially hard for her during the summer months, though Lillian had never heard her complain.

Right now Lillian's attention was focused on the Camaro.

"They located it a few blocks away from where Matt found Rachel," Deborah explained.

Lillian tried to reenact the scene in her mind. "Someone rear-ended them. The air bags deployed. This could explain Rachel's injuries, the impact hitting her in the face and chest. This could absolve Luke."

"It's possible. Then why didn't he tell us there was another vehicle, or what happened to the Camaro?"

Lillian wondered the same. "He's obviously scared. Maybe he recognized the driver as someone Duncan sent after them."

Deborah gave her a look of disbelief. "Let's stick to what we do know, which isn't much. A hit and run. Someone didn't stop to render aid. We need to look for a vehicle with front-end damage. Luke didn't show signs he was injured. Was he out of the Camaro when it was hit? Did he or someone else drive the Camaro away from the scene, leaving Rachel unconscious on the road? We need to find the driver and I'm betting Luke can help us. I don't buy a memory lapse."

Lillian nodded in agreement, but she had another question. "What if the damage to the Camaro happened where it was found?"

Deborah frowned. "You mean, with Luke gone and Rachel taking the car?"

"Something like that. They could have argued and Rachel then could have taken the Camaro and driven a few blocks away."

Deborah shook her head. "Then she would have been found there and not where Matt claims he found her."

"You're right. I wish I could get my head around Luke driving off in the Camaro after it had been hit, and leaving Rachel. The kid's in love with her."

"We need answers. I want you to bring Luke back to the station and this time I want the truth from him. This is new information and you know that Kurt will agree."

"I agree, too," Lillian said. "Luke's lied to us."

So has Rachel.

Deborah said, "I can pick him up now if you can get Kurt to meet us there."

"Wait, let me bring in him. I'll make sure Kurt's available and explain everything. This way we can advise Luke and properly prepare him. If he thinks you're going to throw him in jail again, he might clam up or even try to run."

"I wish you wouldn't do that. I like the idea of surprise." Deborah gave another glance at the Camaro then checked her watch. "Make sure he's at the station in two hours. That should give you enough time."

Lillian called Kurt on her way back to the office and explained the situation.

"Pick him up now and I'll meet you at the station," Kurt said. "I don't want him thinking up lies before he gets there, so tell him very little."

Lillian wasn't surprised that he concurred with Deborah. He sounded put out, and Lillian couldn't blame him. Their client had lied or covered up the truth. Not that clients never lied to their attorneys. Happened all the time. But there was no reason for Luke not to reveal that his car had been hit. Did he think the car wouldn't be discovered in its condition? Stupid criminals.

Lillian had worked herself up to a justified anger that she didn't ordinarily waste on clients. She rarely concerned herself about their guilt or innocence. Her job was to ferret out the truth that would satisfy a judge or jury, and get a "not guilty" verdict.

Luke looked up when she unlocked the motel room door and strode in. Her attitude conveyed more than words. His eyes widened in surprise, then fear.

She was glad to see he had showered and changed into the new clothes she had bought him that morning before checking him into the motel. Evidently expecting dinner out with her.

"Are we going out to eat?" he asked, tentatively.

"No, we're going back to the station. Officer Wallace has more questions for you. Your attorney and I will be there with you."

He gave her a wary look. "How come you keep calling her Officer Wallace? I thought she was your cousin."

"She's you're arresting officer," she said with unusual bluntness. "Let's go."

"Right now?"

"Right now."

They were silent during the ride to the station. Luke kept glancing at her, looking increasingly nervous. Lillian couldn't help wondering what he and Rachel were hiding. And why. Kurt was adamant about not prepping Luke in advance, which was unusual. It was one thing to lie about your innocence. It was another to omit a third party that changed everything they knew so far.

Kurt had arrived before them. He approached and peered at Luke, who acted more nervous than scared.

"I'm here to protect you, Luke. But you haven't been fair with me." When Luke said nothing, Kurt shook his head. "I can't help you until you tell me the truth. We have a few minutes before Officer Wallace talks to you." He motioned toward the empty interrogation room.

Luke stared into it for a long moment then nodded. He sat, and Kurt and Lillian each took a side.

Kurt began. "They found your car."

Luke closed his eyes.

"We know you were rear-ended and the air bag exploded. Tell us exactly what happened."

Luke deflated before them. He opened his eyes but didn't look at either. When he finally spoke, his voice was barely audible. "It was like I told you. Rachel and I were arguing about her going to Matt's. She hit me in the face a few times, and I lost control of the car. We swerved off the road. Just as I got us back and straightened out the car, someone smash us from behind. The sound was horrible. He must have been going really fast. I looked over at Rachel and at first I couldn't see her at all. The airbag covered her. It exploded all over her. I tried to tear it away. When I finally saw her face, I nearly gagged. She fell out and crashed to the ground. I heard her head hit the pavement. I screamed and yelled for help." His voice cracked. "It was the worst day ever."

"Luke," Lillian said, "what about the driver of the car who hit you. Did you see him?"

"I—I don't—I—"

"The truth, Luke," Kurt said, "Either you saw him or you didn't. Did he get out of the car?"

Luke squinted as if seeing it all again. "Yes, he stepped closer. He saw Rachel, but didn't touch her."

"Did he say anything?" Kurt said.

Luke shook his head. 'He got back into his car and backed away. He turned around real quick and left."

Kurt kept his voice even. "What kind of car was it?"

"Black. An SUV but I don't know what kind."

Lillian reached her hand toward him. "It was a man. You're sure?"

Luke nodded.

"I need you to be truthful, Luke. Did you recognize him?" Kurt said.

Luke's eyes cleared. First he turned to Kurt and then to Lillian. He cleared his voice. "His name is Valentine Strong. I think Rachel's dad sent him after her."

Lillian exchanged glances with Kurt.

"Why didn't you tell us this before?" Kurt asked.

"I was scared, man. I didn't want him finding Rachel."

Lillian tapped the table to get his attention. "One more question. Why did you leave with the Camaro?"

Luke, for the first time since the questioning had begun, became animated. "I went after the prick. I was hot, man, really hot. He almost killed her and runs off? What kind of a man does that? Especially a mercenary like him."

"Mercenary?" Lillian repeated.

"He was in Afghanistan. He's a trained killer. I just wanted to see where he was going. Then the Camaro stopped running. I got it to the side of the road and it just stopped. I ran back to be with Rachel. She was gone. I couldn't believe it. I thought she woke up and walked away. I went crazy. I figured the only way to find her was to find Matt, and I was right."

Lillian stood as did Kurt. They left Luke sitting there and went out into the hall. Deborah was waiting for them.

"Good work, you two." She gave a thumbs up. "Got it all on record. Take him back to the motel. We need to find Valentine Strong."

CHAPTER 13

When Matt approached Dallas on I-45, road construction obstructed one lane and traffic clogged the other. Dump trucks cluttered the side of the road and emergency vehicles blinked up ahead. He estimated the delay ate up most of an hour. With an effort, Matt put aside his irritation and concentrated on developing a strategy that would get him in the door that once had been readily open to him.

Elaine's suggestion that he attend the reception at the Omni fit in perfectly with his plans. He'd have a chance to talk to some investors in person. All the better if McAdams or Duncan showed up. Or both. He should be so lucky. He was in the mood for a showdown.

He checked into the Ramada on Regal Row. Nothing fancy but it suited his needs and fit into his budget. A king-sized bed and Internet access were his only requirements. He dropped his suitcase on the floor, freshened up in the small bathroom, and changed his shirt before heading out again.

He parked in the covered garage of the Renaissance Tower and took the lobby elevator to the fifteenth floor. The spacious interior of McAdams' office had the air of inactivity. The reception desk in front was empty. Matt listened for the sounds of computers, copy machines, printers. Nothing. He checked his watch. Almost three-thirty. Did they work half-days on Mondays? Or did they close early today because of the party?

He was about to leave when he heard the click of high heels coming down the hall. An attractive young woman emerged and apparently didn't see him. She looked flushed and slightly breathless. With quick strokes she smoothed wrinkles from her navy short skirt. The top three buttons on her white silk blouse were undone. Her bare legs curved like a dancer's and her feet arched in stilettos. Matt stared at her in rapt admiration. He envied the man she left behind in whatever back room they were in. She was blonde with dark roots and appeared to be in her late twenties or early thirties.

She looked up with a quick intake of breath. "Sir? Do you have an appointment?"

He smiled, hoping to put her at ease. "I just arrived from Houston. I hoped to catch Sterling before he left the office for the reception tonight. We had some unfinished business to discuss."

She slid behind her desk and settled into her chair. "Mr. McAdams left already. I don't expect him back to-day."

"That's okay. I'll see him later at the Omni." He start-ed to turn toward the door.

Her voice stopped him. "You said Houston. Are you with the Rosendekker party?"

Matt tried to hide his surprise. Duncan *was* connected to McAdams. But how did the receptionist connect him with Rosendekker? He laughed to cover his confusion. "You nailed it. I'll catch up with them tonight."

She placed one hand on the phone. "I can call Mr. McAdams and let him know you're on your way."

So much for a surprise visit. "No, don't bother. I'll text him. Thanks again for your help."

Her demeanor changed. "What did you say your name was?"

"That's all right. I want to surprise him. Should I give him a message from you? I can pass on a good word, tell him how much you enjoy your work." He gazed toward the hallway, and even craned his head as if he could see through doors to another late-working employee.

She got his meaning. Instead of showing fear, she glared at him, and picked up the receiver and punched a number on the desk phone.

He quickened his steps and left the office. Before the door swung shut, he heard heavy footsteps getting louder. He reached the elevator banks and punched the down button. He glanced to his right toward the stairwell. Before he could decide on the alternate route, the elevator doors eased open and he hurried inside. As the doors closed, he caught a glimpse of the man coming out of the office. Big and burly. Security? The hot receptionist's lover? He rode the elevator down to the lobby and left by the door to the garage.

The Omni Hotel was not called the Crown Jewel of Downtown for nothing. Located within walking distance of the Dallas Convention Center, the hotel was a favorite of conventioneers. If McAdams was out to connect with big money oil investors, he picked the right place. Matt crawled up the circular drive in front of the hotel and waited for the valet to take his keys.

Once inside he crossed the lobby's glossy tiled floor to the bar area. A few suits sat at the bar. He didn't see McAdams. The man could have reserved one of the many meeting rooms on the second floor, but Matt wasn't about to barge in and interrupt a business meeting. After the disastrous breakfast in Houston, another fiasco would put him on the permanent do-not-call list.

He took a chance that the day's meeting times and

room numbers would be scrolled across a marquee by the elevator banks. He wasn't disappointed. He was reading the scroll when the elevator beside him opened. Several men in suits got out, murmuring to each other. Matt's attention was drawn to them and his chest tightened as he recognized three potential investors who had recently turned him and his company down. They took no notice of him, engrossed as they were in talks of the next big oil gusher.

The last man exiting the elevator was Sterling McAdams. Matt watched him shake the hand of the man next to him followed by a smile of satisfaction when he thought he was finally alone.

"Looks like you had a successful meeting," Matt said from behind him. "I hope Black Gold was the subject of your upcoming plans."

McAdams whirled around. "Matt." His shocked expression quickly disappeared, leaving him with an air of puzzlement. "I didn't know you were going to be here."

"I have friends with the Petroleum Club," Matt said, pasting on a cool smile. "I caught the moldy scent of my former investors. I figured I'd ask them in person why they declined my offer. I don't need a broker to get an explanation."

McAdams gripped Matt's upper arm and attempted to steer him away from the others, several of whom had slowed to look at them. "This is not the place nor the time for this."

Matt dug in his heels. "I disagree. This is the perfect place and time. I'm not going anywhere."

McAdams faked a smile for the men in his company. He waved and called out, "Go ahead. I'll join you shortly." He turned eyes that glittered with annoyance toward Matt and lowered his voice. "How did you know where I'd be?"

"Who said I was looking for you? Oh, I guess you got a call from your receptionist."

"Yvonne."

"Guess she was suspicious. I narrowly missed your security guy."

"What? She sent Brian after you?"

"If he's the bulky giant I saw."

McAdams gave a deep chuckle. "Sorry about that."

"You have enemies?"

"Naw, nothing like that. But it pays to be careful." McAdams glanced toward the bar. "Let's get a drink. People are staring at us."

"Fine," Matt agreed.

McAdams led the way to a secluded corner of the room. They sat in cream-colored leather chairs that flanked a rectangular glass table. Canned music played softly in the background. A waitress, in a short black skirt and matching vest, took their drink order seconds after they settled in their chairs.

McAdams crossed his legs and looked around. "We got a good crowd tonight. The weather is holding up, thank goodness. How was your trip up?"

"I'm not here for small talk," Matt said. "I want to know what happened to the funding. You approved all the specs a month ago. We were all set to sign the papers. With no warning, all your people backed out."

McAdams brought out a thick brown cigar and ran his thumb and forefinger down its length. "It's the economy. The price of oil has plummeted. You read the reports. This is not the time to invest."

"Bullshit. I see some of the investors are here. I'm going to talk to them and find out what spooked our deal."

"Go ahead. But they won't listen to you."

"You've brokered the deal with someone else?" Matt suggested.

"I'm not at liberty to say," McAdams said.

"Who is it? Duncan Rosendekker?"

A look of surprise crossed McAdams's face. "Why would you bring up that name?"

"It would answer most of my questions."

"What questions? Look, Matt, your prospect is not in the best location, and the reports I'm seeing doesn't support an infusion of capital right now."

"Then I'll ask him personally. He's here, isn't he?"

"Not at the moment," McAdams said. "Do you know him well?"

"Well enough." Matt was getting tired of the man's evasive tactics. "Maybe the Petroleum Club has some answers. They look down on any ethics violation. The way I see it, taking business away from me and giving it to my worst and most dishonest competitor would be looked upon as unethical."

McAdams stared at him for a long moment. Then burst into laughter. "You *do* know Duncan."

Matt wasn't sure how to take this sudden reversal of tone. Mentioning the Petroleum Club certainly didn't hurt. Getting on the wrong side of them could ruin a career. "Sure I do. Ever since college. Almost did business with him before. Won't do it again."

McAdams put a hand on Matt's shoulder. "Look, there's been no deal yet and most of the investors will be at the party. Duncan will be there, too. I'm happy to broker any deal that I can work out."

"Glad to hear it," Matt said.

Their drinks arrived and McAdams signed the tab.

Matt sipped his scotch and water. "Shame about what happened to his wife. I only heard about the accident recently."

"Ahhh, yes, Victoria," McAdams nodded. "Such a tragedy. We were all in shock."

"So you knew Victoria?"

"Quite a woman. We all miss her. Did you know her?"

"I'm the one who introduced them. We were in college together. She was the most beautiful woman I'd ever seen. Not just beautiful, but sweet tempered and kind …" Matt stopped himself.

McAdams choked back a laugh. "Are we talking about the same woman? You got the beauty part right. But the Victoria I knew was a spitfire with a temper to match. She turned a lot of men's heads. Shrewd, too. Good head for business. Better than Duncan, in some respects. Don't tell Duncan I said so." He stopped, seeing Matt's face. "I'm sorry she died. Two years now, right? Were you two close? After college, I mean."

Matt swallowed the words that clogged his throat and managed to loosen his fists. He fought the urge to smash McAdams's face before he could speak again, and forced himself to keep his voice calm. "I guess she changed after she married Duncan. I heard they had a daughter."

McAdams squinted at him. "Yes, Rachel. What I've seen, the girl takes after her mother. No offense. Duncan says she's all the way out of control. She takes off on a whim, doesn't tell him anything. Don't envy him at all. The good news is she's turned twenty-one."

Matt needed to change the subject before he said something he couldn't take back. "Did I tell you why I was late to our meeting in Houston? There was an injured and unconscious girl on the road. I had to take her to the hospital. She's recovered except for some bruising."

"Okay." McAdams looked confused. "And you're telling me this…why?"

"Rachel is that girl."

For several moments McAdams didn't speak. Finally, he said, "You're shitting me. Last I heard, she took off and hasn't been seen. All this time she's been with you?"

"That's right."

"Better watch it with Duncan. You can get in real trouble harboring his daughter."

"That was her choice. Like you said, she's twenty-one. She doesn't answer to anyone, and now she has the money to live as she likes."

McAdams's eyes narrowed. "Her inheritance, you mean."

"You seem to know a lot about Duncan and his family. Does he also influence your business decisions?"

"Are you asking me if Duncan had anything to do with the investors pulling out of your deal?"

"It's an honest assumption, given our history. Though it's a mystery as to why he would pick now to screw me over."

"I don't have an answer for you, Matt. Come to the party tonight. Talk to Duncan. I'm sure he'll be relieved to know Rachel is well. I'll do what I can for you. I have nothing to gain by seeing your company lose its funding." He paused then grinned. "Hey, maybe you can get Rachel to pitch in. I hear her trust fund is more than enough to fund several companies. Bet she'd do it just to get even with Duncan. Did she tell you what she thinks? Practically accused him of murder."

Matt stopped listening. *Her trust fund is more than enough to fund several companies.* That hadn't occurred to Matt. McAdams said it in jest, but what if…

CHAPTER 14

Lillian's research found very little documentation on Valentine Strong that would pinpoint his whereabouts. The little bits of information she gleaned from Luke only led her to believe he was either lying or holding back. Rachel must know him but neither she nor Matt were in town.

She returned to the motel and knocked on the door. Luke didn't look happy to see her.

He asked, "I'm not going back to jail, am I?"

"Absolutely not. I promised to take you to out to eat. It's too early for dinner, but I can take you to lunch. How does the Hard Rock Café sound?"

A smile lit his face. "Cool. I'll go for that."

Most of the conversation on the drive over was small talk, with her doing the most talking. His face became animated when he looked up at the huge guitar above the entrance. Inside he became a star struck teenager. A wooden bar took up the middle of the room with booths against both walls. A waitress seated them halfway down the left side in a booth with leather-covered bench seats. The whiff of beer, grilled meat, and fried onions hovered in the air. Decorating the wall were photos and paintings of famous rock stars alongside signed guitars. Luke studied them all until the waiter took their order.

While they waited for their food, Luke went on about the different rock musicians he had seen in Dallas and the CDs he had collected over the years. He only stopped talking when the oversized hamburgers and fries arrived with frosted glasses of Root Beer.

Lillian waited until they finished eating and their glasses were refilled. "Glad you like the place. The food was good, too, wasn't it?"

"The best. Thanks, Miss Wallace."

"Call me Lillian."

He heard the difference in her voice and comprehension overcame his enthusiasm. "There's a catch, isn't there?"

"Not much of one. A little *quid pro quo* is all. As you know, our job is to get the assault charges cleared and off your record. To do that we need to place the blame where it belongs."

His gaze dropped to the table. "What do you mean?"

"Don't play dumb. You know who I'm talking about. Valentine Strong. You brought up his name. Now I need the rest. Who is he and where can I find him?" She watched his reaction. The guy was so easy to read.

Doubt flitted across his face followed by anxiety and finally resignation. "He goes by Val. Nobody calls him Valentine."

"You did," she reminded him. "So tell me about Val."

"Not much to tell. He works part-time for Farley Kittering, Rachel's grandfather. Does stuff like take care of the old man's ranch. Lives there part of the time ever since Mr. Kittering had his stroke. But he's also got an apartment in the city. He used to work on the rigs and do some explosive work. He mostly freelances."

Lillian asked, "Didn't you tell me he was a mercenary?"

Luke swallowed. "He did some contract work in Afghanistan. That's being a mercenary, isn't it? I heard he used to be Special Forces, a SEAL maybe, in the Gulf war. He never talks about it."

"He sounds dangerous. Is that why you didn't tell us about him?"

His head bobbed. "Yeah, that's why. You don't cross the guy. I didn't want to get him involved. I thought Rachel's father sent him after us. I didn't know any other reason Val be following us."

Lillian held up a hand to stop him. "Why would Rachel's father send him?"

Luke blinked rapidly. "I don't know. To stop Rachel from finding Matt? Fuck, I don't know. Ask him."

"I'd like to if I can find him. Do you think Val was trying to stop Rachel when he crashed into your car?"

Luke squirmed. "Shit, I don't know. That's why I got the hell outta there."

"Leaving Rachel behind, knowing she was hurt." She could hear the anger in her tone.

His eyes widened. "No, I led him away from her. I didn't know she was that hurt. I went back after I lost Val but she was gone."

"Where did you go after you dumped your car?"

"I didn't dump my car. Are you kidding? It stopped running." He wiped the sweat off his forehead with his napkin. "The middle of nowhere. I had to hoof it until I found Mr. Langdon's house."

"Let's get back to the crash. You thought Val intended to hurt you and Rachel?"

"Naw. Just stop her. Might knock me around some for driving her. But he'd never hurt her. He was like her godfather, or something, when she was young."

Now Lillian was confused. "So you're saying he only wanted to talk to Rachel. Then why did you run?"

"First of all, I didn't know it was him at first. Couldn't

see through his tinted windows. It was only when he stepped out of the car that I recognized him. He looked really pissed. My first thought was to get the hell outta there. I thought he'd stay there with Rachel, but he took off after me. I figured he went back when he couldn't find me. I thought he took Rachel to the hospital. But it was Mr. Langdon"

"Did Rachel see Val?" Lillian knew she hadn't mentioned Val in her statement.

"I don't know." Luke frowned. "Didn't she say?"

She didn't answer. Instead she asked, "Is Rachel your girlfriend, Luke?"

He put his elbows on the table and dropped his head in his hands. "She was, but now she thinks she's too old for me."

Lillian turned to hide a smile. Did Rachel phrase those words? If so, she was more diplomatic than Lillian remembered. "Any idea where I can find Val?"

Luke shrugged. "No, but my dad might."

Lillian paid for their meal and brought him back to the motel. After seeing him in, she sat in her car and punched Hank Jamison's number in her phone.

He picked up on the second ring. When she explained what she'd learned from his son, he became outraged. "That's the sonofabitch hit his car? Wait 'til I see him."

"Hank, wait. Let me talk to him first. I need him to back up Luke's story. Do you have his number?"

"I got it here somewhere. I can't believe this. He hasn't said a word to me. Hang on." Hank came back on the line a moment later and reeled off the number. "Listen, if you can get to Dallas tonight, he'll be at the Omni Hotel for a reception given by the Petroleum Club. He's scheduled to speak. I can point him out. I'll be at the affair with Duncan. It's black tie. Hadn't been looking forward to going until now. What do you say?"

"I say I'll be there. Tell Val I want to talk him, but don't say why."

Hank chuckled. "If he crashed Luke's car, he'll damn sure know why the attorney's investigator wants to talk to him."

"Then wait until I get there to tell him. That way he won't have a chance to think up a lie."

Two hours later she packed a bag and got back into her car. The sun slipped below the horizon as Lillian drove toward Dallas. To fill the hours she let her imagination play with the information Luke and Hank had told her about Val's background. She pictured him tall with massive muscles, laser-red eyes, maybe a cruel mouth. Someone who would crash into a car and leave an injured girl lying on the street. The thought made her grit her teeth in anger. As the drive along the interstate became more monotonous, she added to his resume Secret Service agent, CIA operative, and hit man.

She laughed to herself. Enough fun and games. Time to plan her strategy with the real Val Strong, whoever he might turn out to be.

She arrived at the hotel and handed her car keys to the valet. It didn't take her long to follow the party noises to the reception. Hank said he'd point out Val, but how would she find Hank? She had only dealt with him over the phone, never in person. As her gaze went from one face to another, she realized she was hoping to see Val, not Hank. She had been too busy letting Val Strong entertain her on the four hour-long drive. She had to deal with reality. He probably didn't look at all like she pictured him.

For this job, she'd chosen to wear a short, black leather skirt and an expensive silver blouse. Her shapely legs were bare and ended with black low-heeled shoes. To complete the look, she'd swept her burgundy hair into a twist with strands curling against her pale skin. She sensed heads turning in her direction as she entered the room. The practiced routine worked every time.

Lillian scanned the groups of men and women, playing their part with drinks in hand, negotiating whatever deals they had come to negotiate. Several bars were set up around the room with guests lined up, waiting for refills. Canned pop music played in the background.

She didn't see anyone who fit her idea of Val Strong. She stepped out of the room and moved to a bank of telephones in one of the corridors. One other person, a man with his back to her, used another phone. She sat on one of the stools, crossed her legs, and opened her contacts for Hank's number.

A raspy voice behind her said, "You must be Lillian Wallace."

She turned and faced the speaker. He was tall and lean, with wide shoulders. His face was weather toughened, pockmarked, with thin lips and sea blue eyes set deep under a shelf of wiry brows. His hair was a mix of black, brown and gray strands, pulled back into a short ponytail.

She worked her throat to swallow. He was sexier looking than her imagination had taken her. "Val Strong?" she asked.

"Yup."

"How did you know I was here?"

"Hank said you wanted to talk to me." Val's gaze swept over her. "His description didn't do you justice."

How did Hank know what she looked like? Then she realized. "He was describing the picture of me on the firm's website. We never met in person."

"I'll bet the picture didn't do you justice. Ninety percent of the women here already hate you."

She laughed "They need to get a life." She looked

down the corridor. "Is there some place private where we can talk?"

He pointed to a room set apart from the reception area. "No one has discovered this haven yet. Won't last that way long."

Inside, she saw a circular bar and several candlelit tables. He led her to the back of the room and to a small round table with two cushioned arm chairs.

"What are you drinking?" he asked.

"I'll take a glass of Riesling."

He went to the bar and came back with her wine and a dark beer for himself. With all the scenarios she had pictured on the drive over, none of them came close to this reality.

He sat across from her and crossed his legs. His eyes seemed to devour her until she became self-conscious.

"Don't do that," she said, her voice barely audible.

He gave a sideways grin. "Do what?"

"Look at me that way," she said.

He shifted slightly to his right. "I didn't mean to make you uncomfortable. I'm just curious. What makes a beautiful woman choose an invasive profession like investigating witnesses and criminals?"

"Wow. That's a mouthful. Do you mean, what makes a woman choose such a profession? Beauty has no relevance here."

He shook his head. "Not true. A beautiful woman can elicit more information from a male subject than could a plain woman or another man. Don't you agree?"

Despite her intention of conducting a reasonable interview with this man, his words and attitude unleashed a barrage of resentment against condescending men that she had kept buried until now. "I have no opinion," she replied. "Whatever is in the eye of the subject beholder should have no relevance to the answers. Either the subject is telling the truth or he's lying. Or he's trying to discredit or distract the interrogator before she has a chance to interrogate."

He sat back, an amused smile spreading across his face and reaching his eyes. "Bravo. Rachel must love you."

She didn't smile. "Rachel should hate you for what you did to her. You should have been behind bars for assault, not Luke."

He frowned and his body went tense. "You are ready to convict me without hearing me out?"

"You made a mockery of me and this meeting, Mr. Strong. I shouldn't have had to come here to Dallas to talk to you. You should have come forward immediately and told the police what happened. Rachel could have died for all you knew or cared."

His lips thinned. "Do I need a lawyer, Miss Wallace?"

"I'm not the police, Mr. Strong." She felt rage so strong it burned her face. She could not see anything but his SUV smashing into the red Camaro and then chasing Luke without knowing or caring how he injured Rachel or if she survived at all. She had to bite her tongue to keep more accusations spewing out. "If I was the police, I'd have you arrested."

He stood, rigid with anger. "I think we're done here. You aren't here to listen, only to convict. You've already made up your mind about me."

He turned and strode out of the bar.

She sat without moving, seeing red dots flash before her eyes. Her head pounded. This did not fucking go the way she intended. She'd totally blown it for Luke. She reached for her wine but her hand shook so hard she withdrew it and pressed her chest. Her hand never shook. Hadn't in all her years working investigations of all types. She had allowed Val Strong to intimidate and overwhelm her. Tears stung her eyes. She saw through blurred vision his glass of beer still untouched. She wanted to brush it off the table and let the glass break and watch the dark liquid spread across the polished wood floor.

Hank would know she failed Luke. He would fire Kurt. Kurt would blame her. The charges of assault would stick on Luke like tar paper. She pressed her knuckles against her mouth to hold back anguished sobs.

She felt a presence behind her. She twisted around and looked up, expecting to find Hank.

Val Strong looked down at her, his face void of emotion. "How is Rachel?"

Without waiting for an answer he returned to his seat and lifted his beer glass to his lips.

She stared at him, feeling her heart slam against her chest. "Better than how you left her."

"I would never hurt her."

"Then someone else must have been driving your black SUV. Does it still have front end damage? Or did you destroy the evidence?" *Like her father did after killing her mom.*

His jaw worked. "What did she say about me?"

"Nothing. If she saw you, she never said. I didn't know about you until Luke told me what happened."

He looked down at his hands. "She probably never saw me. What did Luke say?"

"No way. I want to hear your version if you're willing to tell me."

He nodded slowly. "Fair enough." He looked up. "You wearing a wire?"

She snorted with impatience. "No. This isn't for court. You can testify at his hearing if it comes to that."

His jaw muscles jumped. "Believe it or not, Miss Wallace, I'm not a bad guy. I've looked after Rachel since she was a baby. She's like my own daughter. I knew Victoria before she ever married Duncan. Any suspicions that I could hurt her makes me crazy."

"Why did you come back?"

"I couldn't let my personal feelings hurt Rachel or Luke. You want to hear the truth. I'm here to give it."

Lillian reached for her drink. Her hand was steady this time and she took a long swallow before setting it down. He finished his beer and waved to the bartender, holding up two fingers.

"Hank told me that Luke was driving Rachel to Houston. Duncan was raving like the maniac he is. Luke has known Rachel all her life, but recently his hormones caused him to look at her as a woman, not the tomboy who hiked and swam the creek with him. He would do anything she asked even if it meant defying her father. Hank was concerned about what Duncan might do to Luke if he left with Rachel."

The bartender delivered their drinks. Val signed the tab and waited until they were alone.

"I confronted Rachel and told her not to go. She was adamant. Said there was someone she had to see because her mother told her he could be trusted. I guessed she was looking for Matt."

"You know Matt?" Lillian said.

He gave a half-smile. "Sure. We were both in love with Victoria during our college years. That's why Duncan was so crazy mad Rachel would leave him to go to Matt. When I heard they had left for Houston, I went after them. I didn't tell anyone my plans. Hell, I didn't have a plan. See that Rachel was safe, that's all. I caught up with the Camaro on the interstate and followed them. When he turned off, I lost him. I doubled back and found them on that little shit road. I saw the Camaro coming off the shoulder. Saw it skid to a stop. Saw Luke and Rachel fighting, and that's when I lost it."

"What do you mean, you lost it? So you rammed them?"

"I only intended on bumping their fender. My foot slipped and I hit them harder than I meant to. I got out to see if anyone was hurt, but Luke turned and saw me and gunned the Camaro. He shot out of there and I took off after him. I thought they were both in the car." He slammed his fist on the table making it jump and knocking over Lillian's wine glass.

Lillian didn't take her eyes off Val. "When did you realize Rachel wasn't with Luke?"

"When I found the Camaro. The airbag was deflated on the passenger's side. I saw blood on the steering wheel and the seat. Luke and Rachel weren't in the car. I went back to the crash site. That's when I saw blood on the ground and realized she must have fallen out the car. I swear I didn't see her fall."

"That's not what Luke said. He told me you got out of your car and saw Rachel."

Val frowned. "No, I got out of the car but I didn't see her. I wouldn't have gone after Luke if I'd seen her on the ground. Luke's mistaken. He might have thought I saw her, but I didn't. I didn't know what happened to her. I called the hospitals but no one could tell me anything. There had been no injured female brought in by ambulance."

Lillian studied him. His face looked gray and drawn and miserable. She wanted to believe him. "There was no ambulance because Matt found her and drove her in his car to the medical clinic."

He nodded and wiped his face with his hands.

"I'll need you to write this down in your own words for the court."

"Anything you need. Now tell me about Rachel. I heard she was staying with Matt."

"You heard right. She suffered a few superficial wounds, bruised ribs and a concussion. Serious enough injuries to keep her in the hospital a couple of days. The bruises are still visible, but other than headaches, she's recovered. I'm sure she'd like to see you and get your version of what happened."

"I'll come to Houston and give a formal statement for the court."

"Good." She looked around the room. A few partiers had discovered the quiet bar and the noise level was rising.

He bent down and picked up her empty wine glass. "Can I get you another?"

"No, thanks. I'd like to meet Hank now."

As they stood a woman in a tight red dress rushed up to them. "Darling, what are you doing? Jose is looking for you. You can't just sneak out on us." Her eyes pointed like lasers at Lillian. "Val, who is this woman?"

"Cool it, Karen. Tell him I'll be there in a minute."

"They're getting ready to make the announcement." Karen's searing gaze didn't waver from Lillian. "Dear, you mustn't hog all Val's attention. He has more important things to do than buy whatever you're selling." She looked Lillian up and down as if the sight offended her.

Lillian poured sugar into her voice. "Don't worry, honey. I'm not here to take over your corner."

Val chuckled, which only made Karen's open mouth drop lower. "Karen, darling, go back and tell Jose to keep his pants on. I'll be there on time. Have you seen Hank?"

"You mean King Rosendekker's shadow? They're near the balcony." Karen gave one more poisonous glance at Lillian before sweeping out of the room.

Lillian stared after her. "Who is that woman?"

"Nobody. Unfortunately, she hasn't owned up to that yet."

She eyed him, thinking again of Luke's description. Navy. Army. Special Forces. Mercenary. "What are you doing here, giving hand to hand combat lessons? Checking the room for bombs?"

He grinned. "The Petroleum Club hired me."

"As a bouncer or a spy?"

This time he laughed outright.

They returned to the party where the aroma of perfume, smoke, beer and hot air assailed her. He led her to a man with a thick neck, a running back's shoulders, and ruddy skin. A small mole marked his chin. Black hair shot liberally with gray receded toward the back of his head. He was almost at the tail end of a joke and laughing harder than his audience. When he saw Val, his laugh cut off.

Then he saw Lillian. His gaze rose and fell over her. Every inch of her body felt exposed under the hungry eyes of a predator. A visceral wave of shattered memories came flying back and spiraling in her head. She gripped onto the present with all her strength and let the memories fade. The voice she assumed belonged to Duncan Rosendekker put a rod down her back.

"Who is this?" he said, his voice a drawl.

Val watched her reaction. "Lillian Wallace. She works for Hank's lawyer. Where is Hank? He's usually protecting your back, Duncan."

Duncan glared at him. "I'm always watching his. Watch your tongue." He turned back to Lillian. This time he kept his gaze on her face. "What do you do at the law office, Miss Wallace?"

"I'm his investigator," she said.

"Really? Who are you investigating here?" Duncan

jerked his thumb toward Val. "Of course, it's obvious. You're investigating this rogue. This must be about the accident he caused, the one that hurt my daughter and got Luke arrested." His eyes glittered with malice, but no emotion affected his dry tone. "I hope you know what to do with him."

Before Lillian could respond, a new voice tinted with a Texas twang joined them. He was taller and slimmer than Duncan and looked more like a teacher than an oil-man. "Lillian Wallace, I believe. I see you found Val. I'm Hank, as you've probably guessed."

Val's neck and shoulders relaxed as he faced Hank. Lillian breathed, relieved. She expected any moment to see Val let a fist fly into Duncan's soft mouth. Instead, he was calm.

"I told Miss Wallace I would drive down to Houston and make a formal statement if that will help Luke."

Hank smiled. "I knew you'd do the right thing."

"She's a good negotiator," Val said, looking at Lillian. "She knows how to handle herself, especially in present company. Lillian, very nice to meet you. Let's talk later. I'm due to give a speech in a few minutes. See you, Hank." He paused before Duncan. "Don't make matters worse for Rachel." Val spun on his heel and left Duncan with his mouth open.

Hank steered Lillian away from Duncan. "How's my son? Hanging in there?"

"He's doing well. He'll be free to come home soon."

"That's why I hired Kurt."

Lillian couldn't help posing her next question. "What's wrong with Duncan?"

Hank looked puzzled. "What do you mean?"

"He didn't even ask how his daughter was doing."

"She must have called and reassured him."

Lillian wanted to believe him, but Rachel's attitude

toward her father demonstrated a rebellious and angry relationship.

Hank looked over her shoulder and his eyes widened. "Is that who I think it is? Where is he—Oh, hell no, I've got to stop him. He's heading right for Duncan."

Lillian turned to see who Hank meant. She had a different reaction than Hank's. "I'm not surprised to see him. He's looking for answers to save his company. Most of the investors are in this room. Why are you so worried?"

Hank looked at her in surprise. "I didn't realize you knew Matt that well. He's the guy charging Luke for breaking into his house."

"He's dropping those charges," Lillian said.

Duncan had seen Matt. He inched closer to Hank and Lillian. "Well, what do you know? Another sonofabitch. This place is shitting with the little buggers. Hey, Lillian, did he come with you?"

She barely heard him. Instead, she was seeing Matt's red face. He was aiming at Duncan Rosendekker like a boxer in the main event.

CHAPTER 15

From the moment Matt had stepped into the Omni Hotel and merged with the party, his sole purpose had been to demand answers. The first potential investor he had recognized was Roger Harding, waiting in line in front of a small bar. Matt forced a smile and led with his hand out.

"Roger, thought I might find you here. You got a minute?"

"Matt." Roger looked startled. "Didn't expect to see you tonight."

"McAdams suggested I stop by. Greg tried calling you last week."

Roger looked around as if seeking a way out. "Sorry, Matt. My wife is waiting. Have to run. Can't talk now. Maybe later."

"Sure," Matt said to empty air. He scanned the room. Found another potential investor who hadn't returned his call and marched over to him. "Bill, have a minute?"

The man's eyes widened. "Sorry, Matt, but I have to meet someone. Good seeing you, though. We'll catch up later."

He, too, left Matt standing and feeling like he'd been punched.

Determined now, and growing more desperate, he

moved quickly around the room like a shark sniffing blood. Spotted another on his list. The guy saw him coming and moved away but not fast enough. Matt caught up with him. "Hey, dude, what's up with the knife in my back?"

"What? Jesus, Matt. You talk to McAdams?"

"Yeah. He didn't have much to say, except to suggest I talk to Duncan. Have you seen him?"

"He's over there somewhere."

At that moment, he heard his name. "Matt?" He turned and saw a friendly face.

"Hank, you got to help me." Matt heard the fear in his voice and started again. "I've been trying to talk to these guys. You heard what happened? Investors pulling out, nobody answering the calls. Is Duncan having the same trouble?"

Hank's tone conveyed sympathy as he steered Matt toward the door. "This is a bad time, Matt. You recognize the climate. Oil prices dropping, gas prices lower than ever, everyone's panicking."

Matt worked to steady his breathing. "Not everyone, Hank. Duncan seems to be riding this out on a jet stream. How is he profiting and I'm not? I can't help but wonder if he's stealing investors from me and other companies like mine. You know where I'm coming from, Hank. I'm talking from experience. He screwed me once before."

"You got this all wrong, Matt. Nobody's out to screw you. Let's get together tomorrow and talk. This is not the time or place."

"Talk about what? If you don't have answers, it's all bullshit and you know it. Hey, I got an idea. Maybe Duncan's targeted me because I have his daughter."

Hank shook his head. "I wouldn't bring up Rachel right now, Matt. That's a raw subject with him. Let's keep things civil. This is a party."

Matt ran his hands through his hair. "Sorry, Hank. I know it's not your fault. You got your own troubles. I've met your son, you know. He's really a good kid. He broke into my house to find Rachel. That's why I'm not pressing charges. He thought she was in danger. Think of it, Hank. Duncan's daughter came to me. That must really piss him off."

Hank put his hand on Matt's shoulder. "Matt, you need to leave. This can wait."

Matt shook him off. "You hired the right lawyer for Luke. Kurt's my lawyer, too. Did you know that? Did the paperwork for Black Gold. Even he thinks I'm being screwed."

"Kurt came highly recommended. Did you know his investigator is here tonight?"

Matt stopped cold. He stared at Hank in stunned silence. "Lillian Wallace?"

"She's here to talk to a witness for Luke." Hank looked to his right and waved. "There she is."

Matt looked in time to see her wave back. His prior encounters with the investigator hadn't stood out in his mind as extraordinary, but this Lillian was different from what he remembered. This Lillian was strikingly beautiful. Strange he'd never noticed before.

Lillian traversed the distance between them with surprising calmness. "Matt, I knew you were coming to Dallas, but it's still a surprise to see you here. Did you bring Rachel?"

Hank's head jerked around as if Rachel might be standing behind him.

Matt reassured him. "I took her to Elaine's. She didn't want to be anywhere close to Duncan, and I didn't want to leave her at my house."

Lillian nodded her approval. "Especially with Aaron there."

Hank glanced to his left where Duncan stood in a corner with a group of men. He lowered his voice. "Rachel's staying with Duncan's fiancé?"

"Is that a bad thing?" Lillian asked.

"It is if Duncan finds out," Matt said. "He wouldn't be happy to learn the two women have been communicating for quite a while."

"He's forbidden them to talk to each other?" Lillian sounded incredulous. "He's planning to marry her. She'll be Rachel's stepmother."

"Unless Rachel convinces her otherwise," Matt said.

Hank looked furtively toward Duncan. "Duncan's already seen you. Let me talk to him first." He hurried off.

"Sorry," Matt said to Lillian. "This is feeling awkward."

"No problem," she said. "Are you having any luck reaching the investors?"

"None at all," he admitted. "I seem to be poison around this crowd. What brings you here?"

"Meeting with a witness for Luke's case. I think you know him. Val Strong?"

The name hit him like a splash of ice water. "That's a name out of the past," he said with an uneasy laugh. "How is he a witness? Rachel never mentioned him."

"Deborah found Luke's car. Someone crashed the back. I think the airbags exploded in Rachel's face. That caused Rachel's injuries. Luke never beat her up."

"Let me guess. Val drove the other car. Sonofabitch. He's here right now? I want to talk to him."

"Later." A look of apprehension came over her face. "Until you hear the whole story, don't jump to convict."

"Why didn't he call the police? Did he say? He should have been the one to take her to the hospital."

Lillian kept her voice even. "I know you have questions, and Val will answer them. Suffice it to say, once

Val's statement gets into the record, the charges against Luke will be dropped."

"Not good enough. What will Val be charged with?" Matt demanded, feeling his stomach churn.

"That's up to the DA."

Frustrated again, Matt scanned the room, but saw no one that halfway resembled Val Strong. "It's been years since I saw Val. I probably won't even recognize him."

He had a picture in his head of a young Val in uniform, getting ready to leave for Afghanistan. They were at the Kittering ranch celebrating going to war in a distant land. It was the last time he occupied the same room with Val, Duncan, and Victoria. That was over twenty years ago. The only person missing now was Victoria. He felt the familiar tightening in his chest when he thought of Victoria. He turned away from Lillian and blinked rapidly.

Lillian didn't seem to notice. "I've got what I came for. Val is one of the speakers at the dinner. There's no reason for me to stay."

"Are you getting a room for the night?"

"Not sure yet," she said.

"How about meeting me for a coffee or drink in, say, an hour from now?"

She smiled. "Deal."

He watched her move away. Her hips swayed slightly, unconsciously, naturally. When she was out of sight, he turned back to the reception, hoping to see Val, but looked for McAdams.

He spotted a potential investor he had missed earlier. He took several steps toward the man but was blocked by Duncan's bulk. He'd expected to see him sometime that evening. He didn't expect to have Rachel's accusations shout in his head. He saw a murderer, not the oil executive.

Duncan made the mistake of shoving him. "We got shit to talk about."

Matt instinctively shoved back. "What shit is that, Duncan?"

"I heard Rachel found you."

"That's right. What about it?"

"Why did she go to you?"

"Ask her."

Duncan poked his chest. "I'm fucking asking you, asshole."

The gesture unleashed a flare of anger in Matt. "She doesn't answer to you. She's an adult. She goes wherever she wants."

Duncan's bulbous nose flared. "You've been in touch with her all these years, haven't you?"

Matt laughed. "Sorry, but no."

"Then how did she know about you?"

"Ask your wife. No, wait. Must have been before you shot her head off."

Duncan froze. He didn't speak for several seconds. "What did you just say? You fucking bastard. Rachel said that, didn't she? She's a crazy bitch. Everyone knows Victoria's death was a terrible accident."

"Can't prove otherwise. But you'll never convince her daughter it wasn't murder."

Duncan's eyes flicked sideways. A small crowd gathered to watch them.

He lowered his voice. "I know what's eating you, Langdon. You can't find any investors to fund your prospects. You'd like to blame me. Won't work. Why would I waste my time on you?"

"You tell me. No one else will. Not one investor who originally signed on will go ahead with the deal. They were willing once. Who changed their mind, and why?"

"You think I influenced them? Sorry you're in trouble,

but that's your problem. You're nothing to me. You got nothing I want. Except—" He lowered his face until he was an inch away from Matt's face. "—one. You've got something that belongs to me and I want her returned."

Matt backed away from the fumes that spoiled the air between them. "Rachel. Ah yes. Because she's now fully in control of her trust fund and she won't give you a penny." He watched Duncan's jaw line tense and his eyes get smaller. The sight spurned him on. "She came to me at the perfect time. Think about it, Duncan. I don't need these investors when I've got Rachel." The words flew out of his mouth, surprising him. Had he ever really considered that idea?

Duncan's face turned a reddish orange under the artificial lighting. His words spit at Matt. "Old man Kittering wasn't in his right mind when he formed that trust for Victoria. You think Rachel will give that money to you? Hell no, she'll have it squandered in a year."

"That's really eating you up. The money." Matt lowered his voice so only Duncan could hear him. "Got you mad enough to kill?"

Duncan glared at him. "Fuck you. Nobody is listening to Rachel's lies. It was an accident and the sheriff will back me up."

"Sure, he will. You covered that. Hard to autopsy a cremated body. Evidence gone up in smoke."

Duncan snorted "I was within my rights, asshole." He paused, breathing hard. After a moment, he spoke in a calmer tone, "I don't blame Rachel. Not really. She never got over her mother's death. She's been acting out ever since. She prefers to blame all her bad behavior on me. Did she tell you she was a drug addict? Bet she didn't mention that. She's a liar and a con artist, and she's doing a job on you. You don't know her."

"I know she's royally pissed at you. So pissed off, she

might consider taking investment advice from someone like me."

"Don't count on it, ass wipe. In the end when she comes to her right mind, she'll realize what side her bread is buttered. You think she's going to listen to a loser like you, after all I've given her? She'll come to her senses, and leave you at the bottom of the shithole."

"Don't bet on it," Matt said. "She loved her mother, and you took her away from her. She's got her own opinion about that hunting trip."

"Opinions are like dimes. They get spent and forgotten. Hey, asshole, ever wonder why Victoria told Rachel about you?"

Matt didn't like Duncan's tone. He watched the man's expression turn predatory. "Rachel made that clear enough. Victoria told her we had a special relationship before she married you."

"Special, yeah." Duncan spat on the floor. "Before, during and after. I didn't know Victoria was pregnant when we got married. Did you?" He didn't wait for an answer. "Thought about that a lot over the years. Even made me wonder a few times who Rachel's father really is."

Matt didn't hesitate. "You're her father."

"You sure about that? I raised her, but whose sperm did the deed? Yours? Val's?" He laughed, an unpleasant sound. "Oh, look at your face. You didn't know she slept with Val? Everyone else did."

Matt realized Duncan expected him to yell and scream, maybe throw a punch or two. Not that he wasn't tempted. "Go to hell, Duncan. After all these years, what difference does it make?"

"What difference?" Duncan raged. "Makes a fucking difference to me. Want to know something? I never thought Rachel was mine. Victoria should have married you. Maybe then she wouldn't have turned out to be a drunk and an addict and a slut."

Matt clenched his fists. It took all his control not to use them on Duncan's face. "Shut up. Shut up. Shut up."

Faces turned toward them. The room had gone quiet.

"She wasn't the woman you thought she was." Duncan continued to rant as if Matt hadn't spoken. "Ask anyone. Maybe there's a man here she didn't sleep with, but I doubt it."

"Liar!" Matt grabbed Duncan's shirt at the neck and pulled him forward until he was within inches of his face. "Is that why you killed her? Because she didn't love you? Money and rejection. Powerful motives." He saw Duncan's fist coming up fast but blocked it with his forearm before the blow could connect. Then he shoved Duncan and sent him stumbling backward.

Hands grabbed him from behind. Matt whirled around and saw Hank's reddened face. He shook the man off and marched toward the exit. Duncan's shouts followed him, and the crowd hushed. Out of the corner of his eye he saw Lillian hurrying toward him.

CHAPTER 16

How about that drink?" Lillian said. "You look like you can use one. I'm buying."

Matt's face still showed the flush of unchecked fury from his confrontation with Duncan. She had heard the last part and almost wanted to see Matt smash Duncan's face. But that might land him in jail and she didn't see that happening. He still looked ready to strike out at anyone in his path, but Lillian didn't back off. She had seen security personnel appear and they didn't look friendly. This would not be a safe place for Matt.

She motioned toward the hotel lobby. "Let's get out of here."

He let her lead him out of the building. By the time they reached the street, the red heat faded from Matt's skin, and his breathing returned to normal. They stood, inhaling the humid air.

"Did you decide to stay?" he said, eying the pavement.

"Haven't given it another thought since the last time you asked," she said, urging a smile out of him. "I found out from Val what happened before you found Rachel. He promised to give a recorded statement in Houston."

Matt waved a hand toward the Omni. "If you need to go back, I'm fine out here."

"No, no. You don't understand. I got what I needed. I'm not talking to Val in front of those people. I have his number. That means, for right now I'm free." She pointed toward a small bar at the street corner. "I'm ready for that drink."

He grinned. "Me, too."

The bar was so dark it took several minutes for her eyes to adjust. There was standing room only at the bar, and all the tables were taken. Looking up, she noticed the upstairs was lit and she could see a few empty tables among the ones already occupied. Glasses clinked close to where they were standing. Laughter came from a row of bar stools nearby. A steady murmur of voices underscored the room. The walls were paneled dark wood and decorated with assorted faded photographs that she would examine another time if she had the chance.

Upstairs, the seating arrangements were more varied than the way they looked from below. Booths, circular tables, and sofas were randomly aligned against both the wall and the railing. They walked down the narrow opening until they came to an empty loveseat facing a low table. A waiter appeared two seconds after they made themselves comfortable on the firm cushions.

"Reminds me of a place in Houston," she said.

He grinned, which softened his expression. "The one with the curtained-off back room?"

She could only laugh. "You've been there, too. I won't ask what you were doing, but my excuse is tame. Two gay male friends took me."

"Hah. There's a story behind that."

"I wish. Unfortunately, it was business, so my lips are sealed. Bet that wasn't your excuse."

"I'm a gentleman. I don't kiss and tell."

Her eyelashes fluttered. "I'll have to take you at your word, won't I?"

He raised his hands, palms out. "Have no reason to lie. I'm innocent."

Their drinks arrived and Lillian swirled the cocktail stick in her vodka and tonic. She felt more comfortable with him now as opposed to doing business with him in Houston.

"Tell me what you know about Val. Will his character stand up in court if he had to appear?"

He crossed his legs and leaned back. "I knew him through Victoria. They grew up together and were best of friends. But I'm sure he was in love with her as we all were. Thinking back, I think she was in love with him. But her father was adamant that she marry someone with a future. I was second best, though I didn't think of myself that way. Not then. I thought she loved me the way I loved her. Then she dropped me for Duncan. Looking back at the times, I believe her choice was really for her father. Duncan was the football star, and he was taking over the family oil business. He made the better match. Val tried to talk her out of marrying Duncan. That caused a rift between them that lasted years. He joined the Navy, eventually became a SEAL. That's the last I saw of him before tonight."

His picture of Val fit with her own observations. She hesitated before she asked the next question. "I overheard Duncan tell you Victoria was pregnant when she married him."

He scoffed at the words. "He was just saying that because he knew he could get to me. Don't believe it."

Was he trying to convince himself or her?

He drank more of his Scotch. "You going to tell me what Val did after he smashed into Luke's car?"

She glanced at him. "He said he didn't intend to hit the Camaro that hard. He got out, but Luke saw him and took off. Val thought Rachel was still in the car with Luke. When he realized she must have been hit by the airbags and fell out of the car, he went back. But by then you had already picked her up."

"You believe him?"

"Unless he says otherwise later, I do believe him."

Her cell phone beeped. Looking at the Caller ID, she swore under her breath. "Sorry. I have to take this."

Matt waved his hand in a gesture that said, "Go ahead."

"I'm in Dallas," she said into the phone. "No, everything's fine. *I'm* fine. I'll be back tomorrow. Yes, I'll call you when I get to the office." She ended the call and whispered an apology to Matt.

He smiled. "Your boss checking up on you?"

She shook her head. "My cousin Deborah. She always checks up on me. You'd think I was still twelve. Can you imagine?"

"I think that's a very caring thing to do," he said.

She wondered what he would think if she told him how Deborah's calling her had become a ritual ever since Lillian was raped. No matter how many times she told her cousin that calls weren't necessary and she didn't need looking after, it did no good. The few times she ignored the call, Deborah sent out a police force to hunt her down. Finally, Lillian gave up trying to convince Deborah the past was over. She took the calls, reassured her all was well, and went on to whatever she was doing.

Her phone buzzed, indicating a text. She punched the key harder than necessary. *What now?* She calmed down when she read the words and typed a response. She looked up to see Matt trying to act uninterested. She wanted to laugh, but he might take that the wrong way.

"Val's on his way," she said.

CHAPTER 17

H e's coming here?"

Matt echoed her words but their meaning didn't penetrate right away. While she had been on the phone, his mind returned to the party and he was still hearing Duncan's rants. Was Victoria really pregnant when she married him, or was Duncan messing with him as he used to do in college? Football rivalry was only a small part of the competition Duncan fought with Matt. Taking Victoria away from him was the trophy in the final round.

She had chosen a crude, misogynistic, and ruthless player over him. But was Duncan capable of her cold-blooded murder as Rachel believed?

The abrupt arrival of Val at their table jerked Matt back to the present. He stood and shook hands with Val while he appraised the older version of the young man he remembered. Despite skin weathered with more than age, Val had developed a hardened body any man would envy. He wasn't pretty boy handsome. Matt decided the lines in Val's face gave him character. His eyes held intelligence and a wariness of others. It was easy to see what attracted Lillian. She couldn't take her eyes off the guy.

Matt now had Duncan's last words running through his head.

Victoria had slept with Val while she was seeing Matt and Duncan.

He tried to force the words out of his head because if he believed Duncan, he would be left wondering who had fathered Rachel.

Val held onto his hand with tensile strength. "Didn't expect to see you, ol' buddy. How long has it been? Too many years. But you look great."

"So do you. As if it was yesterday. But hell, I wouldn't go back to those days for love or money."

Val dropped Matt's hand. "Not me either."

Matt finished his drink. "You have business with Lillian. You can have my seat."

"Hey, buddy, don't rush off." Val grabbed an empty chair from another table and sat facing them both. He motioned for Matt to stay put. "I'm glad you're here. I want you involved in this discussion. It concerns Luke and Rachel."

Lillian looked surprised. If this was an ambush, Matt thought, she was a good actress.

Val folded his arms across his chest and turned to Lillian. "Where's Luke?"

"He's staying at a residence motel in Houston until his hearing. Why?"

Instead of answering, Val asked, "Hank's footing the bill?"

"Of course." There was an edge to her tone. "Are you worried about Luke?"

"I'm supporting his story and keeping him out of jail. When's his hearing?"

"The date hasn't been set, but it's usually heard within the month. If we submit your statement to the court, he may not even need to appear. When are you coming to Houston?"

"Soon."

"I told Kurt I'm dropping the B and E charge," Matt said. "With your statement, Luke should be ready to return home. Looks like you got it all tied up." He made a move to get up. "I should get back to the party."

Val reached out a hand and touched his shoulder. "Stay. They don't want you back."

Matt grunted in disgust. "Afraid I'll create another disturbance?"

"Yep. Like that. Lillian and I finished our business earlier this evening. You and I need to catch up."

"Some other time." Matt scooted toward the edge of the loveseat.

"Spare me a few moments," Val said. "For old time's sake."

Matt tried to smile. He felt glued to his seat. "That's a good enough reason not to stick around."

Lillian slid to the opposite edge and stood. "Matt, if I don't see you again before I leave, have a safe trip back to Houston."

"You, too." He watched her go down the aisle, back supple, shoulders set, hips swaying. His gaze lingered until she disappeared down the stairs.

He turned his attention back to Val, who slid into the vacated spot.

"Beautiful woman," Val commented.

"And smart," Matt replied. "Her cousin is the cop who arrested Luke at my house."

"I wondered at the names," Val said. "Let's talk about Rachel. Where is she?"

"I took her to Elaine's. Do you know her?" He was having second thoughts about this decision. What if Duncan decided to visit and caught her there?

Val scowled. "Duncan's girl friend? Sure. Rachel's good with staying with her?"

"She thought someone should warn her about Duncan before she marries him."

"Rachel still believes Duncan killed Victoria."

Matt raised his eyebrows. "You don't?"

"Not for me to say. I'll tell you this, Rachel keeps messing with Duncan, and he'll go after her, too."

"Duncan said something about old man Kittering. I think he wants him declared incompetent to make the trust he willed to Victoria invalid."

Val snorted. "Fat chance. Farley is sharper than Duncan ever was."

"I haven't seen Farley in years."

The corners of Val's mouth twitched. "You want to see him? I'll take you."

Matt perked up. "When?"

eoeo

The next morning, Val's Jeep bounced over the rutted, red dirt road and jumped back onto pavement that curved in front of Farley's ranch house.

Matt looked around. Old memories stirred. Victoria had grown up here. The place had changed little since Matt's college years. Except for the added extension.

He let out a low whistle. "I thought he was in a nursing home." *And why didn't you tell me up front he was home?*

"He moved back here about six weeks ago," Val said. "He's a tough old bird. As soon as Farley's brother Frank learned he was starting to regain his speech, he moved him home. Hired nurses around the clock. They're paid extra to keep their mouths shut. He's still partially paralyzed on one side. His speech is garbled, but he's improving with therapy."

"Has Rachel been told?"

"No one has."

"Why the secrecy?"

Val turned off the ignition. Heat enveloped them. "Let's go inside."

Matt kept up with Val as they mounted the stairs to the wide, wraparound porch. Val extracted a key from a chain looped in his belt buckle. A woman, wearing a calico dress that stopped below her knees, and her steel-gray hair wrapped in a bun, came into the room. Matt felt her sharp eyes pierce him. She didn't change her sour expression.

"Who you bringing here, Val?"

Matt spoke up. "I'm not surprised you don't recognize me, Mrs. Kittering. It's been almost twenty years."

Reba Kittering squinted at him and moved closer. "Matt? Matt Langdon? Why, of course, I recognize you. Nothing wrong with my memory. What're you doing here?"

She looked to Val, expecting him to answer.

Val ignored her question. "Where's Frank?"

"At the office. Where do you think he'd be this time of day?" She looked back at Matt, who had the impression she could flip through the years like the pages of a book and read what he'd become.

"We're paying a visit to the old man," Val said.

"I assumed as much," she said. "You'll want iced tea."

Val waved his hand. "Later."

Matt nodded to Reba Kittering, but she turned and marched out of the room. He followed Val down a hall to the back of the house.

A man in a white jacket stepped out of a room. He stopped when he saw the men approaching. His gaze paused at Matt before he nodded to Val. "Mornin', Mr. Val."

"How's he doing, Billy?"

"A little agitated."

Val smiled. "I always believed he had a sixth sense. This is Matt Langdon. He knew Farley a long time ago."

"Well, keep the visit short," Billy advised. "His blood pressure's up."

"We will," Val promised.

They stepped into a room that smelled like a hospital. An adjustable bed sat next to a window with the curtains half opened. On the left was a dresser holding bottles of pills and packaged syringes. Two chairs were near the bed.

Matt expected a shrunken shadow of the man he remembered as a larger-than-life powerhouse whose non-stop energy was fueled by a temper that put shivers in lesser giants. His booming voice could be heard over the machines pumping out gushers of oil while he delivered orders to his men. The first time Matt met him, however, was not on the oil fields but at the Kittering ranch, meeting his fiancé's father for the first time. Farley Kittering might have huffed, shouted and bullied Matt if Victoria hadn't stuck up for him.

Matt did his best to show the old man what he was made of, but Kittering had someone else in mind for his daughter. A football star whose ambitions, Matt knew, far exceeded his abilities. But Duncan had convinced the old man, and Matt looked like second best. Not good enough for his daughter.

Matt took in the wrinkled brown skin of the man who had spent most of his years outdoors, but now showed a tinge of gray. The watery blue eyes held Matt in a fierce gaze. They seemed to say, *I'm not dead yet. Don't blow me off.*

"Mr. Kittering," Matt began. "Do you know who I am?"

"Of course I do." The words came out with a forced

quaver. "Matthew Langdon. Sit." He lowered his gaze to indicate the chair by the bed.

"You look good, sir," Matt said once he was seated.

A cough erupted from the old man. "Don't bullshit an old man."

"Not wasting away, I see. I expect you'll be walking next time I see you."

"Next time." The old man fixed his gaze on Matt. "You got Rachel?"

"She found me."

"She's got her money?"

"That's what she told me."

Kittering tried to raise his head. "Don't let Duncan get it."

Matt reached out to him, falling short of touching the old man's forehead. "Don't worry about Duncan. He might be her father, but she wants nothing to do with him."

He let his hand slide down as Kittering fell back into his pillow.

"Don't trust the bastard. Keep him away from her," Kittering said. Tension bled into his voice. A pulse throbbed at his temples.

"You're worried about Duncan harming her?"

"He killed my daughter." He coughed and gasped for air. When Matt looked around the room for the nurse, Kittering grabbed his hand and forced his attention back to him. In a voice that sounded like gravel, he said, "It's my fault. All my fault."

Matt swallowed, apprehension filling him. "What's your fault?"

Kittering's fingers curled into a claw and dug into his sheet. "I did what I could for my girls. But it killed my poor Vic. You got to look after Rachel. Keep her alive."

The old man must have lost his mind, Matt thought.

Talking gibberish. Killing Rachel would be like turning a spotlight on Duncan.

"Where's Luke?" Kittering's weak voice broke into Matt's thoughts.

"Houston. He's safe," Matt said, wondering why the old man would be interested in him, too.

"Good. Keep him there," Kittering demanded in a tone that started strong and fell off at the end.

Matt noticed that Kittering seemed to be struggling for breath. He turned to Val. "Call the nurse in," he said.

"He's okay," Val said, coming closer. "He's overexcited, that's all."

"You're not a doctor," Matt said. He was about to get up when the man in the white uniform came in.

Val motioned for Matt to follow him out, which he did gratefully. Matt needed fresh air. He kept walking, increasing his speed as he passed through the front door and stepped off the porch. He didn't stop until he stood under an oak tree. He desperately wanted a cigarette, even though he'd given up the habit years ago.

Val caught up to him. "What's wrong?"

"You tell me," Matt said. "What makes him think Rachel is my business?"

"You have to ask?" Val said, with a hint of amusement in his tone.

Remembering again Duncan's drunken accusation that Matt could be Rachel's father, he shook his head. "She's not my daughter."

"Probably not."

Matt's head spun. "Duncan thinks you're another candidate for fatherhood. I recall Farley thinking you weren't good enough for her either. Did you sleep with her while she was engaged to me? You can tell me. She's dead. What does it matter now?"

He tried to read Val's expression, but the man's face showed nothing.

"I know you were seeing Victoria before I met her," Matt continued. "Thinking back on those days now, I don't think she ever stopped loving you even after we were engaged."

Matt saw the pain come into Val's eyes. So it was true.

"Be careful what you say about her," Val growled.

Matt didn't listen. "I was going to marry her. It's one thing for her to leave me for Duncan and his money. I can understand that. But even when she said she loved only me, she couldn't stay away from you, or you from her. Admit it, Val. Rachel could be yours."

Val turned to him. The veins in his temples jumped. "Anything's possible."

Anything's possible?

Matt laughed with bitterness. "What gets me is this. If Victoria knew she was carrying a child, why the hell did she pick Duncan to be the father?"

CHAPTER 18

Lillian sat in her boss's office and turned her chair to face Deborah. "You're telling Kurt and me that Luke told you there was a witness to the hunting accident? What brought this on?"

Deborah spoke in her usual clipped tone. "He called me because he couldn't reach you. He wanted me to drop the charges and let him go. I explained that wasn't going to happen. He stays where he's at or he waits in jail until the judge gives the order."

Kurt leaned forward and put his elbows on his desk. "How did the conversation turn to Victoria's death?"

"He wanted to be released because he believes he's in danger. He says he knows the person's identity. I told him he was safe as long as he was in custody. Do you know what he's talking about?"

Lillian shook her head. "No, I haven't heard any of this from him. He didn't name the witness?"

"Nope."

Lillian ran her fingers over her skirt. "Rachel is convinced it was murder and says the sheriff covered for Duncan. Is Luke implying Rachel is the witness?"

"If she's the witness, then why didn't she come forward two years ago?" Deborah said. "She's been very vocal about what she believes. I don't think she would've hesitated to go to the sheriff."

Lillian wasn't so sure. "She was a minor at the time, living under Duncan's roof and being supported by him. Maybe she was afraid to go against him."

Kurt interjected. "That's not the case now that she's an adult and come into her inheritance. She's out of his control."

Deborah stood and wandered to the window. "From what I've learned, the sheriff had no choice but to take Duncan's word that her death was an accident. There's no evidence to support an investigation. No body, just ashes." She turned and faced them. "No witness came out of the woods and pointed a finger at Duncan and accused him of murderous intent."

"What if I have a talk with Sheriff Tandy?" Lillian said. Even before Kurt and Deborah shook their heads in unison, she knew they were right. Bringing up a two-year-old death certificate that was on the books as accidental would not reopen the case. Even if a credible eye-witness came forth now, it might be too late. It would be Duncan's word against the so-called witness, who could bring nothing to substantiate the charge. "So what *do* we do?"

Kurt shuffled papers on his desk. "Luke's hearing is coming up in a few days. We need to protect him until his case is dismissed and he can return home. If word gets out to Duncan about what Luke is saying, we don't know what might happen. If Duncan's innocent, he should dismiss any accusation as gossip. The same applies if he's guilty."

"I've met the man and he is quick to anger," Lillian said. "Luke is right to be afraid of him. Duncan is irrational. You should have heard him with Matt Langdon. They had to break them apart."

"Matt Langdon was there?" Deborah asked, her voice raised in alarm.

Lillian wished she'd kept her mouth shut about Matt. Too late now. "He was looking for answers about the investors who backed out of funding his company."

"He thought Duncan would help him? Matt has his daughter. Is Duncan cool about that?"

"Not really, but there's history between them that has nothing to do with Luke." Lillian hoped her explanation would suffice.

Deborah didn't look convinced and seemed about to ask more questions.

"Val Strong is the reason I went to Dallas," Lillian said. "I found him and he's coming here to give his statement."

Deborah's eyes narrowed. "Yes, you told us he's the driver of the SUV who hit Luke's car. Did you buy his story?"

"It made sense to me. He should arrive sometime today."

The mention of Val's name brought on a physical sensation Lillian couldn't explain. She squirmed in her chair and finally stood. "I have to use the restroom," she told Deborah. "Be right back."

She hurried down the hall to the door marked *Ladies* and went into the first stall. Her heart pounded and her hands were shaking. What was wrong with her? The last time she saw him, they had met at the hotel after she decided to stay over a night. They had a nightcap and Val walked her to her door. It had taken all her strength not to invite him in, even though his body had brushed against hers and his lips had touched the inside of her ear lobe and traveled to her neck. He had frozen her in place. Well, frozen wasn't the right word. Liquid heat better described the way she felt.

Then a panic attack took over and jolted her back in time to a place of terror and pain. She shoved him aside and escaped to her room. There the shabbiness, stale air, and cold unfamiliarity gave her no comfort. Inescapable fear threatened as images, sounds, even the feel of her own skin burning seemed all too real. She had dug inside her overnight bag until she found the pint bottle of Scotch. Gripping it tightly to her bosom, she willed herself back to reality. No one could see her this way, weak and unsure. She was not a scared victim any more.

She heard Val's persistent knocking, and the concern in his voice asking her if she was all right. For one terrifying moment, she questioned what she had felt. What if she had imagined his body so close to hers, touching her? What if desire and need had brought those feelings to life and not his touch? Her voice was shaky but she had managed to answer him through the locked door. She was fine. She would see him in Houston.

"Lillian? Lillian! Are you all right?" Deborah's voice penetrated through the stall door.

Lillian flushed and opened the door to see the worried look on her cousin. She forced a smile. "I'm fine. Just had to pee."

Deborah looked uncertain. Lillian again reassured her.

"Your face went bright pink when you mentioned Val Strong," Deborah said. "Did that man do anything to you?"

"No, of course not." Lillian forced her eyes to look into her cousin's. "Don't worry so much. I can take care of myself."

Deborah seemed placated, though she continued to eye Lillian as they returned to the office.

Kurt looked up. "Everything okay?"

Lillian nodded. Her skin felt normal again and her heart beat steadily.

Kurt's landline on his desk buzzed once. He hit the intercom. "Yes?"

The receptionist's voice came through the speakers. "There's a gentleman here to see you. Val Strong? Says he's expected."

"Show him in, please," Kurt said.

Lillian tensed. The door opened and she glanced at the man who stepped inside. He was dressed casually in jeans and a black turtleneck with an unbuttoned blue jacket. He gave a cursory nod to Lillian before going straight to Kurt and shaking his hand.

"Glad to finally meet Luke's lawyer," Val said.

"Thank you for coming," Kurt said. "You've met my investigator, Lillian. The officer is Deborah Wallace. She arrested Luke. I'm told you're here to make a witness statement."

Deborah stood. "You work for Duncan Rosendekker?"

"No, ma'am. I do contract work for several different oil and gas companies. I've done some business with Rosendekker Exploration in the past but not recently."

Kurt nodded. "We appreciate you giving up your time to help Luke."

Val turned to him. "You can answer something for me first. Why wasn't Luke released after the bond was paid? He should have been free to go wherever he wanted as long as he was back in court for his hearing."

"That's up to our client. Hank Jamison is paying us to make sure he stays in Houston where we can watch him."

"Why?"

"You'll have to ask our client."

Val glanced at Lillian but his expression didn't change. "When's the court date?"

"Three days from now. All we need is for the judge to get your written statement."

"What about the B and E charge?"

"Mr. Langdon has agreed to drop all charges," Kurt said. "We're ready as soon as you are."

"I have to see Luke first."

A look passed between Kurt and Deborah. Lillian sat rigid, as the tension squeezed her neck and shoulders. The only person in the room who seemed in command was Val Strong.

Deborah spoke to Val first. "I can't let you see him alone."

Lillian couldn't believe what she was hearing. What red flags had Luke raised the night before? Did they believe Val was dangerous?

"Why?" Val's tone demanded a fast answer.

"Security reasons," was all Deborah would say.

"I need to *see* Luke," Val repeated, jaw tightening.

Lillian stood. "I'll take him."

Deborah gave her a sharp look, but Lillian ignored her.

"Come with me, Mr. Strong." She moved quickly past him into the hallway.

"It's Val, remember?" he said softly and followed her to the elevator.

CHAPTER 19

Matt arrived at the sheriff's office in Riverton County the morning following his visit with Farley Kittering. He convinced the deputy in charge that he was originally from the Dallas area and knew Duncan Rosendekker. If the deputy assumed his association with the oilman was friendly, well so be it. He gained admission to Sheriff Tandy's inner sanctum.

The sheriff was on the phone, and waved at Matt. While the sheriff was occupied, Matt wandered around the room, examining the décor. The sheriff's office had accumulated dozens of personal items from the many years he had served. A moose's head and a multi-antlered buck's head hung on the wall behind his desk. There were more pictures of Tandy standing or shaking hands with celebrities on his book shelves than there were books. One photo showed Tandy with the current governor. Matt recognized several Country/Western singers in the photos. Matt stopped in front of a picture that showed the sheriff as a young man, standing with Duncan in his high school football uniform. Another one showed Duncan, the oilman, shaking the sheriff's hand.

Sheriff Tandy slammed the phone down and folded his arms on his desk. He was in his sixties and looked every minute of those passing years. His weather-tanned face had grooves instead of wrinkles. Gray dominated his thinning hair combed back to his neckline. Bushy eyebrows and mustache overpowered his watery blue eyes and thin lips.

"That's one of my favorites," the sheriff said, acknowledging the photo of Duncan, the football star that seemed to have captured his visitor's attention. "I always said he should've made the pros." He pointed a fat finger at Matt. "I remember you back then, too. You played with him, didn't you?"

Matt sat in the wooden chair opposite the desk. "Just that one year."

Tandy appeared to relax while his eyes narrowed in on Matt. "Those were the good old days. When greatness meant something. You been to see him?"

"We were both at the Petroleum Club's event Monday night."

A smoldering cigar rested on a dish and filled Matt's nostrils with its stink. Tandy ground out the offending cigar but kept holding it. "That boy's sure done right well for himself. Employs most of the town. Now then, tell me, son, what can I do you for?"

This wasn't going to be easy, Matt knew. "I heard about how Victoria died two years ago. We were close in college."

Tandy stroked his thick mustache. "A terrible shame, that was. Poor man was beside himself. Such a pity."

"How did she die?"

Tandy looked surprised. "You said you heard about it."

"I wanted to get your version, Sheriff."

Tandy scowled. "There's no version. Hunting accident, simple as that. Ask anyone."

"There are some who believed the shot was intentional."

"Says who?" He snorted. "His daughter?"

Matt kept his voice even. "Did you look into it?"

"Of course I did. Duncan told me exactly what happened. I had no reason to believe anything else."

"You two are good friends. I heard he got you elected."

Tandy's tanned face turned a shade of red, but otherwise he didn't move. "What are you saying, boy?"

"Just that there might be another explanation for her death."

"You accusing Duncan of lying? Or worse, accusing me of covering up a crime?" He tapped the cigar on the edge of his desk and chuckled. "Oh, I've heard the same accusations from Rachel. It don't bother me none. I understand. She was close to her mother. We all look for explanations past the simple ones."

"You never suspected he was hiding something when he had her cremated so soon?"

Tandy planted his elbows on his desk. "Men like Duncan don't like the idea of death. It's too close to the skin. Know what I mean? You want to get rid of the stench and reality as soon as you can. Victoria put it in her will she wanted to be cremated. Duncan did the right thing." He chuckled again. "I'm not saying he was the perfect husband, or she was the perfect wife. They were like any other couple. You know what a marriage without problems is called? The honeymoon. Most honeymoons only last a week at best."

"I heard rumors," Matt said.

Tandy laughed outright. "Rumors! Gossip! You know the one I like best? That Duncan preferred his sheep more'n he liked screwing his wife. Haven't seen that for myself, mind you. Don't know anyone else can verify it either. That's what rumors are, boy."

Matt held his temper in check through strength of will.

Talking about Victoria and screwing sheep in the same sentence made him want to choke the sheriff. He was sure Tandy was trying to goad him into doing something stupid. He waited for Matt to throw a punch. Matt kept his voice steady. "What if it's more than a rumor?"

"You give me a witness that says otherwise, and I'll take a look into it again. Mind you, it's been two years. No one's come forward with a story that proves Duncan did what his daughter's accused him of. Even if a so-called witness showed up now, it would be their word against Duncan's. Need more than that." He squinted at Matt. "Don't even think about making trouble in my town. Go on back to Houston where you belong."

Matt stood. "Thank you for your time, sheriff."

"You have a safe trip home now, boy."

Outside the building Matt breathed in the open air and absently watched the orange and red leaves of an early fall drift to the ground. The deputy who had let him in earlier was leaning against the building, smoking a cigarette, making a show of watching Matt.

Matt got into his car and headed toward Dallas. He wasn't ready to head home yet. He had one more stop to make. He pulled over and made a call to Rosendekker Exploration and was told the office was closed for the rest of the week. No explanation. A quick call to Kurt's office got him Hank's home address in Frisco, a few miles outside of Dallas. He took a chance Hank would be at home. His hunch proved right.

Hank's wife, Crystal, answered the door. Dressed in jeans and a crisp white shirt, the petite woman with short blond hair looked ten years younger than her husband.

"Hank told me about you," she said as she led him past a room containing a large quilting machine and mountains of fabric. "You caused quite a ruckus at the party the other night."

"Were you there?"

"Yes, but I must have been out of the room at the time." She stopped abruptly in the hallway. "Do you know my son?"

Matt tried to keep his surprise from showing. She wasn't aware he was the reason Luke had been arrested? "Yes, ma'am, I've met Luke. He's seems like a good boy."

"He's obsessed with Duncan's girl, Rachel. That girl's bad news. My son is a decent, good-hearted young man. He doesn't belong in jail."

"I'm confident all charges will be dropped," Matt reassured her.

"They better be. I don't like to talk badly about another person, but Rachel's involved Luke in her problems, and that's not right."

"What problems?"

"Drugs, alcohol, you name it. Staying out all night doing God knows what. She's a sorry influence. Now that she's turned twenty-one, no telling what kind of trouble she'll stir up. I feel sorry for her father."

At that moment, a door opened down the hall and Hank appeared. "Crystal? Who are you talking to?" He frowned when he saw Matt. "What're you doing here?"

"Sorry for not calling first," Matt said. "Can I talk to you a minute?"

Hank hesitated, his gaze shifting to his wife.

"I'm done," Crystal said. "I'm going back to my quilting."

Hank led Matt back to a room with a bench and work table. Miniature ships in bottles, and ships in different stages of construction covered the table. "My hobby. Keeps me sane in my spare time. Crystal has her quilting. This is my thing."

"Very nice." Matt tried to sound interested, and gave the art work a cursory glance. He couldn't care less about how the man spent his spare time. He sat in the only other chair in the room. "I'm sorry about Monday night. I was out of line."

Hank shrugged. "Duncan had a lot to drink before you saw him. Look, Matt, I know you're having problems with funding. We all are. Did you talk to McAdams?"

"Missed him. I didn't go back after I was thrown out."

"That shouldn't have happened. No one had the guts to throw out Duncan." His laugh was a deep-throated rumble that shook his shoulders.

Matt leaned toward him. "Have you heard anything, Hank? Did someone talk to the investors and persuade them not to sign on?"

Hank sighed. "I can only tell you what you already know. Oil prices have taken a swan dive. Everyone is hesitant to invest right now. You know that."

Matt was through with being polite. "Who's pulling strings?"

"Listen to yourself, Matt. You sound paranoid."

"I have a right. One day the investors are ready to sign. The next day all of them drop out. No explanation. No return calls. I'm supposed to believe the dip in oil prices is to blame?"

"Talk to McAdams again," Hank said.

"What good would that do? He's avoiding me. What's Duncan's opinion?"

"I thought you had that conversation last night." Hank turned his attention back to his miniature ships.

Matt crossed his legs and watched Hank pick up a tiny sliver of wood with a pair of tweezers. "I'm asking you."

Hank sighed and turned back to him. "Duncan has other matters on his mind. He's getting married again. Did you know that?"

"So I heard. Elaine is a very lovely, wealthy woman. Is he hurting for money? A goldmine for him if he becomes a widower again."

Hank almost choked on a burst of laughter. "We're back to Victoria now, are we? I heard about your accusations. Got it from Rachel, I presume. Nonsense, all of it,"

"You haven't asked me about your son."

"No," he drawled. "Has anything changed besides Val coming to the rescue?"

Matt sighed. "No, nothing's changed. The hearing's in a few days. He'll be out and back home with you." Hank's expression changed and became more withdrawn. Matt wondered why. "Isn't that what you want?"

"Of course," Hank said.

But he didn't sound convincing. Matt pressed him. "Why didn't you want him home while waiting for his hearing?"

Hank didn't look at him. "Kurt advised me to keep him in Houston in case the hearing was moved up. Made sense to me."

"Were you afraid he would run away?"

"Not at all. I agreed he should stayed there for the court appearance." Hank moved around the table and rubbed his hands. "Is he all right?"

Matt watched him. The man had no reason to be nervous, so why did he feel Hank was holding something back? "Why wouldn't he be?"

"No reason. He's being kept at the residence motel, right? Better than jail." He came to a stop in front of Matt. "Sorry I couldn't be more help. Hope you get the funding. Seriously."

Matt rose to his feet. "Thanks. You hear anything that might help my company, I'd appreciate it if you'd let me know."

Hank walked Matt to the door. "Sorry about Victoria.

You should have been notified two years ago when she died. Wasn't right."

"Rachel thinks there are many aspects of her death that aren't right."

Hank glanced at him. "She's a mixed-up kid. Don't take everything she says seriously."

Matt hesitated, wondering why Hank was so quick to dismiss Rachel. "You never considered the possibility she might be right?"

Hank gave an uneasy laugh. "Whatever really happened, we'll probably never know. Two years, a cremation, water under the bridge. Luke used to go with him and help carry his equipment. I'm just grateful he wasn't along that time."

This was news to Matt. "Maybe if he had, things would have turned out differently for Victoria."

Hank reached for the doorknob and the door swung open. "Guess we'll never know. Good seeing you, Matt. Stop in any time you're in the neighborhood."

"Thanks for your time. I'll check in with Luke. Any message you want me to give him."

"Tell him I love him, and this will be over soon." Hank shut the door.

Matt stared at the house. Was there a hidden meaning behind Hank's words? *This will be over soon.*

Before he had a chance to mull this over, his phone rang.

Forty-five minutes later he entered Rogers Cafe, a place known for its BBQ. He found Duncan seated by himself in the back room with a beer bottle in front of him. He was dressed casual in jeans and a button-down, long-sleeve shirt despite the hot weather.

"You saw Big Ray," Duncan said when Matt slid onto the bench seat opposite him.

Matt hadn't heard Sheriff Raymond Tandy called that

by anyone other than Duncan. It only showed how deep their friendship went. Deep enough that the sheriff would cover up for his buddy?

"I wanted to know what happened to Victoria," Matt said.

"I told you already."

"So you did."

A waitress stopped at their table. Matt shook his head.

"Bring me another Coors," Duncan ordered without taking his eyes off Matt. "You sure you don't want anything? Shiner? Scotch, maybe?"

"I'm good," Matt said. "You closed the office this week?"

"Yeah, we worked our asses off for the Petroleum Club conference. Most of my guys are still at the hotel in meetings. Nothing going on at the office." He sat back and stared at Matt with hooded eyes. "You're looking into ancient history. Is that because you're pissed off that your business is going into the toilet? Hey, I understand that. I'd be pissed, too, in your place. But why come after me? You're accusing me of what? Murder?"

"I haven't accused you of anything, Duncan."

"It doesn't feel that way, old buddy. Look at what I'm going through. You got my daughter and turned her against me. The son of my best friend and landman is in jail—custody, same thing, you know what I mean."

"Last night you were denying Rachel is your daughter."

"Never said that. Never. That's bullshit." He took a long gulp from his bottle. "You need my help, buddy, so I'll make a deal with you."

Matt felt his insides grind but managed to keep silent. He wanted to hear the man out.

"I'll talk to those investors. See what's up and figure a solution. You bring Rachel home where she belongs. Oh, and get Luke free. I'm getting married again, and I want my family together at my wedding."

"When are you planning to get married?"

"Soon. I'm moving up the date."

"Elaine know that?"

Duncan looked at him suspiciously. "How do you know Elaine?"

Matt couldn't resist grinning. "Haven't dated her, if that's what you're asking."

Duncan's tone lowered with an underscore of menace. "I'm asking how you know her."

"Rachel brought up her name. Look, Duncan, I don't have any control over your daughter. She's an adult now."

Matt felt a shiver down his spine as soulless blue eyes stared back at him. It was the kind of look Duncan used to give his opponent on the football field before tackling him to the ground and making sure it hurt.

Duncan finished his beer in one swallow, and banged the bottle on the table. "These are my conditions, Matt. Get me what I want, or your company won't be worth the paper it's written on." He slid out of his chair and stood. "You know what I'm capable of."

With these final words, Duncan strode out of the cafe. A few minutes later, the waitress brought the check and set it in front of Matt.

CHAPTER 20

What are we going to do?" Greg's agitated voice came over the speaker phone in Matt's car. The landman hadn't stopped ranting over Matt's recitation of the events in Dallas. "Duncan is crazy. He can't do this to us."

Matt turned left onto the road leading to his house. "We'll figure something out. I'm almost home. The only plan I have for the rest of the night is checking on Aaron, taking a shower, and drinking a cold beer, in that order."

"I'm tearing my hair out here. We can't afford to lose this well. Where are we going to find the money?"

"Immediate answers aren't rushing at me right now. I'm dead tired, my eyes feel like they're on fire, and my bones ache. I can't solve the world's problems tonight."

"How about solving our own freakin' problems. Soon. I'm coming over for breakfast. We need a plan."

Matt groaned. Before he could respond, the line went dead. He cursed loudly, which he could do because he was alone. He could listen to Greg swear and rant all day, something Matt rarely did in public. He considered the F-bomb part of the lazy man's vocabulary. Tonight, as worn down as he felt, any effort would feel like running a marathon with an elephant strapped to his back.

Apprehension reawakened as his home came into

view. A strange object blocked his driveway. Beside Carrie's red Mazda was an unfamiliar red and black Harley-Davidson. He parked on the street.

The door opened before he reached for the knob. Carrie stood there in jeans and a skintight black T-shirt. She looked wide-awake.

"About damn time," she said by way of greeting. "Rachel's back."

"What?" Thoughts of sleep in the near future crashed and burned.

She stepped aside to let him in. "I was only going to stay to keep Aaron company, but then she showed up and I didn't dare leave. I think she's on something. Anyway, Aaron fell asleep playing video games. I'm telling you, that girl's a mess. She's also an expert at manipulation. Must take after her father."

He watch her stride out the door. As she reached her car she turned back to wave at him. "Good luck."

What the hell did I come home to? He waited while she climbed into the Mazda and cranked the engine. He winced at the screech of tires as she shot out of the driveway. When she disappeared around the corner, he tossed his overnight bag in the hallway and faced the living room. Carrie's words filled him with dread. Rachel, back at his house, instead of at Elaine's where he'd left her. Their parting had not been without rancor. He told himself he was too tired for another confrontation. He would dismiss her with as few words as possible and head for the bedroom.

She wore tight, black leather pants with a matching vest, and she had streaked her blond hair purple. She stood by the fireplace holding a half-empty bottle of Bohemia, Matt's favorite beer, in one hand, a cigarette in the other. Her eyelids were heavily outlined. She wet her lips before pursing them in a playful pout.

What was this? A new act? Was she coming on to him?

"What are you doing here, Rachel?" He spoke with an effort and sank onto the sofa. "You were supposed to stay at Elaine's."

She blew a plume of smoke toward the ceiling and tossed the cigarette butt in the fireplace. "I got bored. I couldn't talk her out of marrying Duncan so I came back here."

Matt's gaze strayed to the Bohemia and dismissed the temptation. He needed to stay alert around this new Rachel.

"I talked to Duncan," he said. "He's very upset with you. Wants you home in time for the wedding."

Rachel's hand tightened around the bottle, but her tone remained casual. "I thought it was planned for next year."

"He's moving up the date."

She turned away from him and drank from the bottle. "Elaine really believes he loves her. Says she's not worried."

He heard the bitterness edging into her voice as well as a hint of resignation. "When did you get the motorcycle?"

When she faced him again, a bold smile showed brilliant white teeth. "Before I left Elaine's. Had to get some transport. Do you like it? Aaron said you used to ride a Harley."

Not just her words but the way she said them made him wary. She was trying too hard to attach herself to him.

Her tongue slid over her lower lip. "Did you expect me to stay there until you came around again? I missed you and Aaron."

He grew more uneasy at her tone. "You should have called me first."

She dismissed this with a flip of her hand and finished off her beer. She put the bottle on the end table and sat next to him. "We need to think about Luke. What do you say about us hitting the road with him until all this blows over?"

Us? What's with that? Matt's head jerked up, any ideas of sleep evaporating. "Luke stays until his court date."

"That's days away," she said. "He must be bored out of his skull. A change of scene wouldn't hurt any of us. We would be back in time."

"*We* are not doing anything of the sort." Matt's thought lingered on the Bohemia in his fridge. "Luke is fine where he is. You got him in enough trouble without talking him into another getaway adventure nonsense."

Eyes flashed angrily. "Oh, give me a break. Legally, he's an adult. It's not like he's my boyfriend." As if she regretted her outburst, she added, in a throaty tone, "I prefer older men who know what they're doing." She delivered a knowing wink and touched her lips with her tongue.

Damn! She looked just like Victoria at that moment. The same sensuous expression that used to drive him nuts. Duncan's accusation at the party slammed him. *No. Duncan would make up any story to throw me off balance. Get a grip, man. Don't let this girl get to you. She's nothing but a spoiled brat.* He thought of Carrie's warning. Was Rachel on drugs?

Matt looked away from her and inched closer to the edge of his seat. He planted his elbows on his knees. "So did you lie when you told me you've had sex with Luke?"

She shrugged. "Why would I lie? I admit it. I let him seduce me when I was under the influence. And it was only one time."

Are you under the influence now? Matt forced himself

to look at her. Her eyes were clear. "He's still in lust with you. You're playing a dangerous game."

She scooted closer to him. "He's young. He'll get over it."

Matt leaned away from her. He had to turn her attention in another direction. "Something Hank told me about Luke got me thinking. He said his son usually accompanied Duncan when he went deer hunting. Is that right?"

She blinked at the shift in topic. She seemed to tense. "Yeah. Why?"

"He said the day Duncan took Victoria hunting, he didn't want Luke to tag along. Was that unusual?"

"Not really. Sometimes he went hunting with business partners or potential investors and didn't need Luke. Why do you ask? "

"So as far as you know, Luke didn't go with Duncan and Victoria that day."

Rachel hesitated, but then stared straight at him. "No, he didn't."

"Or follow him?"

"No."

She looked over his shoulder. A look that Matt swore to be pure relief transformed her features. He turned to see Aaron in the doorway. His hair was askew. He wore a bathrobe over his shorts.

"Hey, Dad, when did you get home?"

Rachel left Matt's side and rushed over to Aaron. "Good, you're awake. I'm so glad to see you. Tell your dad what you said."

For a second, Aaron looked confused. He was prompted by Rachel. "Okay, yeah. Hey, Dad, I told her she can stay in the guest room. Is that okay?"

Rachel pulled his head toward hers and pecked him on the cheek. She rushed over to Matt and wound her arms around him in a hug. "I don't know what I would do without you both." She raised her head to look into his eyes, her lips parting.

Realizing she was going for a kiss, he shoved her away. "Stop it!" he ordered.

Her eyes widened, then squeezed shut and turned into a faucet of tears. She covered her face.

Dismayed at her reaction, Matt lifted her chin and forced her to look at him. "What are you doing, Rachel? What is the matter with you, acting like this?"

She let out a strangled cry and wrenched away from him. Before he could stop her, she ran out of the room.

Father and son stared at each other in shocked silence. The next sound they heard was the motorcycle's engine roaring to life and screaming away from the house.

"Christ," Matt muttered. For a second, he was relieved she was gone.

Aaron stood still, staring at the door and then at Matt, as if waiting for his father to react. When Matt didn't move, he started for the door. "I'm going after her."

"Dammit, no," Matt said, as if shaken awake. "You stay here in case she comes back."

He grabbed his keys and ran outside. No sign of her.

Matt jumped in his Jeep, jammed in the key and pulled out onto the street. Where would she go? Rachel hadn't been in town long enough to know the area well. Overhead, dark clouds moved over the moon. Distant lightning splintered the sky. He wound through the streets, straining to listen for the rise and fall of the motorcycle's engine, letting him know how close he was or wasn't. He went up and down back streets. Surely, she wouldn't get on the freeway. She would stay close, but it would be easy for her to get lost.

She has no place to go, he told himself, as he continued to search neighborhood streets. He tried to imagine what it had been like for her, growing up as Duncan and

Victoria's child. It was natural to yearn for acceptance and a show of love from her parents. Instead she knew only that her mother was miserable in her marriage, maybe escaping into affairs, as Duncan had hinted. Duncan, meanwhile, either pushed his daughter away, or did something worse. Did Duncan really believe Rachel wasn't his, and he could do whatever he wanted to her? The thought made Matt sick.

Then there was the "what if" question that had nagged at him since Rachel showed up. Duncan had flung the question at his face. *What if* Rachel was his daughter? If he thought hard enough and rationalized long enough, he had to concede that the timing was right. Victoria had slept with Duncan about the same time she was engaged to Matt. And he couldn't forget about Val Strong. He never denied being her lover. Had there been others as well?

He had to stop thinking of Rachel that way. Not as a possible daughter. He hadn't known she existed until he found her on the road. He only knew what she had told him. She was a multi-millionaire at age twenty-one because Victoria had unexpectedly died. But before she died, Victoria had pointed Rachel in his direction for reasons he had yet to understand.

Poor Victoria. She must have thought she was free when she inherited her trust fund. Was she planning to leave him? Duncan wasn't the type to let her go, not with all that money. He would do everything possible to keep the money. Even if it meant killing her. *Did Victoria have someone who would have helped her escape? A lover maybe? Did Duncan suspect someone? If he did, the man's life would be worthless.*

Or maybe she was planning to find Matt to tell him she loved only him.

A pale light on the horizon announced a new dawn despite the heavy clouds that bunched in clusters and began to spit. Fat drops fell on his windshield, a chill wind blew in, but Matt didn't want to roll up the windows yet. He wanted to hear the sound of the motorcycle, see the flash of red and black zoom down the street. See a purple-streaked blonde riding toward him. So far, nothing. The drops came hard and more frequent. He turned the wipers on high. Had she ever ridden a bike before? Ridden in the rain?

Rachel couldn't have gone far. Was that an engine sputtering nearby? He raced toward the sound but it turned out to be a car pulling out of a driveway.

Then he saw her and his heart sped up in alarm. The bike was down, laid on its side. Rachel sat on the curb, rain drenched. She didn't even try to cover herself up as the rain continued to soak her.

He rolled up next to her and opened the passenger's door. She looked up. Tears mixed with rain streaked her face.

She looked so pathetic with her make-up smeared and her hair in her face, he couldn't hold on to his anger. "You okay? Are you hurt?"

She rubbed her leg and gave a shrug.

"Get in," he said.

She pointed to her bike. "What about this?"

"We'll get it later. Get in the car."

She wiped her hand across her face then slowly got up and slid into the passenger's seat.

"Your seat will be all wet," she whimpered.

"It'll dry."

"Sorry." She looked down at her clasped hands, then gazed up at him.

He searched her face. She looked and sounded sincere for the first time that night. "We'll talk later. Right now, I'm taking you back to the house."

Aaron stood on the porch as they drove up. He brought an umbrella to the car and held it over Rachel as she slid out. Aaron held her arm as she limped through the rain to the house.

Matt ducked his head and dashed after them.

"Good thing Mom took her shopping," Aaron quipped after he brought Rachel a towel to rub herself dry. No one smiled at his attempt to lighten the mood.

Rachel looked more embarrassed and miserable than grateful as Aaron wrapped the towel around her shoulders and led her to a chair in the kitchen.

Matt knelt in front of her and slipped off her left boot and felt her body tense. "Is it your leg?" It was impossible to tell what was under the tight leather that encased her legs.

"No big thing," Rachel said. "I need to check on the Harley. We skidded and I laid it down."

"Leave it to me. I'm more worried about you," Matt said. "You don't have to run from me, Rachel. You don't have to put on an act for me either. Just be yourself."

"Whoever that is," Rachel said with some bitterness.

He offered an encouraging smile. "You'll figure it out. Meanwhile, you can have the guest room until you decide your next move." She twisted and grimaced when he pulled off her right boot. "There's ointment and bandages in the bathroom. If you need to go to the ER—"

"I'm fine," she said. "I want to get my bike and see Luke."

"I'll take you to visit Luke tomorrow."

She stood, wincing slightly. "If you don't mind, I'd still like to get my bike now."

"I said I would take care of it," he said, his tone sharp with impatience. "You know where to find the bathroom and guest room. Your clothes are there. I'm not telling you what to do, but going back out in the rain is not the wisest option right now." He wanted to add, *Try acting like an adult.*

Her lips trembled but she didn't argue. She jutted out her chin and lifted her head and made an effort to walk out of the kitchen in her stocking feet without a limp, but not quite succeeding.

When he was sure Rachel had shut the guest room door behind her, he turned to Aaron "Come on. Let's go pick up the bike."

CHAPTER 21

Lillian drove with her gaze steady on the road. She barely looked at Val, slouched in the passenger seat next to her. She didn't want to think about whatever happened, or didn't happen, between them in Dallas. All she wanted to do was arrive at the apartment, make sure Val wasn't planning to harm Luke—not that she believed he would—and see that the talk between them stayed civil. After that she would return to her office, write up her Dallas report, and invoice Kurt. Her part was then done.

She rolled her shoulders and tilted her head to relieve the tension. Seeing Val for the first time since leaving Dallas left her with mixed emotions. No matter how hard she tried, she couldn't forget her last night at the hotel. She still believed Val had made a pass at her.

The panic attack she experienced afterward she attributed to a flashback of the trauma she'd experienced fifteen years ago.

Val interrupted her thoughts. "Did I offend you?"

His question, seeming to come out of nowhere, made her wonder if she'd spoken her thoughts aloud. "What do you mean?"

"Your attitude changed." Val glanced at her. "You're different than the woman I saw in Dallas. My guess is, you needed something from me and put on an act to get it."

His choice of words stung. *What I needed?* She hadn't needed anything more than a written statement from him to exonerate Luke. *I haven't changed. Only, what the hell happened in front of the hotel room?* Memory flashed in and out like a fantasy film. Had she only imagined him trying to kiss her? She would die before she would ask him. Instead, with a bitterness that matched his tone, she said, "You always make snap judgments? Or only with women?"

He twisted around to face her. "I am not a misogynist. I saw a confident career professional who had a job to do. I also caught a glimpse of you, the woman, who may be afraid to show her emotions."

Lillian's grip on the steering wheel tightened until her fingers felt paralyzed. "Oh, really! Well, I saw a pompous man who thinks he's God's gift to women."

To her dismay, he laughed. When he saw her expression, his eyes softened. "I'm sorry. Did you think I was pushing myself onto you that night? Is that why you're acting so strange?"

She pressed her lips together and didn't answer.

"I think you misunderstood what was really going on. I wasn't coming on to you. Though the idea was tempting, it would have been very unprofessional of me. Not my style. What actually happened, Lil, was this. You had a spider on your hair and I was trying to get it off without scaring you."

She shot a quick look at him. A burst of laughter wanted to explode from her. She swallowed hard to hold it in. Was he serious, blaming a spider? Her cheeks did a slow burn as she pictured the scene once again. Seeing it from Val's point of view made it worse.

"Well, did you?" she snapped back. Despite her efforts, out came choking bouts of laughter she could no longer hold in. She sputtered. "Did you get the damn spider off me?"

He laughed with her, looking relieved. "I did. I was going to show you the little bug but you bolted inside before I could."

She tried to scowl, but the ridiculousness of the situation brought more laughter. "You should have told me before you reached for it," she managed to say. "I'm not afraid of spiders."

This made him laugh harder. "Or anything else, I assume."

She shook her head, unable to speak, and turned her attention back to the road and pushed the gas pedal.

"If I can be serious for a minute," he said. "I'd like to make an observation, hopefully without destroying our precarious business relationship. I think someone once hurt you badly, and you're not quite recovered. You try to hide the flashbacks, but haven't learned yet how to deal with those occurrences. Isn't that what really happened?"

His words slapped her in the face. She no longer felt like laughing. She wanted to pull over and stop the car, get out and scream. Instead she kept her voice even and the car within the speed limit. "You're a psychologist now?"

"If I'm out of bounds, just say so. If not, I have experience in that area. I can help."

"No thanks, and you are out of bounds." She gripped the steering wheel tighter. "Shouldn't we be talking about Luke?"

He grinned. "Maybe, but you're far more interesting."

A part of her glowed, just a little. She turned away. "I think we should change the subject."

"I'm making you uncomfortable?"

"Not at all." She showed him her fake smile.

He chuckled. "Good. Luke tell you anything?"

She jerked to look at him. "Why? Are you changing your testimony?"

He met her gaze. "No."

"You scared him when you hit his car."

"He has no reason to fear me."

"But you hit his car."

"Yep." He glanced at her. "That's why Luke will talk to me."

"Fine," she said. *Don't mind me. I don't need to understand. Asshole. But you better not have lied to me.*

Twenty minutes later she parked under a tree behind the motel. "If he doesn't want to see you, we're leaving." She marched up the walkway to the door. She knocked twice before using her key.

Luke scrambled off the sofa when the door opened. Lillian walked in first, watched the young man tense, fists pressed against his sides. Val stepped in and moved past her into the room, sure-footed, towering over her. Luke straightened. His shoulders relaxed. "Knew you'd come."

"You okay?"

"Yeah. Sure. Great," Luke said. "I'm, like, a prisoner here, but the digs are sorta cool. You gonna spring me outta here?"

"Soon," Val said. "Need to get a couple of things straight first. This lady thinks you're scared of me."

Luke looked surprised. "That's crap. I ain't scared of nobody. But why'd you crash my car, man? Not cool."

Lillian crossed her arms. *Yeah, why did you do that, Val?*

"You hit her."

"That's bullshit," Luke said. "What you saw? We was just arguing. We always argue. She hit me a bunch of times."

"You saying you didn't hit her?" Val said.

"I might have slapped her once, but I didn't *hurt* her. *You* did that when you slammed into the back. The damn air bag went off in her face. Ask her."

"I got a question," Lillian said. "Why were you following him?"

"Not him," Val said. "Rachel."

"For Duncan?" she persisted.

"Hell, no." Val turned and faced her. "What I told you in Dallas is the absolute truth. Duncan never cared about her until she got the big bucks. I've known Rachel all her life. I'm the one who's always been there for her."

"'Cause you work for her granddaddy," Luke said.

"That's not the only reason," Val said.

"Rachel said her grandfather's in a nursing home recovering from a stroke," Lillian said.

"He's recovering at home now. In fact, I took Matt to visit him last week. Old man Kittering is worried about his granddaughter. He feels partly responsible for Victoria's death. He set up the trust fund as her separate property and he's convinced that's the reason Duncan killed her."

"Is that what you think, too?" Lillian said.

"Damn right," Val said. "But Duncan underestimated Victoria and he didn't know jack shit about trust funds. For instance, you can have a trust fund set up so a named person can never touch those funds. That's how Farley set up the trust. He eliminated Duncan. Victoria did the same with a second trust. Both trusts would only go to Rachel in the event of her mother's death. I laughed my ass off when I found out Rachel inherited it all. But then I got to thinking, if Rachel dies, would the money go to Duncan? Farley said no. The trusts specifically states Duncan would not get a penny."

"Hope he knows that," Lillian said.

Val turned back to Luke. "Let's get back to what happened on the road. Did Duncan call or text you while you were driving Rachel?"

"Yeah," Luke said. "He demanded I bring Rachel home. I told him to fuck off."

"Why?" Val said. "You always followed his orders before. You'd sit up and bark if he told you to."

"No frigging way. I'm done with him." Luke's voice shook.

"What changed?" Val said.

Luke backed away. "I don't answer to you."

Lillian knew why Luke was holding back. He'd told Deborah he knew about a witness that he was afraid to name. But such information was dangerous. She wasn't that sure about Val's motives. She was about to change the subject when a knock on the door saved her the trouble. Val squinted at Luke. "You expecting company?"

"Not me," Luke said.

Lillian crossed to the door and peered through the peephole. "Such timing," she murmured as she opened the door for Rachel and Matt. "What a surprise."

"I'm playing chauffeur." Matt stepped inside after the girl. "Rachel wanted to see Luke."

Rachel looked unhappy at Val's presence. She pointedly ignored him, went directly to Luke, and gave him a hug. "You all right?"

Val's voice took on an edge. "He's fine, Rachel. Haven't heard from you since before the accident. Not like you. Still angry?"

Rachel didn't answer. She squeezed Luke's hand.

"I'm good, Rach," Luke assured her.

"I'll make sure you stay that way," Rachel said.

Lillian heard a sisterly quality to Rachel's tone. Poor Luke just looked at his friend with puppy dog eyes. *Rocky road ahead for those two,* she thought.

Matt moved into her line of vision. "Good to see you again, Lil."

Lillian noted the tired smile, the lines around his eyes and mouth, the sprouts of gray above his ears, and tried not to compare him to the other man in the room.

"Did you just get home?" she asked.

"I took a couple of days to do some investigating on my own."

"Oh? Care to share?"

"Later."

She suppressed her impatience. "Can I get you a Coke? I think there's some in the fridge."

"No thanks." His gaze swept the room, registering the clothes strewn across furniture, several empty bottles and encrusted plates on the tables. "This room reminds me of my son's."

"Aaron's sloppy, too?" Lillian said. "How is he?"

"He's good."

Rachel bristled. "At least Aaron isn't locked up in his room."

Lillian gave her a friendly smile. "When did you get back in town, Rachel? I thought you were staying with Elaine Westerfelt."

"Only one night," Rachel said. "Matt says I can stay with him."

Val's head jerked up and his gaze found Matt. "You didn't tell me that. You said she was staying with Elaine."

Matt shrugged. "Change of plans."

"I've been at Matt's since he rescued me from the accident *you* caused," Rachel said.

"I never saw you. I swear, I thought you were in Luke's car. That's why I went after Luke. If I'd seen you on the ground, I would have stopped and taken care of you."

She shook her head in disgust. "Sure. Did you even look?"

"Your grandfather's not in the nursing home anymore," Val said. "He's recovering at the ranch. His speech has even improved. He'd be glad to see you."

"Mother thought I should look up Matt if I was in trouble."

Val paled. "Victoria said—what? When did she tell you that?"

"Obviously before she died." Rachel rolled her eyes.

Lillian stole a glance at Val who looked as if he'd been struck.

Forget him, Lil. He's still got a thing for a dead woman.

Val recovered quicker than Lillian anticipated. He turned on Matt. "This arrangement suits you?"

"It's had its moments—" Matt winked at Rachel. "—but we've more or less come to an understanding."

Val jammed a finger at him. "What was that? A wink?"

"Cool it," Matt said.

"Don't tell me to cool it," Val said, scowling.

No way was this going any further, Lillian decided. "Val, we need to go back to the office and attend to business. We're finished."

"Not quite," Val said without taking his eyes off Matt. "Say, Matt, when's the last time you saw Victoria? I should have asked you the other night."

Oh, boy. Here we go. Again.

Rachel shook her head and tugged on Luke's arm. "Come on. I'm craving a Coke. Show me the kitchen." She pushed Luke ahead of her.

Matt waited until they were gone before answering Val. "Last time? About twenty years ago, Where are you going with this?"

"Why did she tell Rachel to go to you?"

"And not to you? I don't know," Matt said. "Too bad she's not here to explain herself."

"How did Victoria know where you lived?"

"Hey, man, I'm on the Internet. I'm not hard to find."

"I think you're lying," Val said. "Did you go to Dallas for your trysts, or did she come here?"

Matt looked incredulous. "Jealous, Val? You think she was seeing both of us at the same time? Again?"

For one terrible moment, Lillian was sure a fight would erupt. "Stop this juvenile talk right now."

They ignored her.

Matt stepped closer to Val. "She never contacted me. I see now what was really going on. She was leaving Duncan for you. Admit it. You got her killed."

CHAPTER 22

N

o." The word spat out of Val's mouth. "Duncan killed her for the money. He didn't care who she slept with as long as he held the purse strings."

"That's enough." Lillian gave both men a shove. "Victoria is dead. Nothing will change that fact. Without evidence there is no way to establish murder. Now is the time you should be thinking of Rachel. Look at her."

Both men turned. Rachel stood three feet from Val. Her eyes searched his. "You were seeing Mom? I knew it. Duncan knew it, too. Matt's right. That's why he killed her."

Val stepped closer to her. "Sweetheart, I loved your mother. I hated the way Duncan treated her. I wanted her to have a better life. If you think that makes me a villain, Rachel, so be it. I believe she cared for me, but she would not have left Duncan until you turned twenty-one. You were the only one she truly loved."

"If you loved her, if you love me, then prove she was murdered," Rachel said.

The room went still.

Rachel pushed further. "Look what Duncan's doing to Matt. He's gone after his company. He won't stop until Matt's bankrupt. Tell him, Matt."

Val turned to Matt. "That's why you were in Dallas."

Matt nodded. "He did threaten to destroy my company if I didn't bring Rachel and Luke home. But the investors were backing off before Rachel and Luke came to me. Why ruin me?"

"Jealousy," Val said.

"What?" Matt choked out a laugh. "What does that sonofabitch have to be jealous of?"

"Think about your last business deal with him. Went sour, right?"

"Bastard tried to screw me and I backed out. So what?"

"You cut him off."

"You bet I did."

"The deal almost bankrupted him. Investors listened to you. Other contractors refused to work with him. He made a few dirty deals to get back on track. Take my word for it, anyone who crosses him gets slashed."

Including his wife and daughter? Lillian flashed on the man she'd met in Dallas. His party persona seemed superficial at best. No, the man was hard. He cared for no one but himself, and he held grudges. Not a man to go up against.

Would she go against him for Rachel and Luke's sake? *No, no, no, not your job.*

Matt frowned. "Duncan's not poor. I looked him up. He's buying prospects. That's just the beginning."

Val didn't seem to hear him. "You don't know him like I do. When Rachel left home and he found out where she was going and why, he blamed you, Matt. All it would take is a phone call from him to McAdams and every investor would back out of your deal. Never mind that you didn't even know Rachel at the time. In his mind, you stopped him from getting the trust fund money he'd killed for. So you had to pay. That's how he thinks. He couldn't kill you but he could destroy you."

"See?" Rachel said. "If he can bankrupt Matt, how far will he go to silence a witness?"

Lillian turned to stare at her. Had Luke told her he knew about a witness? Or was that witness Rachel herself? "Honey, do you know something nobody else knows?"

Rachel met her eyes and Lillian held her breath.

"I'm just sayin', what if there was a witness and that person could prove Duncan killed Mom on purpose?"

No one spoke.

Then Luke came out of the kitchen. "Goddamnit, Rachel. Don't say things like that."

Matt's cell phone shattered the tension. He walked a few steps away, and answered.

"This is Matt." He listened, while everyone else in the room stared at him. "Calm down, Elaine. If you really need me, I can be there in a few hours." He paused. "No, that's fine. Tomorrow would work. I can leave first thing in the morning."

"What's wrong?" Rachel tried to snatch the phone from his grasp, but he punched off and evaded the movement.

"She wouldn't say," Matt said.

"You have to take me with you," Rachel said.

"She doesn't want you there."

Color came into Rachel's cheeks. She bit her lower lip and turned to Lillian. "Then you go with him. You're a PI. What's your time worth?" Before Lillian could open her mouth to object," Rachel said, "I'll pay you five thousand dollars to stop a wedding."

CHAPTER 23

Lillian shook Elaine's outstretched hand before entering her ranch house. Nothing about the woman met Lillian's expectations. Elaine looked casually elegant in brushed silk pants and a flowing pink top. If she expected to see Matt, she didn't show disappointment in the change of plans.

Elaine gave Lillian an approving once-over. "I've met a couple of investigators in my time, but none of them with your looks and youth."

"If that's a compliment, thanks," Lillian said. "Depending on the case, looks and youth can be an advantage." She checked out the feminine furnishings in the pastel living room as they went through. She couldn't imagine Duncan living here.

"I would never make a good investigator," Elaine said. "I'm too outspoken. I hope Matt's in good health. He sounded tired over the phone. Next time you see him, tell him I enjoyed meeting him and to bring Rachel back anytime."

"He wanted to come himself, but he was needed at his office," Lillian said. "I offered to come in his place. I suggested he bring Rachel to work with him. Wouldn't hurt her to learn more about the business."

"Great idea. That girl needs direction from a competent adult. She has what I'd call a case of adolescent de-linquency, in addition to suffering a grief hangover."

"To put it mildly," Lillian said. "Remember, she still believes her mother was murdered."

"That's a lot to cope with," Elaine said. "I have iced tea set up on the patio. I'm designing a new flower ar-rangement for my garden club. We can talk while I work."

Elaine led the way through the French doors off the living room to a spacious flagstone patio. Lillian paused to admire the lush garden that extended out to a pool complete with fountain and waterfall. Elaine waited for her at a table set up with an oval pitcher of iced tea, tall Waterford glasses, and a matching sugar bowl. Two Adi-rondack chairs flanked the table and faced the pool.

"You must be thirsty after such a long drive," Elaine said, pouring the tea. "I should feel guilty for bringing you all this way, but the truth is, I needed reassurance."

Lillian perched on the chair's edge and tasted the tea. Strong the way she like it. "Matt said you sounded pan-icky."

"I suppose I did. His fault for making me doubt my judgment." She reached into a wooden crate next to her chair and brought out a bunch of yellow and lavender flowers. After she laid them on the table, she pulled out green sheets of wrapping paper. "You know that I'm a widow. I was a good wife to Henry up until the day he died of cancer. I nursed him at home through most of his final year. I've been single for five years now and content with my life. The only reason I'm bringing this up is so you'll understand my decision to marry Duncan. I've missed having a companion to share my days and nights. He stepped in and convinced me I could be happy with a man again." A worry frown crinkled her perfect skin.

"But?"

Elaine picked up a scissors and clipped the ends of two flower stems. "When Duncan called the other day and informed me he was moving up our wedding day, I started shaking. Understand that I'm not by nature a shaker. Was I letting rumors and supposition affect my decisions? Or was it a sign? I couldn't let him know that I wasn't jumping with excitement, not thrilled until my teeth hurt, and not anxious to be a bride again. *His* bride."

She didn't look the type to be easily ruffled. Everything surrounding the woman spoke of thoughtful preparation. Her clothes, her house, even her white blond hair, lifted and twirled and pinned so close to her head not even a hair strayed.

"Did you ever question him about Victoria's death?" Lillian asked.

"I met with him after that phone call and demanded the truth about Victoria. I told him I couldn't marry him until he could assure me of his innocence. He was furious. He blamed Matt. He said Matt has never gotten over Victoria and would do anything to destroy him. Is that true?"

Lillian took a long swallow of tea before putting down the glass. "I've known Matt for over three years professionally. He's ethical, hard-working, and devoted to his son. Since Rachel came into his life, he's been trying to help her."

"That was my immediate impression of him. I never doubted Duncan before, but I kept looking at that mole on his chin, turning darker and uglier." Elaine plucked a violet from the box. The stem shook in her hands and she dropped it. "I knew Duncan Rosendekker as the successful head of an oil company, one of the best competitors in the business. He was the typical ex-football star and woman magnet. No one questioned him, except Rachel.

Anyway, Sheriff Tandy ruled Victoria's death accidental. What else could he do?"

"Just out of curiosity, how many deputies does the sheriff employ?"

"Hmmm, let's see. My Henry was a member of the city council for a number of years. During that time, Trampas, Jericho, and Zachary worked out of the sheriff's office. I imagine they still do. Maybe a fourth, not sure. It's not a large county. What are you getting at?"

"Maybe not everyone is a fan of Duncan's. Do you know these men personally?"

Elaine arranged the flowers in the vase. "Not personally. Only when they sat in on council meetings. His deputies were always loyal to Tandy." She set the vase aside. "Except for one. Sheriff Tandy fired Jennings last July."

Not too long after Victoria's death. "Why?"

Elaine shrugged. "Never made the papers. That's strange for these parts."

"Any idea where Jennings is now?"

"Couldn't say." Elaine's eyes narrowed. "Let me make a few calls. Have some more tea while I'm gone."

Lillian watched the other woman disappear into the house. She looked around at the perfect garden, the pristine pool, the bright sunshine sparkling on the water, and tried to put herself in Elaine's place. A wealthy widow running a successful company about to merge with a widower with a competing business couldn't feel more alien to her. On the other hand, she did feel empathy for a lonely woman who felt there was a piece missing from her life, and who thought she had finally found a compatible partner. If she didn't look too deep into his soul.

Elaine returned with a smug look on her face, holding a slip of paper. "Chris Jennings is with the state police now and works out of Austin."

Lillian felt a smile spread across her face. "Doing what?"

"Hey, I can't do all the work for you," Elaine said. "Meanwhile, what am I going to do about Duncan? I can't shut down the wedding without a good reason."

"Try to hold him off. Give him some excuse that won't leave him feeling suspicious."

"Not sure what that will be, but I'll try."

"Tell him you need to see a doctor. Or your elderly aunt is sick, and you have to take care of her. Or there's an emergency with one of the oil wells. You'll figure it out. I have absolute confidence in you, Elaine."

Elaine grasped her hand and her expression was troubled. "Do you really think he's capable of murder?"

Lillian rested her hand over the other woman's. "I wouldn't marry the mole."

Elaine burst out laughing. "His mole. He'd be handsome if he'd just cut off the damn thing."

"Sorry. I shouldn't have brought it up. But it's the first thing I noticed when I met him."

"He does have a big one. Did you see that one hair sticking out? Oh dear, what am I saying? You're the only person I know who's dared to mention it."

"I'm sorry," Lillian said again, trying to put on a straight face, but not succeeding.

Elaine waved at her words. "No, don't be. I shouldn't have called Matt. It was a rash decision done in a moment of weakness. You needn't have come. In fact, I was surprised that anyone took me seriously. Matt and Rachel put suspicions in my head I wasn't ready to deal with. I'm really not afraid of Duncan. I'm not—as long as I have my gun." The last was said with a grin and a twirl of her forefinger as if spinning a gun in the trigger guard.

Lillian raised an eyebrow. "Ah, your gun. Well, don't let him grab it away from you."

Elaine turned serious. "Never happen. Not ever." She walked her to the front door and swung it open.

Lillian stepped out, and froze. A sheriff's patrol car was parked outside. A deputy stuck his head out the window.

"Everything all right, Miss Elaine?"

Lillian whipped around to face Elaine. "You called them?"

"I had to," Elaine said.

CHAPTER 24

Yes, I called." Elaine wore a pained expression. "How else could I come up with Chris Jennings's whereabouts? I never expected Sheriff Tandy to send his deputy out here."

The deputy's appearance made Lillian uncomfortable. *What is really going on?*

"Tell him you're fine before he decides to arrest me. I was just leaving."

Elaine waved to the deputy. "It's all right, Zachary. You didn't have to come out here."

Zachary's attention was riveted on Lillian as he got out of the patrol car. "Who's your friend, Miss Elaine? Don't think I've seen her around these parts." Zachary's hostile stare sent a shiver down Lillian's spine.

Elaine laughed uneasily. "Come off it, Zach. Are you questioning my visitors? You can't be serious. I don't think the sheriff would appreciate you harassing me."

Lillian wondered why the sheriff was watching Elaine's place. After Matt and Rachel, she was the third person to drop in on her within a week. *Are we putting her in danger?*

The deputy didn't crack a smile. "Miss Elaine, the sheriff told me to check out your house."

For what? Any joviality on Elaine's face disappeared.

Lillian could see from her frown that this visit was not routine.

"As you can plainly see, Zach," Elaine said in crisp, biting words, "I'm in no danger and no law has been broken. Please inform the sheriff he needn't have bothered to send you. I suggest you turn around and leave."

Lillian wanted to rush past Zachary, who stood between her and her car. Get Elaine's house and the deputy out of her sight. She could *feel* the menacing glare shooting her way from the deputy's laser-like eyes.

"Sorry, Miss Elaine," the deputy said. "Need to ask a few questions."

Elaine put her hands on her hips. "What questions?"

"The sheriff wants to know why you asked about Chris Jennings."

"*What?* Tell him it's none of his damn business. I'm sure my fiancé would like to know why Sheriff Tandy is so interested in what I do and who I see. You do know who my fiancé is, don't you?"

The beginnings of a grin appeared and wiped off his face before he drawled, "Don't mean no disrespect, ma'am. Fact is, it was Mr. Rosendekker who requested we look in on you and report anything out of the ordinary."

"Is that so?" Elaine said. "And my asking about Jennings defines 'out of the ordinary'"?

"Yes, ma'am, Miss Elaine."

"So Sheriff Tandy tattled on me to Mr. Rosendekker?"

Did her voice sound shaky? Only with anger, Lillian hoped.

"I wouldn't know about that, ma'am." The deputy's tone revealed nothing.

This a load of crap. If she stood in Elaine's shoes, there would be no marriage. First hearing that her fiancé might have murdered his first wife, and now he was *spy-*

ing on her? No way would she stay with this guy. But then, she wasn't in Elaine's shoes.

With difficulty, Lillian held her tongue. No sense in causing a scene and making the situation worse for the woman. There was nothing the sheriff could legally do to Lillian. *Legally.* That was the key word.

Elaine's eyes flashed and her cheeks pinked. When she spoke, her voice no longer shook. "You tell the sheriff to call Mr. Rosendekker back and inform him I'm perfectly capable of taking care of myself. Tell him if he wants the wedding to go on as scheduled, he'd better not be checking up on me like I was a child or an employee. I know you're only doing your duty, but I'm asking you to leave. Now."

Zachary shot a parting glance at Lillian then tipped his hat to Elaine. "Yes, ma'am."

Lillian watched him return to his car. She stood by Elaine until the car disappeared.

"Let's go back in," Elaine said.

Door shut, Elaine put a shaking hand out to steady herself on the wall, then made a beeline for the bar. "I'm having a brandy. Want a shot?"

Lillian was tempted. "I better not. I'm driving. Will you be okay after I leave?"

"Okay?" Elaine said. "I'm angry, no, furious at Duncan. If he thinks he can control what I do, and who I see, he doesn't know me at all. I'm calling off the marriage." She picked up a round squat bottle of amber liquid, twisted the cork off and poured a shot into a whiskey sour glass. She downed the liquor in one gulp and poured a second.

"This may not be the time to make important decisions," Lillian said.

She was all for Elaine calling off the wedding—or, as Elaine put it, the marriage—but the woman was only reacting to what the deputy said. A few hours from now, or when she talked to Duncan, she might change her mind.

"I know what you're thinking," Elaine said, watching her over the rim of her glass. "But I won't change my mind. Breaking the engagement, though, timing is critical. I have to be ready."

"Ready?"

Elaine drank a third shot and put away the bottle. "When I confirm with Duncan that he talked to Tandy." She coughed into her hand. "Look, I can't take that deputy's word that my fiancé is having me watched. It could be Tandy, lying about Duncan."

So much for not changing her mind. "I'll be going now, Elaine. Sure you'll be all right?"

"Don't you worry about me," Elaine said. "Worry about yourself. You be careful on the road."

Elaine's last words came back to Lillian fifteen minutes later when she saw the deputy's car behind her. They had her license tags and knew by now who she was.

She was coming up on the exit to Austin and slowed. She could be back in Houston in a few short hours. Or, she could be in Austin in less time and, hopefully, getting answers from the one person who might not be in Rosendekker's pocket. If Sheriff Tandy fired Chris Jennings, the former deputy might be willing to tell her what the sheriff wouldn't.

She had no idea what Jennings did with the state police. He could be driving one of the black and white patrol cars she'd seen on the highway. One simple phone call now could save her a trip. Another glance at the rearview told her Deputy Zachary still had her in his sights. Wouldn't be smart to telegraph her intentions, she decided. Instead, she continued south toward Houston. The deputy's car stayed on the feeder and disappeared under the overpass. She drove another twenty miles before she

turned around and headed for Austin and the Texas Department of Public Safety building.

It turned out that Investigator Christina Jennings
worked in the DPS Criminal Intelligence Service.

"Are you sure?" Lillian asked the officer behind the
Information Desk. "We're talking about the same person?"

The officer looked up at a wall clock that read four-
fifty-five. He fielded a new call and Lillian tapped her
foot while she waited. She had barely made it inside before the building began to shut down. She doubted that
Jennings would see her this late, but she could hope. So
many questions. According to Elaine's information, Investigator Jennings had been fired a little more than a
year ago. How did she get to be an investigator for the
DPS, or get any job in law enforcement, after being fired?
That couldn't happen. Maybe she got the name wrong.
The officer was still talking. Several minutes passed.

"Miss Wallace?"

Lillian turned toward the voice and faced a woman in
a gray suit. If she had to guess, she would place the woman in her mid-forties. Her ash-colored hair, pulled back
into a knot, made her facial skin taut. She wore black-
rimmed glasses and no makeup.

"You wanted to see me?" Jennings sounded on edge.

"If you're Chris Jennings," Lillian said. "I took a
chance—" She glanced at the clock. It was five after five.

Jennings nodded. "Come up to my office. We can talk
there."

Lillian tried to hide her surprise as she hurriedly followed Jennings into an elevator. When the doors slid
open again, she was in a long hallway. Jennings's office
was the third door on her right. She sat in the only visitor's chair in front of the walnut desk. The walls were
lined with file cabinets and little else.

"I'm a PI with a criminal defense firm," Lillian began.

"Yes," Jennings said. "I know."

Lillian stared at her, stunned. "How—"

"I got a call about an hour ago. I didn't expect to see you this soon."

"I don't understand," Lillian said, trying not to stammer. "Sheriff Tandy called you?"

Jennings gave her a cool smile. "I didn't say *he* called."

Lillian frowned, confused. "If not the sheriff, then who?"

"You had a friend ask about me, remember?"

"I was told you worked for the state police." Lillian's head buzzed. "Did Elaine call you?"

Jennings waved away the question. "It doesn't matter who called. You're here now."

Why the secrecy? "I wanted to see for myself the person who allegedly got fired from one department only to land a promotion with DPS. Love to know your secret."

Jennings didn't comment. Not even a twitch moved her lips.

"Is it true you were fired?" Lillian persisted. She couldn't help herself. This woman in front of her sat like a sculpture. A yes or no would suffice. For now.

Jennings glanced at her watch. "You're wasting my time, Miss Wallace. Get to the point. Why are you here?"

Lillian changed gears after a moment's inner struggle. "We have a client who asked us to investigate the death of Victoria Rosendekker. Were you working for the sheriff's department at that time?"

"If you're referring to the hunting accident that caused the death of Victoria Rosendekker, then yes, I was working with the sheriff then."

"Did you ever question the cause of death?"

Jennings shook her head. "She was cremated. There was no autopsy."

That didn't answer her question. "Did you say he could go ahead with the cremation?"

"Mr. Rosendekker did not come to us for our approval. He notified us after he had her cremated. Why are you bringing up her death? Do you have new evidence?"

"Not yet," Lillian said.

"Can you give me the name of your client?"

"You know I can't."

Jennings reached for a card off her desk and stood. "I really can't help you, Miss Wallace. I'm afraid you made the trip for nothing. Here's my card with my cell number if you come across information that could be useful."

Useful to what? She'd just said there was no investigation. Lillian sat in her car after leaving the building, contemplating what she had or hadn't learned from the investigator. Even if Jennings wasn't fired, it was a big jump going from a small county sheriff's department to working with Criminal Intelligence. Victoria Rosendekker's death might not be the real issue, but it was obvious Investigator Jennings wouldn't tell her squat. Still, Lillian had other ways of finding the truth.

CHAPTER 25

Lillian arrived in Houston shortly after seven that evening. Tired and sore from the trip, a shower and a hot meal sounded like heaven. She put aside the temptation. More pressing matters needed her attention first. Judging by the day's work so far, the five thousand dollar retainer Rachel had insisted upon paying wouldn't go far. Mileage and Lillian's time ate a good portion.

She plopped her butt at her desk, slipped off her shoes, and opened her laptop. She clicked on Rachel's file and entered her notes. Not satisfied, she added her overall impressions of Elaine and Jennings. No detail was too small. She did the same with every case she worked. She never knew what might be important or which telling remark would later get a client off a criminal charge.

Rachel's case was unique, and Lillian found herself in virgin territory. She had to prevent a possible murder and, in the process, prove the commission of a crime nobody believed happened. A total waste of Rachel's money, Lillian admitted to herself. Duncan Rosendekker was too rich, too powerful, and the incident too damn cold to be called a case.

Yet Lillian had agreed to take the girl's money, overriding her boss's objections. As Kurt pointed out, she had no evidence, no corroboration, only a gut feeling that Rachel was right all along.

Years ago, nobody had believed Lillian's story at first. Somehow she was able to convince her cousin Deborah, then a rookie patrol cop, to arrest the two young men who drugged and raped her. She refused to accept she was a victim and testified in court. If she hadn't done that, she wouldn't be the woman she was today. Those young men had all the power over Lillian that money and politics could buy and they terrified her. It took all her strength to focus her rage and fury to fight them in court. She saw the same strength of purpose in Rachel. That young woman would not back down and she wouldn't either.

Lillian's watch read ten to nine when she hit the save button. She squeezed her burning eyes shut for several seconds, and rolled her shoulders. *Hell with it.* There was no reason to rush home to an empty apartment at this hour. She reached into the bottom desk drawer and brought out a bottle of single malt Scotch and grabbed the glass nestled in the corner. She poured two fingers, leaned back into her chair, and put her stocking feet up on her desk. She mentally went through the day's interviews.

She got stuck on Deputy Zachary. He said the sheriff sent him. Then he said Rosendekker gave the orders. Tandy and Rosendekker colluded two years ago to prevent an investigation into Victoria's death. Today, two years later, they were still conspiring to hide the truth. *Why are they so worried about Elaine's visitors?*

Then there was Christina Jennings, who had worked as Sheriff Tandy's deputy at the time Victoria died. Jennings either got fired or quit, only to become an investigator with Criminal Intelligence. *How had that happened?* Her questions kept coming.

Lillian swept her feet off the desk and sat up. She used her cell to make a call.

Deborah answered after the third ring. "Are you back in town?"

"Got in a couple of hours ago. Got a minute? Have a question for you."

"Shoot."

"Do you know any investigators with DPS?"

"That's a broad question. I know you, Lil. You like to take the long route home. You have a name?"

"Christina Jennings with Criminal Intelligence. Is the name familiar?"

"Why are you interested in Jennings?"

"Before she became an investigator for CI, she was a deputy sheriff. Supposedly she got fired by the sheriff last July. I want to know how she got her current job under that set of circumstances."

Deborah was silent for several seconds. Lillian paced while she waited.

"There could be several reasons," Deborah said finally. "But unless I know specifics, I won't have an answer."

"If I told you in confidence, would you discreetly look into it?"

"In other words, you want me to spy for you."

"In a manner of speaking," Lillian conceded. "I mean, wouldn't you be curious? If you got fired tomorrow, you wouldn't be able to step into a job with the FBI or CI. Even if the reason was bogus, you have to admit it would take a mountain of paperwork and political pressure."

"How important is this information to your case?"

Lillian thought hard. "It would answer several questions."

"Who's the sheriff?"

"Wilbur Tandy. Riverton County." Lillian held her breath and waited for Deborah to connect the county and its sheriff with Rachel's story.

Deborah took her time answering. "I'll get back to you."

When the call disconnected, Lillian remained at her desk. She knew Deborah would get back to her one way or another, but she also knew it could take days or weeks. She felt the walls close in on her. No longer tired. Her skin tingled as if she had drunk a pot of coffee instead of a double shot of scotch. The brief buzz had come and gone. She still didn't feel like going home. The idea of calling Val Strong at his hotel grabbed her and gave her a tug, but she resisted. Val was off limits. Finally she grabbed her purse and headed out to her car.

She drove fast, just above the speed limit, and headed south. She tuned the radio to the jazz station and emptied her thoughts. An hour later she parked along the beach on the far side of Galveston. With her windows down and the radio off, she listened to the soft splash of waves hitting the hard wet sand. There was a quiet rhythm to the sound that matched the beating of her heart. The wind picked up and blew on her face. Feeling the soft slap and caress of the salty sea air, she obeyed the call and slid out of her car. She followed the path down to the gritty sand, took off her shoes and wiggled her toes. With no destination in mind, she walked, occasionally hopping through the frothy white surf, skirting around seaweed that tried to ensnare her. The crab shells caught her attention and she picked up a couple, felt their smooth touch, before returning them to the sea.

She chased away thoughts of Rachel, Duncan, and Elaine. She struggled briefly with Jennings, but no answer was forthcoming and she let the puzzle fade and drift to the back of her mind. She sucked in air and let the sand work the muscles in her feet and calves. The night was clear and the stars were scattered in the sky as if tossed there by the gods.

Loud laughter and shrill voices shattered the peace. She'd almost run into a beach party. Awakened abruptly from her dream-like state, she stared at the young people. Those who stared back made faces and whispered to one another as if they were being invaded. They pointed and laughed. Or maybe she imagined cruelty where there was none. Maybe they weren't seeing her but playing some kind of game. She might be only a vision in the night, not real to any of them. She didn't feel real. Sometimes she pictured herself in a movie that had no plot.

Lillian turned away and quickened her step, leaving the party behind her. She realized she had walked longer and farther than she'd intended. She must have rounded a corner because she couldn't see her car. Houses overlooking the beach became shadows against the darkened night. The wind at her back pushed her into a jog, then a sprint. She lowered her head and forged forward.

When she looked up again, she saw her car right where she left it. But another car with a row of rolling blue lights on top purred behind hers. She bounded up the stairs to the street.

The uniformed officer was typing on his digital tablet.

"Officer," she said, breathing heavily. "This is my car."

The policeman looked up, taking a second to assess her appearance. "Were you aware you parked illegally?" He pointed to a faded No Parking sign.

"No, sir." She looked down the street. There were a few parked cars farther down the beach.

"I'm writing you a ticket. In the future you need to watch the signs."

"I'll be more careful next time."

He looked at her again, this time more intently. "Ma'am, have you been drinking?"

"Drinking? No, sir." Then she remembered the scotch

back at her office. That had been more than two hours ago.

"If I gave you a breathalyzer test, would you pass?"

"I'm sure I would."

"I need to see your license and insurance card."

"Certainly. May I get my purse from the car?" She stood poised next to her car door, her hands up where he could see them. "I'm from Houston. An investigator from a law firm. Just needed some air." She was babbling. Couldn't help it. She shivered from a sudden gust of cold wind that came off the sea. The cop would no doubt assume she had been drinking. Did her breath still smell like scotch? Her hands shook.

"Are you planning on driving back tonight?" the cop asked.

"Yes," she said, trying to sound strong.

He motioned to the front seat. "Get your purse, but keep your hands where I can see them."

She nodded and opened the car door. She raised her purse in front of him and opened the clasp. Slowly she pulled out her wallet and loosened her ID from its plastic holder and handed it to him. "My insurance card is in the glove compartment. You want me to get it?"

He took her license and typed in the numbers on his tablet. She waited until he gave her permission to open the glove compartment.

She took a deep breath after he returned both pieces to her. He turned the tablet toward her and showed her where to sign.

"Maybe you should get a motel room for the night," he said when she finished signing. "Are you sure you're okay to drive?"

"Thanks for your concern, Officer," she said, relieved that she sounded alert and firm. "I'm awake. Getting a ticket gave me a jolt of adrenaline. A perfect end to this day. Guess I should thank you." She gave him a big smile and flung her purse to the passenger's seat. Without a backward look, she slid in behind the wheel and shut the door.

She felt him watching her as she turned the key in the ignition. Nothing. A jolt went through her. *No, this can't happen.* She tried again. Still nothing. Could be the battery, she thought. Or the alternator, or starter. Wouldn't get fixed tonight. Would she be taking the officer's advice and checking into a Galveston motel room? No. She counted to three and turned the key again. This time the engine roared to life. She giggled with relief. The officer's worried expression relaxed to a grin. She gave him two thumbs up and gripped the wheel. She turned onto the street, leaving him standing in front of his car.

She turned up the volume on the jazz station, savoring the night air with the windows rolled down. The wind cleared her head. Her thoughts were focused as she reviewed the day with all its strikes and misses. She lingered on the Galveston officer and the way he had stood next to her car and stared at her. Reminded her of Deputy Zachary. Her mind jumped ahead to Jennings. While Lillian puzzled over the investigator's promotion, a thought hit her. She needed to talk to Deborah again.

CHAPTER 26

Any information on Jennings?" Lillian stuck her fork in the salad and heard the satisfying crunch of fresh radishes and cucumber. She invariably ordered the salad with the vinaigrette dressing at Baba Yega Café, a favorite Montrose restaurant.

She and Deborah sat at a table with their backs against the wall.

Lillian shared her cousin's insistence on facing all entrances and exits when they ate out. The open air atmosphere still allowed her a view of the colorful caged parrots on the patio.

"I haven't had the spare time to look into this," Deborah said. "What are you expecting to find about Jennings employment record?"

"I don't know," Lillian admitted. She took a sip of iced tea then put down the glass. "There're two possibilities. Either Jennings was working undercover when she worked at the sheriff's office, or she bribed someone, like a politician, to get where she is with DPS."

Deborah gave a startled laugh. "That's a leap, even for you. Either way, no one's going to spill any dirt to me."

"So who investigates the sheriff they suspect of taking bribes? DPS?"

Deborah eyed her. "That's what this is about? You

think Rosendekker paid off the sheriff to falsify evidence in the hunting accident?"

Lillian shrugged. "Rachel said Tandy got a new truck afterward."

Deborah rolled her eyes. "So Rachel said? I wouldn't take that girl's word for anything."

"Even about her mother?"

"Especially about her mother. She has no proof. Why are you still obsessed with her story?"

Good question. "I believe her. Plus, she's paying me."

Her cell rang, and she looked at the caller ID. With an apologetic shrug, she stood. "I have to take this."

Lillian stepped to the patio and spoke into the phone. "It's me. What's up?" She listened and felt her face go hot. "Give me two minutes and call me back. I'm on my way."

She returned to the table and took several bills from her wallet. "Sorry, Deb. I have to go,"

"I'll get the check," Deborah said, standing. "You go ahead. Call me later."

Lillian gave her cousin a quick hug. "Feels funny, me getting the urgent calls instead of you."

"Take care of business, girl."

Lillian's phone rang again when she reached her car. She snatched it up. "Damnit, Kurt, are you sure he's not in the apartment?"

"I just checked. He was here when I brought him McDonald's this morning. I stopped by to see if he wanted dinner. No Luke. Everything's a mess. Can't tell if he took anything with him. You've talked to him. Any ideas where he might go?"

"Only one place I can think of. I'll check there first."

She ended the call and started up the car. Hitting the speed limit and beyond, she reached her destination twenty minutes later and parked in the driveway.

She pounded the door several times before Matt appeared. Before he could speak, she pushed past him. In the living room she whirled around to face him. "Where is he?"

"What the hell, Lillian?" he demanded. "I just got home from the office. Where is who?"

"Luke. He's not at the motel."

"You're telling me you lost your client?"

She didn't need the needle jab. "Looks like it."

"Why do you think he'd come here?"

"Because this is where he'd expect to find Rachel. Where is she, by the way?"

"She's not here and neither is he. Look around if you don't believe me."

"I will." She glanced around but the search seemed fruitless. "You haven't heard from Luke at all?"

"I told you I've been at the office. I only came home for lunch."

"Where's Aaron?"

She saw a flicker of irritation cross across his face. "He's not here."

"Did you see them when you first got home?" Lillian said.

"They're adults," Matt said. "At least Rachel is. They don't tell me their every move."

"Then how do you know Luke's not here?"

"I've been home for thirty minutes. I would know."

Thought you just got here. "Can I check the rest of the house?"

"Help yourself." He followed her while she did a cursory search. "How long has he been gone?"

"He was at the apartment when Kurt came by with breakfast from McDonalds. That was about eight."

He glanced at his watch. "Seven hours ago." He took his cell phone from his pocket and made two calls. He turned to her. "Aaron's not answering. Rachel didn't pick up either."

"They have him," she concluded miserably. "They could be in Mexico by now."

"Don't jump to conclusions. Aaron wouldn't take off without telling me."

Lillian wanted to argue, tell him he was naïve, but the worry etched on Matt's face changed her mind. Instead, she asked, "Does Rachel have a car?"

"No, a Harley." His eyes met hers, and they both rushed out the door. There was no sign of Rachel's motorcycle. He reached for his phone again.

She put out a hand to stay him. "Don't call the cops. If Luke's jumped bail, a warrant will be issued for his arrest."

He put away his cell. "Next you'll be telling me the kids will be arrested if they're with him."

"A minute ago, they were adults."

He didn't seem to hear her. "Maybe Hank picked him up."

She stared at him. "Why? Luke has to be here for the hearing."

He opened his phone. "I have Hank's number somewhere."

He dialed and held the phone out so she could listen in. Voicemail came on and Matt left a message with his number.

"Now what?" he asked Lillian.

She felt more angry than helpless. She had another thought and punched a button on her phone.

Val answered on the third ring. "Hey, beautiful. Been a while."

"Have you seen Luke?"

"He's gone? Shit. I knew this would happen. Guess you're worried he won't make it to court. Listen, my statement is good, isn't it? Maybe you won't need him."

"If he's jumped bail, the cops will be looking for him. I don't want to see him go to jail."

"Yeah, okay. I got it. You haven't called the police?"

"Of course not."

"Give me a couple of hours. I'll track him down."

"That's not why I called you. I can handle this."

"I know the kid. Let me help."

"I don't need your help unless you can tell me right now where he is."

He laughed. Then he must have realized she was serious because his voice lost any trace of humor. "You don't trust me?"

"I didn't say that."

"Good, because my word is gold. I don't have Luke."

"If you see him before I do, you better call me right away. Get it?"

The call disconnected with a loud click in her ear.

She turned to find Matt looking at her with wry amusement. "What?" she demanded.

He shrugged. "Val's not a man who takes orders well."

Not from a woman, you mean. "Wasn't an order." Thinking back, maybe it was the way she said it. *Screw him.* If he couldn't take her words at face value, that was on him. "If you see Rachel, tell her to call me."

She stalked to her car.

Lillian stewed as she started the engine. She didn't need Mr. Val Hotshot getting in her way. If he knew what Luke planned to do, he should have told her. *Why did Luke run?* That was the big question. He wasn't worried about the hearing. There was no question the judge would release him. She and Kurt went over the proceedings with him several times until he understood. What did Val know that she didn't? *Screw him.* She didn't need him.

She drove straight to the motel. *Stupid kid. What hair got up his ass? Boredom? Not a good reason. Then why?*

Just as she found a place to park, Val's black SUV swerved in front of her and stopped. Lillian wasn't surprised. She realized she had been expecting him to show. They reached the sidewalk at the same time. Lillian looked up and down the empty streets, and at the darkened windows in the nearby apartment buildings. The few businesses in the area showed no activity. She saw no movement anywhere. Mid-afternoon in mid-town. The sun hung like a pale globe in the bleached blue sky.

"We had the same plan, I see," Val said.

With difficulty Lillian kept her temper in check. "I told you to mind your own business."

"Luke is my business. He's why I'm in Houston."

She dug out her key ring and strode to the stairs. He stayed behind her. Close. She could almost feel his breath on her neck.

The place was in the same condition as she remembered from her first visit. Clothes were tossed in a pile. Dirty dishes and glasses covered the coffee table and kitchen sink. Video games were strewn on the floor around the TV. Only when she got to the bathroom did she call out to Val.

When she felt him behind her, she pointed to the edge of the bathtub. "Blood. Just a smear, but this could mean he's been hurt. Or abducted." With steady hands she found the camera app on her phone and snapped pictures of the area.

"Let's not jump to conclusions," Val said. "I'll check the rest of the apartment for trace."

"I better call Deborah." She hadn't wanted to, but the blood changed the story.

They both heard the apartment door crash open. Lillian got to her feet, her heart pounding. *Luke?* Val pulled her back. When she yanked free, he put a finger to his lips. She shook her head in protest.

A female voice shouted, "Luke! Answer me."

"That's Rachel," Lillian said.

Val beat her out the bathroom door but Lillian squeezed past him in the hallway. Together they almost collided with Rachel in the front room.

When she saw Lillian, Rachel drew a sharp intake of breath. "What are you doing here? I thought you were at Elaine's."

"Got back last night. Luke's not here. Have you heard from him?

"Yes, that's why I rushed over. I told him—" She broke off and ran toward the hall. "Luke! Where are you? It's me."

Lillian exchanged glances with Val. They found Rachel in the bathroom, staring down at the blood smear. She let out a strangled cry. "I knew it. He took Luke."

"Who took him?" Lillian said.

Rachel's lower lip trembled. "Duncan. Had to be."

"Duncan's in Houston?" Lillian said, surprised.

"Yes, I saw him this morning."

"Where?"

Rachel flashed a glance at Val before answering. "I went looking for Matt. I went to his office, but didn't see his car. I was about to leave when I saw Duncan pull into the parking lot."

"Did he see you?" Val asked.

She shook her head. "If he did, he wouldn't have recognized me. I had on my helmet with the visor covering my face. I took off in the Harley."

Lillian was trying to put the two incidents together. "You said Luke called you. Was that before or after you saw Duncan."

"After. At least an hour, maybe two."

"What did he say?"

"That he got a threatening call. I told him to do nothing until I got here."

"What kind of threat?" Val said.

"That he'd never make it to court." She covered her face with her hands and let out a sob. "Now he's gone, and I'm scared."

CHAPTER 27

"Did you let the police know about the threatening call?" Lillian asked.

Rachel stood, trembling. She looked imploringly at Val, who put his arm around her shoulders. "Luke didn't recognize the voice. The cops probably wouldn't believe us anyway."

Lillian glanced at Val who frowned. Rachel's story was weak. He knew it, too.

"Let me get this straight," Val said. "You and Luke think the caller was Duncan, but you're not sure. Wouldn't Luke know Duncan's voice?"

"Yeah, but the sound was muffled, like a cloth covering the mic. Duncan would go to any lengths to keep Luke from telling what he knows."

"What does he know?" Lillian said.

Rachel glared at her. "Like I've been telling you. Duncan murdered my mother." She turned and gripped Val's arm. "Please, Val, you have to stop Duncan. You know what he's capable of."

Victoria, again. Rachel was never going to give up. She would do anything for revenge, maybe even talk Luke into disappearing if she could point to Duncan as a kidnapper.

"Rachel, look at me." Lillian waited until Rachel

turned bloodshot eyes to her. "What does Luke know that would hurt Duncan?"

Rachel stared back at her but no words came out.

Lillian had one more card to play. "I have to call the police. Luke is missing. There's blood in the apartment. And he's been threatened."

Rachel's eyes widened. "Would they arrest Duncan then?"

Lillian was startled by the question. "Not without evidence of a crime. Meanwhile, Luke's bail will be forfeit and he'll be arrested when he's found and kept in jail until the hearing. His father will lose the bail money he had Kurt put up. Right now we can't even prove he got a threatening call, because the cell phone is gone. So Duncan won't even be questioned."

Rachel's cheeks bloomed red. "This is how you handle a kidnapping case? I thought you cared."

"I do care, but we don't know if he's been kidnapped or just run away. That's why I need to call nine-one-one."

Rachel grabbed Lillian's arm. "He followed Mom and Duncan into the woods the day she died."

No one spoke.

"Luke saw the shooting?" Val demanded.

"No one would listen when I said Duncan murdered her." Rachel twisted her hands. "But I saw Luke go into the woods behind them."

Lillian wanted to shake her. "Did Luke tell you he saw the shooting? Just because you saw him follow Duncan and Victoria doesn't mean he caught up with them. Even if he did and saw Duncan shoot your mother, how could he tell whether the shooting was accidental or deliberate?"

Rachel leveled her gaze at her. "He told me Duncan aimed right at my mother."

"Goddamnit, Rachel." Val gripped her arm and turned her to face him. "He told you this when?"

"On the way to Matt's house." Rachel looked increasingly agitated. "That's why we were fighting. I wanted him to tell the police, or Matt, anyone, what he saw. He's sacred of Duncan."

Val let her go. His face turned a shade of gray. Lillian saw his fingernails bite into his palms. He had also loved Victoria.

"If Luke had told this story to the sheriff two years ago," he said, "Duncan might be in prison now."

"Like the sheriff would take his word," Rachel scoffed. "That's funny. More likely, Sheriff Tandy would go straight to Duncan, and Luke would disappear for good. You know it as well as I do. Look what's happening now."

"You could have told me. I would have listened," Val said.

An angry flush crept up Rachel's face. "I couldn't just come out and say there was a witness. Do you think I wanted to get Luke killed?"

Lillian had heard enough. She took out her phone. "We have to get Deborah involved."

Val clamped his hand around her wrist. "Wait. Don't call yet. I have an idea where I can find Duncan. He usually stays at the Omni when he's in Houston. He'll talk to me. Believe me, he won't want the cops involved. If he made that call to Luke or knows where he is, he'll tell me."

Lillian jerked her arm away. "Don't ever do that again," she said between clenched teeth.

He raised his both hands in surrender.

Rachel's expression was mixed. A shadow of fear passed over her face, followed by hope. "Yes, please, Lillian. Listen to Val. Wait before you call the cops. I don't want Luke to go to jail. Please?" She grasped Lillian hands and put them against her chest. She dropped to her knees. "Please, I'm begging you. Don't call the police. Not yet."

Lillian looked down at her. She didn't pull her hands away. She couldn't help but admire Rachel's theatrics. "I'll wait until five tonight, by which time Val should know something." She turned and looked pointedly at him. "You will call me after you find Luke, won't you? If I don't hear anything, I'm calling Deborah."

Tears shimmered in Rachel's eyes. "Val, you can put a scare into Duncan. If anyone can, it'd be you. Maybe Luke just got scared and ran. He might come back on his own."

Yeah, maybe. And maybe you already know where he is and you'll make sure he comes back. She never did trust theatrics.

She watched Rachel and Val leave together. Lillian went through the apartment one more time then locked the door when she left.

The Harley was gone when Lillian got to the street. To her surprise, Val stood by her car.

"You were good with her," he said. "I wanted to thank you. She's had a hard time."

"She's manipulating us," Lillian said, meeting his eyes.

"I know."

Lillian clicked the locks open on her car. She stood without moving. "If Luke saw Duncan murder his wife, why would he stay silent all these years?"

Val shrugged. "Remember, Luke's father has been with Duncan's company since conception. They're like brothers. Luke's not going to take the risk of going against the man who could destroy his family."

"So it's possible a murderer has walked away free and clear," Lillian said.

"If that's what Luke really saw, or thinks he saw." He gave her a sad smile, and started to walk toward a Toyota 4Runner.

"You will tell me what you find out from Duncan," she said. "I meant what I said in there."

He gave a short nod. She watched him get in the SUV. Seconds later he pulled out of the parking lot and drove away.

Damn! Did she want to believe Duncan Rosendekker was guilty? She didn't like him, but that didn't make him a killer. She really wanted to believe Rachel was wrong, for the girl's own sake. She wanted Rachel to believe her parents were only human, made mistakes, not that her father was a murderer. That her mother didn't sleep around. She felt sorry for Rachel, who had been suffering for two hate-filled years since her mother died. The only solution Lillian could come up with to satisfy Rachel, and herself, was to close the case once and for all.

❧❦❧

Matt strode to the door where the insistent pounding demanded attention. He couldn't have been more shocked to find Duncan Rosendekker on his porch, fist raised and hovering to strike again.

Before Matt uttered a word, Duncan forced his way inside.

"Where is the little punk rat?" he demanded.

"Now listen here," Matt began, automatically glancing toward Aaron's bedroom. If Duncan so much as touched a hair on his son's head, Matt would send him off in an ambulance, or a hearse. *Where the hell* was *Aaron? And what had he done to fire up Duncan?*

Duncan's next words didn't cool down Matt's fear or his anger. "Give him to me or I'll say you molested him."

"What?!" Matt's jaw dropped. *Aaron? Molested*? No, he had to mean Luke. "The hell you talking about? Luke's not here. I haven't seen him in days."

"I'll look for myself." Duncan didn't wait for an answer but plowed past Matt and stormed into the living room. Doors slammed, boots marched on hardwood, windows opened and banged shut. The more racket Matt heard, the hotter his anger boiled. He thought about his bat in the hall closet. How satisfying it would sound cracking Duncan's skull right that second. He'd do the next best thing. He pulled out his cell phone and dialed Deborah.

A minute later Duncan thundered back into the living room. e pulled

"Where is he?"

Matt tossed the phone on the nearby chair. "If you didn't find him, I guess that means he isn't here," Matt said, holding his fury inside.

"Fucking smartass. How long have you been messing with that kid?"

"Look, asshole, I don't know where you're getting this crap, but someone's shitting you. Get out of my house."

"You got a son, too. I hear you pulled him out of college. Won't look good for you. The law will catch up to you, but I'll get you first."

"Let's go outside," Matt said, feeling the heat burn his cheeks.

"Don't want to mess up your pretty house, you fag?"

"Get it on, you murdering bastard. Not enough that you killed your wife, now you're going to smear me?"

"I murdered nobody. But you make me sick."

"You lied about Victoria and you're lying now."

They circled, moved close and danced back.

"Where's Luke?" Duncan didn't wait for an answer but clipped Matt's chin.

Matt worked his jaw. Nothing broken. He returned a punch aimed at Duncan's stomach but he might as well have hit wood. Duncan snarled.

"Why so anxious to find him?" Matt said, backing away from the other man.

Duncan didn't answer but swung at Matt, who ducked.

Matt's fist dove into Duncan's soft belly and was rewarded by a satisfying "woof" from the man. Duncan was big and he had power behind his swings, but he was out of shape. Too much bourbon and red meat. Matt ran five miles a day, hit the gym at least twice a week and watched his diet. His strong point was speed. If Duncan wasn't holding back, Matt could take the ex-football player.

He didn't see the balled up fist before he felt the blow to the left side of his head. Lights popped in front of his eyes. A leg wrapped around the back of his knee. He was down, wondering what happened, how he had missed the sudden change in Duncan's attack. He wasn't flat on his back, though. He squatted, and with knees bent, he thrust upward, driving Duncan back until he toppled on the coffee table. Matt heard the wood split under the man's weight. Matt kicked out and drove his heel into the other man's chest.

He didn't hear anything but a buzzing in his head. He didn't hear the front door open. He concentrated his mind and energy on keeping Duncan down. With all his strength he punched Duncan in the face again and again.

He barely registered the noise in the room that hadn't been there before.

Duncan stopped fighting. That was when Matt heard his son yelling at him, heard boots on the floor. When he looked up, he saw Aaron, red-faced, with tears streaking his face. Behind him, uniformed officers had their guns out, pointed at him. Deborah stood behind them.

CHAPTER 28

Two hours later Matt left police headquarters and slid into the passenger seat of the black Mercedes. "Thanks for picking me up. I couldn't get ahold of Aaron. He's got my car."

Kurt drove out of the Riesner Street parking lot and glanced over at Matt. "You're lucky Duncan didn't press charges. You might have broken his nose."

"He bullied his way into my house, looking for Luke, even threatening to accuse me of molesting the boy if I didn't produce him. I should have pressed charges against *him*."

"You want to stop and get something to eat?"

Matt leaned his head back and closed his eyes for several seconds. "All I want to do is get home and smooth things over with my son. He's never seen me that angry."

"He'll understand. Mind if we stop at my office first? Won't take long."

Matt raised his hand slightly, signaling assent. He didn't care at this point. He wanted to forget the entire morning. He almost didn't hear Matt's question. "What did you say?"

"How in the world did Duncan come up with molestation?" Kurt repeated.

"Hell if I know," Matt said, only half listening. A

moment later he jerked up in his seat, the words echoing in his head. "Jesus, you didn't take him seriously, did you? Damnit, man, he's talking out of his ass. Ask my ex-wife, my son, my partner. Hell, ask Luke. He'll tell you I never touched him. I am not a child molester."

"I believe you," Kurt said. "But Duncan made good with his threat, didn't he? He planted a kernel of suspicion in the DA's office. With Luke missing, who are they going to look at? You, that's who."

Matt felt heat on his face. "Duncan planned this. Don't you see what he's doing? He knows Rachel is telling people he abducted Luke to silence him for something. He's simply shifting the spotlight on me by making up some ridiculous story. I don't know where Luke is. Probably somewhere out of the way where he can't hurt Duncan. Throwing accusations at me is one of Duncan's tricks he pulls when he's scared or cornered."

"What does Luke have on him?"

"The hell should I know? We have to find him."

"Lil's working on it. Too bad the cops had to find out he skipped bail. He'll go to jail unless I can figure a way out of it."

"Yeah, I know, poor kid," Matt said. "About Lillian, are you sure she's up to this investigation?"

"Stop right there," Kurt said. "Lil has proven to be the best investigator I've ever had. She went through the same training as her cousin. Nobody's more tenacious and inventive. She'll find the boy and the truth will come out."

A new and terrible realization broke over Matt. The idea that his neighbors, his business partners, people he considered his friends, even his family would even consider Duncan's accusations crushed him. "I would never touch Luke or any other kid that way," he said, his voice breaking. "Ask Luke." The weight of the accusation hit him like a runaway train. His body shook with rage. His eyes watered. "Goddamn Duncan."

"I believe you. Shit, how long have we known each other? Someone got to Duncan. He must be scared that Luke knows something that can hurt him. He thinks you're to blame. Why else would he go after you?"

Kurt's words barely registered. Matt stared out the car's window and realized they had come to a stop in front of Kurt's office building. *Where was Aaron?* The police wouldn't let Aaron ride along in the patrol car when they took Matt downtown. Deborah wouldn't answer any of Matt's questions, but had plenty of her own. He told her he didn't know why Duncan attacked him or threatened him with lies. They had to let him go.

There was no sign of Aaron in front of the police station. A call to his cell phone elicited voicemail. A call to his partner also went to voicemail. Alone, shaken and dazed from his ordeal, he had been surprised to see Kurt waiting for him after he was released. He gratefully accepted the lawyer's offer of a ride.

"Come inside," Kurt said, cutting off the engine. "I won't be long."

"I need to find Aaron." Matt's voice came out weak. As he pushed open the car door and dragged himself out to the sidewalk, he felt all his energy seep out of him. Each footstep seemed to stick to the ground. His chest felt heavy and his head hurt.

Kurt had already reached the building. He turned and saw Matt leaning against the car. "Hey, you okay?" He hurried to Matt's side and slid his arm under one shoulder to steady him. "Don't give out on me now."

"Dad! Dad! I'm over here. Dad!"

The sound of his son's voice and the sight of him running toward him revived Matt. His throat caught and he swallowed hard.

He felt lighter when Aaron reached him and took his other arm and squeezed lightly.

"That asshole Duncan," Aaron said to Kurt. "Dad took some hard punches, before he hit back. You should have seen him, Mr. Pasternack. My dad's got some moves."

"Let's get him inside," Kurt said.

In the lobby, Matt sucked in several deep breaths of refrigerated air. He straightened and attempted a smile for his son. "I'm okay. How did you know I'd be here?"

"I waited outside the police station. I tried to call but got static. When I saw you come out of the garage in the Mercedes, I followed. Dad, you scared me."

Matt grimaced. "Sorry, son. I wish you hadn't seen the fight." *Had Aaron heard Duncan's accusations?*

They took the elevator to the third floor. Kurt unlocked the door to his office and turned on the light. A desk, a sofa and two chairs filled the small reception area. Through an open door, Matt could see Kurt's familiar spacious inner office. It had been a long time since he'd needed Kurt other than to draw up oil leases. He checked the door to his left. Lillian's office. Closed.

"Have a seat," Kurt said. "Can I get you guys a Coke or something?"

Matt eased onto the sofa. "Don't bother."

Aaron leaned toward him. "Dad, you need some caffeine. I'll get us each a can."

Kurt pointed to the refrigerator behind the reception desk. "Get me one, too, will you?"

Aaron retrieved three cans and gave one to his father and one to Kurt.

Matt took a long swallow and felt the sugary liquid coat his throat. He raised his eyes to Kurt. "What did you find at the apartment?"

"Funny you mentioned that. Lil says there was blood on the bathtub. Not a lot. More like smear."

"DNA," Matt said. "Did they test it?"

Kurt frowned. "Against whom?"

"Whoever abducted him," Matt said. "Duncan's blood is probably still in my living room. Check that." When Kurt didn't respond, he added, "You got another explanation why he would disappear two days before his hearing?"

"They'll probably test it against your DNA," Kurt said, then quickly added, "Only for elimination purposes. I assume they took a swab."

"That's not funny, Kurt."

"Not meant to be. Think about it. You don't want questions raised over your innocence. You have nothing to hide. Do you?"

"No." Matt wiped sweat from his forehead. His skin felt clammy. "But innocent people are railroaded every day."

"Stop worrying."

"What's he talking about, dad?" Aaron asked, frowning.

"A stupid lie," Matt said, hoping that would satisfy him, but knowing it wouldn't. He looked away and took another long swallow of his Coke. His cell phone rang. The sound filled the room. He squinted at the caller ID. "It's Greg," he said aloud. "I'm a little busy right now, Greg," he said into the phone.

"You're going to get a lot busier, partner. We've had a blowout. Someone set the Dennis Number Two on fire. I'm at the site. I need you here. Now."

CHAPTER 29

Without waiting for the elevator doors to open, Matt raced down three flights of stairs and out the lobby door. He tuned out everything but the urgency of what awaited him at the wellsite. Aaron kept up with him and tossed him the car keys as they reached the Subaru. They hit the evening rush. Matt expertly swerved in and out of traffic, watching the road while talking to Greg on the speaker phone.

By the time they arrived at the lease in Chambers County, all they could see were black smoke and flames shooting into the darkening sky. Oil well firefighters surrounded the wellhead. A fire engine with the Boots and Coots logo was parked nearby. The air thickened with the smell of oil.

Aaron got out of the car after Matt. Within minutes a fit of coughing overtook him.

Matt turned to him. "See the trailer over there? That's our office. Get inside and stay there. I don't want you anywhere near the well. Understood?"

It took several frantic moments for Matt to locate Greg. He finally found him standing behind the firefighters and talking with several men in hardhats. He recognized them from OSCHA. Matt caught up with them.

"What happened?" Matt yelled over the noise.

"Beats me, but it looks bad," Greg shouted. He motioned toward the trailer where Aaron had entered moments before. "Let's get inside."

In the onsite office, the noise dimmed to a level where they could hear each other talk. Oily smoke stuck in Matt's nostrils and throat. Greg's face was smeared black.

Greg grabbed two bottled waters and handed one to Aaron. He drank half of his, wiped his mouth with the back of his hand, and faced Matt. "Hate to tell you this, but it's looking more and more like arson."

Matt's chest tightened. "But you're not sure?"

"Evidence points that way. The arson investigator from Boots and Coots agrees. They'll go over everything once they get the fire under control. Sorry, Matt."

"Anyone see what happened?" Matt asked.

Greg shook his head. "They weren't drilling at the time."

Aaron peered out the window. "How long do we have to stay here?"

Matt gave him a grim look. "We'll be here all night, son. Welcome to the oil business."

"I want to help," Aaron said.

Matt's eyes softened. "Watch and learn. They're setting the dynamite right now."

He ran through the procedure in his head. In fighting a fire at a wellhead, dynamite was most often used to create a shockwave to push the burning fuel and oxygen away from the well, similar to blowing out a candle. Once this was accomplished, the wellhead would be capped to stop the flow of oil. But this is where the threat of danger increased. One small spark from a steel or iron tool striking a stone might re-ignite the oil. Greg handed Matt a hardhat that matched his own. Matt cautioned Aaron to stay inside then headed out toward the well with Greg.

"How in the hell could this happen?" Matt's eyes were already burning from the smoke.

"Hell's got nothing to do with this action. This is man-made shit."

Matt wanted to punch someone. Someone in particular. "Duncan did it." He wished Duncan would materialize in front of him now. The fight they had earlier would look like child's play.

"I knew it," Greg said. "Sonofabitch has been behind all this crap we're having. Didn't I tell you that already?"

You don't know the latest. "All this shit happened after I met with the investors. He wants to ruin me and I don't understand why. But I'm going to find out. In the meantime, what are we going to tell the investors who have put good money into this well?"

"Don't worry," Greg said. "I'll document everything that's happened."

Everything except Duncan's hand in this until we can prove his guilt. For now Matt had to concentrate on what lay ahead of him. He spotted the arson investigator. They headed his way. A few of the OSCHA guys joined them with a list compiled of everything that had gone wrong. But still no one had an explanation for how it started. A movement to his right made him turn. He recognized the owner of the land, a fiftyish man with gray hair and leathery skin.

"Hell of a sight," the man said, peering at the fire.

"Mr. Rogert, I'm Matt Langdon. This is my landman, Greg Jertize."

"Yes, I know who you are," Rogert said. "A few of my guys were out here around the time it started. Thought you might want to talk to them."

"Sure," Matt said, curious as to what they could provide.

Rogert seemed to sense his hesitancy. "They saw a

young man hanging around just before the well fire started. A stranger. Not from around these parts."

Matt exchanged glances with Greg. "I sure do want to
talk to your guys."

Two hours later they were back in the trailer. Matt
took off his hardhat and tossed it on the sofa next to
where Aaron had fallen asleep.

"You heard them," Matt said. "The description they
gave could fit any young man."

"But you think it could be Luke," Greg said.

Matt nodded, angry and disappointed at the same time.
He couldn't explain his feelings to himself, let alone to
Greg. He barely knew Luke. The kid had broken into his
home, true, but he had a reason. Rachel. They had grown
up together. She stood up for him, defended him, and was
possibly hiding him. Or at least he suspected she had. He
liked Luke. He didn't seem that different from his own
son. Only nineteen, hormones racing, first love, identity
confusion, future unsure. He, himself, once possessed
those traits and felt the emotional uncertainty.

Aaron sat up, rubbing his eyes. "What about Luke?"

Greg filled him in. "Someone looking like him might
have set the fire."

"No shit? You catch him?" Aaron said.

"Gone with the smoke," Greg said. "No trace of him."

"He wouldn't do this on his own," Matt said after a
moment. "If the arsonist was really Luke. Could be
someone who looked like him."

"Now you're not making sense," Greg said.

"He has no motive." Even as he spoke, Matt thought
of Duncan's accusation. Was that the second part of the
plan to destroy Matt? He looked at Greg. "I'm being set
up."

"For what?" Greg stared at him. "Why—"

He never finished. The explosion shook the trailer.

Pots, dishes, glasses, and computers rattled, jumped, crashed. Matt gripped the counter top. Greg fell into a chair. Aaron dropped to the floor and covered his ears.

When the trailer settled, Matt turned to check on Aaron who got to his feet, still shaking. "It's okay, son. That explosion means everything is going as scheduled. Unless something else happens to set off another fire, they'll cap the well."

Aaron laughed with relief. "Can we go home now?"

"Not yet. We have more work to do. Might as well get some sleep."

"Uh-uh. I'm wide awake. I want to help."

"Okay, you asked for it." He put a hand on Aaron's shoulder. "Let's get a move on so we can leave before dawn."

CHAPTER 30

After spending the night working at the well site with Greg, Matt and Aaron left at dawn. Greg stayed behind to finish the follow-up paper work after catching a few hours of sleep on the sofa.

Matt found them a motel room in the nearby town. He let Aaron clean up first then jumped in the shower. He scrubbed away the grime and stink of oil, gas and smoke fumes and fell into bed. Aaron, already asleep next to him, emitted soft snoring sounds. Normally after an all-nighter at the well site, sleep would have overtaken Matt the second his body relaxed. Not this time. His mind jumped from one thought to another. He was shaken to think that anyone would deliberately set fire to his most promising well. He doubted even Duncan's twisted mind would lead him to do something so vile.

But if not Duncan, then who? Matt could think of no one. The voices argued in his head until he faded into a restless sleep. He awoke just before the noon check-out time and roused Aaron. After fortifying themselves with coffee and breakfast at the diner next door, they were back on the road and in Houston by mid-afternoon.

Matt stopped at home to drop Aaron off and change his clothes before heading to the office. The boy looked groggy, but he raided the refrigerator as soon as they hit the door. Matt stared at the broken coffee table, a lamp overturned, and broken glass on the floor leftover from his fight with Duncan.

Aaron came out of the kitchen. "Don't worry, Dad. I'll take care of the mess."

"Just leave it. I'll deal with this later."

"Hey, I live here, too." Aaron picked up the lamp and set it aside. He stared at the broken coffee table. "What do you want to do with this?"

"I said leave it. It's junk now." He looked up to see a hurt expression on Aaron's face. "We have bigger problems to worry about. I have to get to the office."

"I said I'd clean it up, Dad. I wish I could do more."

His words hit Matt deep in his gut. He hadn't spent this much time with his son since the boy was ten and he had taken him on his first fishing weekend. For most of Aaron's teen years they had been at odds. A shift had taken place since he'd brought Aaron home. But what was best for his son? "You should go back to school."

A look of disappointment crossed Aaron's face. "And leave you in your time of need?"

"I've been through worse. I'll survive this. I'd feel better knowing you're not in the middle of my mess."

"*I* wouldn't," Aaron said. "You can't make me. Dad, I know you think that's best for me, but it isn't. Not right now. I'm not deserting you. I'll go back next year."

When there'll be another excuse for not going. Matt gave up the argument. It would be a useless exercise and he'd lose in the end. Truth be told, he was touched by Aaron's support, and even more surprised by the realization. Matt didn't have anyone else. Even as the thought crossed his mind, he chided himself. Was he being selfish? Watching his son made him even more conflicted.

"Dad? Aren't you going to the office?"

Matt laughed uneasily. "I am. Get some rest. I'll try to be home for dinner."

"That's all right. Can we eat out?"

"We'll see."

He arrived at the office twenty minutes later and picked up his messages from Betsy at the front desk. He was soon caught up in paperwork, and the hours passed quickly. He didn't hear his office door open and wasn't aware of his visitor until he heard her voice.

"Have a minute? I need to talk to you."

Matt looked up. Rachel closed the door behind her and approached his desk. He saved his work and pushed his chair back to observe her. She was dressed for the summer weather in shorts that showed off her tiny waist and long legs.

A loose black and white cotton blouse with lace trim showed off a tattoo of an oil rig on her left upper arm. She stood with an attitude of resolve with a hint of defiance in her eyes.

Her arms hung loosely at her side, but Matt noticed how her fingers curled and uncurled.

"You want to sit?" he offered, leaning back and giving her his full attention.

"I'm good," she said. "I heard about the fire."

Matt wondered how, but realized it might have made the news. "It's under control now."

"Luke didn't do it. I want you to know that."

"What makes you think he'd be accused?"

She faltered for a second. "I thought—didn't someone think they saw him at the scene?"

Again Matt wondered where she got her information. "Greg checked. They found a man about the same size and age. They're talking to him now. Not Luke. Mind telling me how you knew?"

She rubbed her hands together. "Hank called me. He's

been worried about Luke and heard about the arson at the well."

"That means Duncan knows," Matt said.

"Oh, yeah." She leaned forward and put her hands on his desk. "You think he set the fire?"

"Duncan was in Houston."

"He could have arranged it," she said. "I'm sure you thought the same thing."

"What's about a motive?"

"I've been wondering the same thing. I've been shooting my mouth off about Mom's death. You believe me. So do others."

Matt interrupted her. "This couldn't be about Victoria. No matter what you, me, or other people believe, he's never going to be charged with her murder."

"I know," she said. "It's more than that. It's about the money."

Matt scoffed. "He doesn't have enough?"

"Mom got her hooks in one or more of his secret accounts. She siphoned off a big portion, put it in a separate trust fund, and willed it all to me. He's furious. What's more important, he's exposed."

Matt stared at her. "What are you saying?"

"I'm saying that the shit's about to hit the fan. The motive for killing her is about to become public knowledge."

"You're talking crazy. I don't understand."

"I didn't either until Val took me to see my grandfather earlier today. He explained how the trust he gave mom tripled in value. I benefited because she had the foresight to will that trust to me, as well as set up a separate trust in my name with the money she took from him. Duncan can never touch those funds. It's mine. She died because of that money and because he knew that its source would follow him to hell. That's one of the reason

I'm here. I want to invest thirty million dollars in Black Gold's next project."

Matt's head spun. Her words felt like a tsunami slamming him before he could recover from the well fire. She smiled. Triumphant. Smug. Maybe she wasn't so different from the father she hated.

"Thirty million?" he repeated.

"I want to turn the money over to you now. I have a cashier check made out to Black Gold Corporation, or you could give me the company's wiring information."

Matt raised his hand as if to ward her off. "Wait. This is insane. You haven't had a chance to think this through. Why are you so interested in funding my project with your inheritance? That's like throwing the money away."

"I'm a risk taker. I believe in you, Matt. Your company needs investors. I want to help. I'm not going to change my mind. Besides, I have more where that came from."

Why was he hesitating? Free money when he needed it most. Maybe that was the problem, he thought. Nobody offered this kind of money without wanting something in return.

"One more thing," she said. "This must be an anonymous investment. No one can know where the money came from."

Matt laughed out loud at the sheer lunacy, or was it ignorance, of her suggestion. "That's impossible, if only for tax reasons. What do you want out of this, Rachel?"

She looked disappointed. "I thought you'd jump at the chance. Your company's going down the tubes. Thirty million will help get you out of the hole."

He watched her silently.

"The cashier's check is real. Or I could wire the funds, if that's safer."

"You want to buy me out?"

"I don't want your company."

"No one makes an investment like that without expecting a return."

She gave him a blank stare. That worried Matt even more. She hadn't thought beyond giving away her inheritance?

"Rachel, what do you know about the oil business?"

He saw uncertainty in her eyes. Then, as if an idea occurred to her, she leaned forward. "I want to learn the business. To learn from the bottom up. You don't have to pay me. I'll be a..." She searched for the word. "Intern. I'll be investing in my future. Who knows? Maybe one day I *will* own your company."

Matt slowly shook his head. "What's the real reason?"

"I just told you."

"You should think about this a while longer. I'm sure you have other interests better suited to your wants and needs."

Her face twisted in anger. She stiffened her back and this time there was no hesitancy in her answer. "I'm offering you a lifeline. Take it, Matt, or I *will* buy you out. I can do that easily right now because of the shape your company is in. I've talked to lawyers. I'm not as stupid as you seem to think."

"Or as you've pretended to be," he said with caustic overtones.

She pretended not to hear him. "What's it to be, Matt? Your investors backed out because of Duncan. I'm the only one willing to come forward. What choice do you have?" She reached into her purse and brought out the cashier's check. She tossed the paper on his desk. "If you still want a better explanation for the money, you should talk to my grandfather. He can explain better than I can. He's quite lucid these days."

She stood and turned toward the door.

He got to his feet. "Where's Luke?"

She faced him and smiled. "He's in a safe place."

I knew it. She's hidden him all along. Matt was furious. She had them all running around like lunatics. "The hearing's Monday. Since he's already skipped bail, he can be arrested."

"Kurt's talked to the prosecutor and the judge. Luke will get off." She returned to his desk. "Will you be there?"

"I've already dropped the B and E charge. I don't have to appear."

"You should be there anyway, to support Luke."

"What about your father? Should he support him, too?"

She smiled, a wicked glint in her eyes. She returned to his desk. "I almost forgot the other reason I'm here. To give you advance warning." Her eyes hardened. "Duncan's finished. You should bank that check in a trust account today. Don't wait until tomorrow. By morning, Duncan's name will be all over the news."

He was almost afraid to ask. "Why?"

"Because Duncan will be in prison."

CHAPTER 31

Lillian arrived at her office shortly after ten on Monday morning. As usual the Houston Chronicle was left on the floor in front of the office. She picked it up and mulled over how thin and light the written news felt in her hand. Not the heft the paper used to be. Tossing her jacket on the stuffed chair in the corner, she dropped the Chronicle on her desk and thought no more about it, except to glance at the front page briefly. She made a note of the headlines about a football star, and skimmed the teaser column. Her gaze moved down to the second paragraph and stopped when she saw the words *Rosendekker* and *arrest warrant*. Farther down, the article instructed, "See full article on A3."

Her boss filled her doorway. "Luke's in the conference room. He's free to go home."

"He showed up at the hearing?"

"He did. Rachel brought him. Hank Jamison called to say he's on his way to pick him up."

"Where has Luke been all this time?"

"Safely ensconced at Rachel's grandfather's ranch."

Lillian rolled her eyes. "After she led us to believe he was in danger and sent us all on a wild goose chase. That manipulating little bitch."

"I'm happy to be done with both of them," Kurt said.

Molly, their receptionist, appeared in the hall. She made a production of shutting the door to the reception area before approaching them. "There's an Investigator Jennings here to see Miss Wallace," she said in a lowered voice.

It took Lillian a moment before she connected the name with her side trip to Austin. What possible reason did the investigator from Criminal Intelligence have for coming all this way to see her? Especially after giving her the brush-off in Austin? She glanced down at the newspaper. She wished there was time to read the article before meeting with Jennings. There had to be a connection.

"What do you want me to tell her?" Molly said, looking nervous.

"You better see her," Kurt advised Lillian. "I'll be in my office if you need me."

"Bring her into my office," she told Molly and returned to her desk. The newspaper lay unopened next to her desk blotter.

Jennings stepped into Lillian's inner office. She wore a black suit with only an inch of white blouse showing. Her ash-gray hair wound into a tight bun on top of her head.

Lillian acknowledged her with a cool stare. "I didn't think I'd be seeing you again this soon. Please, have a seat."

Jennings ignored the invitation. "I'm here about Duncan Rosendekker." Her gaze brushed across the Chronicle. "I assume you've read the papers."

"Not yet. Don't tell me he's been arrested for Victoria's murder?" She wasn't serious, but if Jennings wanted to make her guess, that's what she got.

Jennings gave her a thin smile. "He's been arrested, but not for murder."

When she didn't elaborate, Lillian grew irritated. "I'll bite. What are the charges?"

"Fraud, embezzlement, SEC violations, among others."

Lillian stared back at her. Speech was not forthcoming right away as her mind spun back to her visit in Austin. When she finally found her voice, she said, "This is what you couldn't tell me in Austin?"

Now Jennings sat down across from her, watching her reaction. "That's right."

"Did Sheriff Tandy know what you were doing?" Hadn't Jennings worked for the sheriff's office and been fired? Or was that all a lie? Evidently, it was.

"The misdirection was needed at the time," Jennings said. "Sheriff Tandy was working with me and the Texas Rangers."

She should have guessed. But how? "So you were never fired, because you weren't really employed by him or his office. You still worked for the Criminal Intelligence branch of CPS."

"That's correct," Jennings said.

"Now that you've cleared that up, can you tell me a little more about the case? I deserve that much."

Jennings sat back and crossed her legs. "The evidence will come out in trial. Suffice it to say that millions were stolen from his investors. We suspect Rosendekker put the funds into an offshore account after his wife discovered the local accounts. Duncan Rosendekker's company and personal assets have been frozen."

Lillian's mouth felt dry. "Does that mean you haven't found the offshore account?"

"We're still investigating."

"What brings you here?"

"Rachel Rosendekker and Matt Langdon. I need to interview them."

"Matt?" Lillian understood why Rachel would be questioned. "Rosendekker was going after Black Gold Exploration. I'm sure Matt had no knowledge of what he was really up to."

"We're questioning all of Rosendekker's business associates. It's possible that Mr. Langdon was also a victim."

"I wouldn't call Matt a business associate. Rosendekker did everything he could to cut off the funding of Matt's company. Are you aware of that?"

"I'm aware," Jennings said.

"Do you think Rachel knew what her father was doing? All she talked about was how she believed he killed her mother."

"Please, Miss Wallace. I can't go into details with you."

"Fine. Why do you need me?"

"You've had dealings with both of them. Your office is local, and time is running short. I need your help in expediting a meeting with them."

"When?"

"This afternoon."

Lillian's mind raced. Luke sat in the conference room down the hall waiting for his father to show up. She didn't want him involved. Outside of meeting with Hank Jamison, her calendar could easily be cleared. Getting in touch with both Rachel and Matt, and getting them to her office on a moment's notice was another story.

"I'm sure they'll want to cooperate. They must have heard the news of the arrest."

"Can you reach them?" Jennings said.

"I'll try. Would you please wait out front while I make the calls? Molly will be glad to bring you a bottle of water or coffee."

"Of course," Jennings said.

Rachel answered on the third ring. "Lillian? Is everything all right with Luke?"

"He's fine, Rachel. We're waiting for Hank to get here. You can see him for yourself. When you get here, there's an investigator from Austin who wants to talk to you about your father."

"I wondered when he'd get to me. I saw the news last night. I expected it. Honestly, don't know why it took so long. Is he the arresting officer?"

"Ask her yourself. The investigator is a woman. You knew he was going to be arrested?"

"Not at first, but I figured it out."

Lillian mind spun. She was stunned. Rachel never ceased to surprise her. "Have you seen Matt?"

"Last I saw him he was at his office. What's he got to do with the investigation?"

"Have no clue. How soon can you be here?"

"You mean, right now? I don't know. I guess I can be there within the hour."

"Good. I'll tell her."

"Wait a minute. I just got one of my brilliant ideas."

Lillian groaned.

"I'll talk to her on one condition," Rachel went on. "She talks to Luke first."

Damn. Lillian wanted to reach through the phone and slap her. "You can't make conditions or deals, Rachel. Investigator Jennings is with Criminal Intelligence. If she wants to talk to you, it's best you comply. She's working to put Duncan away. Isn't that what you want?"

"For murdering my mother."

"Why do you want her to talk to Luke?"

"Because only he knows what happened to Mom."

Lillian rolled her eyes, glad Rachel couldn't see her. "Rachel, Jennings isn't here to talk about your murder theory."

"If she wants info on dear old dad from me, she'll have to hear Luke first."

"Isn't that up to Luke? Maybe he doesn't want to talk to her."

"He will if I tell him to. He needs to tell the investigator or someone with authority what really happened to my mom. He's the only one who knows the truth and is willing to tell it. I can be at your office in ten minutes if she agrees to talk to him."

Lillian clenched the phone. "I'll discuss it with Jennings."

"Call me back." The line went dead.

Lillian called Matt next and a few minutes later met Jennings in the reception area and relayed Rachel's ultimatum.

Jennings looked confused. "Who's Luke?"

"He came here with Rachel." Lillian realized that Jennings had no reason to know about Luke. "He's the son of Rosendekker's landman, Hank Jamison. He's here waiting for his father to pick him up."

Jennings looked interested. "Hank Jamison is coming here?"

"That's right." She had a sudden, terrible thought. "Wait. Is Hank under suspicion, too?"

Jennings almost smiled. "No. He's been cleared."

What did that mean? Lillian was glad to hear that Luke didn't have that to worry about his dad. "That's a relief."

"Explain to me something. Why does Rachel insist I talk to Luke?"

"She's convinced that Luke saw Duncan murder his wife. I know that's not your case, but there could be a connection that's relevant."

"I doubt that, Miss Wallace. I know what Rachel's agenda is, and I don't appreciate being manipulated into another left turn. Any evidence should have been turned over two years ago. I may need to talk to Luke some time, but not today."

"Rachel is waiting for my call," Lillian said. "I don't like what she's doing any more than you do, but I understand why she's doing it. If Luke can provide proof, isn't it worth a listen? Thirty minutes of your time while Luke is here is all she's asking. After that, you can ask her anything."

"Blackmail," Jennings said, but without venom in her tone. "A little late, isn't it? Why now?"

"Because he was scared. But with Duncan in jail, Luke would feel safe." Lillian knew she was probably wasting her time, but she had one more card left to play. "I haven't heard the story directly from Luke, but in light of the new charges against Rosendekker, isn't it possible Victoria knew what he was doing and threatened to expose him? That's motive."

Jennings sighed. She sipped from the coffee cup Molly had provided. "I'm more interested in the millions Rachel has in her possession. Money that could legally belong to the investors."

Lillian thought of the investors' money Duncan took away from Matt Langdon and his company. Or stole it. "Should I make the call to Rachel?"

"Make the call. She wins this time. I'll listen to what Luke has to say if his father agrees to be present."

Lillian held up a hand. "Luke's nineteen. Legally he's an adult. He doesn't need his father's consent. He very well may not want him there."

"His father may insist," Jennings said. "I need everyone's cooperation. Did you find Matt Langdon?"

"Yes, he'll be here this afternoon."

Matt had not sounded surprised when he answered from his office where he had been working since dawn.

He had already seen the papers and guessed why the investigator wanted to talk to him. He said as much to Lillian.

Lillian walked Jennings back to her office and made the call to Rachel.

As promised, Rachel arrived ten minutes later, dressed in jeans and a red cashmere sweater. She demanded to see Luke in the conference room before meeting with Jennings.

"We're going to wait for his father," Lillian told her when she came back from conferring with Luke.

Rachel shook her head and faced Jennings. "Luke's ready now. You want to talk to me? Fine. I'll tell you everything I know. First we go into the conference room where you can record Luke." She shot Lillian an accusing glare. "You said she's agreed to the deal."

Lillian felt like a pawn being rolled over and flattened by a cement truck. She turned to Jennings. "You want cooperation? Up to you. I've done my part."

Jennings didn't look happy, but gave in to Rachel.

Luke stood by the window looking as though he'd rather be anywhere else but in the conference room. A recent haircut and the black suit pants and crisp white shirt was supposed to make Luke look older, but instead had the opposite effect. More like a teenager in a man's suit, even if the law treated nineteen-year-olds as an adult.

Rachel strode to his side and nudged him toward the table. "It's cool, bro. This is Investigator Jennings. She's the one who arrested Duncan this morning."

Luke eyes were questioning as he gazed at Jennings. "Yeah? For real?"

"For real, Luke." Jennings tendered a smile. "This is an informal meeting, at your friend Rachel's request. You are under no obligation to disclose anything. You are not under arrest or under suspicion of any wrong doing. Do you understand?"

He nodded and sat down. "Yes, Rachel told me."

"We can wait until your father gets here so he can sit in," Jennings said.

Luke shook his head and shot an anxious look at Rachel. "No, I don't want him here."

"See?" Rachel turned to Jennings with an I-told-you-so look then back to Luke. "Tell her, like we agreed, Luke."

He hesitated, staring at Jennings. "Did you arrest Mr. D for her mom's murder?"

Jennings started to speak, but Rachel blurted, "No, I told you, Luke, he got caught for other stuff, like stealing from the company. This is the only chance we have to tell her the truth about my mom."

Luke's eyes filled with sadness. "But it won't matter, Rach. He'll still get away with murder, won't he?"

Rachel looked about to burst with frustration. "I don't know, Luke, but this is the one time they'll have to listen to the truth, even if it goes no further. Just tell them. And we're going to record your statement so it's, like, official."

Jennings started to object, but when she saw Rachel press her hands together as if in prayer, she said instead, "Is this what you want, Luke?"

He nodded. "Can Miss Lillian and Rachel stay?"

"If that's what you want. Let's get started," Jennings said.

Luke took a deep breath and stared at the recorder. "That happened two years ago. Nobody believed me before. What if Mr. D finds out?"

"He's in jail. He can't hurt you anymore than he has already," Rachel reminded him. She turned to Jennings. "He has nightmares."

"Telling this kind of shit to cops won't help, Rach," Luke protested.

"You're right, Luke," Jennings said. "We have no evidence of murder. But the nightmares might go away."

Lillian turned on the recorder and gave the date and time and let Jennings take over. Once the preliminaries were over, Luke took a deep breath and recited how he came to follow Duncan and Victoria into the woods.

"Duncan had always taken me before, not to shoot, but to carry stuff for him. This time he told me I couldn't go. That really sucked, man. I was pissed. Who was going to do the carrying for him and Miss Victoria? I went anyway, but kept my distance. I can track. Mr. D taught me how."

"Why did you decide to follow them?" Jennings asked.

Luke looked uncomfortable. "I heard him and Miss Victoria arguing earlier. She didn't seem real happy about going hunting. Not like her at all. I got this funny feeling in my stomach like something was off."

He cast a sideways glance at Rachel before continuing.

"So they got to this clearing. He had Miss Victoria walk ahead of him. She stopped when he told her to look up at the branches."

Lillian was concentrating on Luke so intensely she almost didn't catch Rachel's expression. Rachel was so tightly contained that when she cringed in anticipation of what was coming, the movement caused a shudder. Lillian reflexively leaned toward the girl, but stopped herself.

Luke choked out a sob before he forced out the words. "He fucking shot her in the head."

Silence fell over the room.

Luke's voice rose higher. "I couldn't believe it, man. I just froze. He carried her to his truck, then tossed her in the back like she was a doe. I stayed in the woods long after the truck left. When I finally got back to the ranch, I learned Mr. D had Miss Victoria cremated. The asshole was telling everyone about the terrible accident that had happened."

"You didn't tell the sheriff what you saw?" Jennings asked.

"I was scared, lady. Wouldn't you be? Everybody believed him. After a while Mr. D started giving me these strange looks, like he was reading my mind or something. It creeped me out. I made excuses for not doing the odd jobs I used to do. I didn't want to have anything to do with him. I wanted to run away, but I couldn't. I had to pretend nothing happened. I wish I'd never gone into those woods."

"When did you tell Rachel?" Jennings said.

"Not until we got to Houston. But I guess she knew already. She said she saw me follow them."

"Could you have possibly mistaken his actions? Could it have been an accident and not murder?" Jennings said.

Luke shook his head. "No, ma'am. Like I said, he aimed right at her." A look of panic crossed his face. "I won't have to testify in court, will I? He'll come after me. He never forgets."

"Duncan's not on trial for murder," Jennings said.

"Yeah, that's right. He just ruined the company," Luke muttered. "My dad's gonna lose his job."

"The company is shut down," Jennings said. "Mr. Rosendekker's assets are frozen."

Molly stuck her head in the door. "Hank Jamison is here."

"Just in time," Lillian said. "Thank you, Luke. You're a very brave young man."

Jennings stuck her hand out to him. "Yes, you are. I don't know if we'll ever be able to use this, but we'll have your statement on record."

"How long will you be in town?" Lillian asked her.

"At least a couple of days. Rosendekker's bail hearing is day after tomorrow."

"Bail hearing?" Rachel and Luke's voice rang out simultaneously.

CHAPTER 32

e's entitled to bail," Jennings said over Rachel's and Luke's cries of outrage.

Lillian wasn't surprised at their reaction. "It's procedure."

"Doesn't he have to stay in jail until his trial?" Luke's voice cracked. "I thought his accounts were frozen."

Rachel looked agitated. "Can't you argue against bail? He's got rich friends, He could get on a plane and go anywhere he wants."

"The prosecutor can present arguments, but more likely the judge will set an amount and if he can't come up with the money, he'll remain in jail," Jennings said.

Lillian admired the investigator's cool demeanor in the midst of the chaos she had caused. There was a time she had seriously considered applying to one of the law enforcement branches, and follow in the footsteps of her cousin and the rest of that side of her family. She respected them for their dedication to the law. As a child Lillian dreamed of catching bad guys and seeing justice met, but her own nature called for a less confining profession.

Hank Jamison walked into the conference room. He strode past Rachel, who had moved toward the door, and reached Luke's side. He put a restraining hand on his son's shoulder. "Are you okay?"

"Yeah, I'm okay. But I really need to talk to you."

Rachel slipped out the door and Lillian had the impression that she wanted to avoid a face-to-face with Luke's father. Lillian wanted to follow her out of the room, but Hank motioned to her.

"I left a check with Kurt," he told her when she approached him. "Stick around. I want to talk to you." She nodded and took the chair next to Jennings.

"Dad," Luke tried again.

Hank put up his hand. "In a minute." He turned to Jennings. "Investigator Jennings, we meet again. I heard you arrested Duncan."

Jennings stood. "You heard correctly. Can we have a few words? It won't take long."

Hank acknowledged her but not before he gave a reassuring nod to Luke. "Is this about my son?"

"No," Jennings said. "This is about the company."

"Have you been talking to Luke without me?"

"Dad," Luke protested. "Listen to me. I want to stay here in Houston."

Hank slowly turned, giving him his full attention. "What are you talking about?"

"I don't want to go back to the ranch."

Anger flashed across Hank's face. "Is that so? Who's going to support you? Rachel? Do you have a job? Money for an apartment? What have you been telling people?"

"Nothing," Luke said, taking an involuntary step backward.

"After all the trouble you've caused these people, breaking into a home, wrecking a car, you think they are going to take you in and protect you? Why, you would be in jail today if I hadn't hired a lawyer."

"I've learned my lesson. I can manage on my own," Luke protested.

Hank went on as if Luke hadn't spoken. "Your mother and I had plans for you. You were supposed to go to college. You have a scholarship that you earned. Don't throw that away. Think about your future. Think of what I've sacrificed for you."

"Dad," Luke began, but Hank cut him off.

"You say you'll manage. How? You young folks think you can snap your fingers and you get what you want. I've worked hard all my life to see that you have all you need, not to see you live on the street." Hank paused to wipe his eyes, which had become moist. His voice cracked. "You're breaking your mother's heart."

Lillian forced herself to remain quiet when she saw Luke about to cry. Red-faced, he bowed his head. "Dad, don't. I'll come home for now, but I won't stay."

Hank put his hand on his son's shoulder. "I knew you'd see it my way. Give me a moment. I have to talk to the investigator, then we can leave." He motioned to Jennings. "Can we talk in another office?"

"You can go into mine," Lillian volunteered.

She watched them leave the room before she went up to Luke. "You okay?"

Luke ground his teeth. "He treats me like a kid."

"He's concerned about you, like a father should be." She hesitated. "Does he know what you talked about to Jennings?"

Luke met her gaze. "I think he suspects, but he doesn't want to believe Duncan's a murderer. They've known each other forever. My dad told me stories of when he worked for old man Kittering before Duncan took over his business. They go way back."

She let his words sink in as she mentally reviewed her research of Rosendekker Exploration. Hank Jamison was the company's landman, and his title was Vice President of Land, making him second in command after Duncan.

As the title suggested, he was in charge of procuring the land for the oil wells. He drew up lease agreements and negotiated with the land owners. He was in charge of the oil rigs and the wells, worked with the Railroad Commission, and all the different entities that made the oil business run. He worked with the accountants who paid the landowners their share from the profits.

Now she was learning that Duncan hadn't hired Hank Jamison. He was part of the Kittering Exploration package. This also meant he knew Victoria long before Duncan met her. Hank came with the experience and expertise that Duncan didn't have. Perhaps Duncan should have made him a partner. But Duncan Rosendekker didn't have partners. Even his board members were not close alliances.

Lillian thought of Hank in her office with Jennings and wondered how much information Hank had already contributed to Jennings. She thought back to the first and only time she met Hank in person. She was in Dallas at the party looking for Val. The only interaction she witnessed that stuck out was Hank breaking up a fight between Duncan and Matt. She hadn't sensed any great animosity on Hank's part, but maybe Hank had been carrying years of resentment for what Duncan did to his previous employer. Or, maybe Victoria's suspicious death been the final brick to fall from the crumbling house of Rosendekker to hasten its demise.

There was a problem with her speculation, though. What did Hank have to gain now that the company was shut down? He didn't have a job. What were the benefits? This was not a good time for oil companies right now with the oil prices down and getting lower every day. Layoffs were far more frequent than new hires. What company was going to pay their overblown salaries now when contract work paid far less?

CHAPTER 33

Lillian slid onto the bench seat at the back of the courtroom where Rachel and Matt sat in pensive silence.

Rachel leaned toward her. "They haven't called him yet. It's been one bail hearing after another. He's probably going to be last. I got to pee. Come with me?"

Matt turned to frown at her, but Rachel ignored him. She pushed Lillian toward the aisle. Once they were outside the courtroom, Rachel half ran to the restrooms. Lillian wanted to ask why she had waited so long.

When she came out again, Rachel pulled at her short skirt. "He's got a lawyer. Not the company mouthpiece either."

"Did you get a name?"

"No," Rachel said, looking jumpy and nervous. "He's short and thin. Never saw him before."

"How did the interview go with Jennings?"

"Don't think she was happy with what I told her. But what could I say? I didn't know my dad took all that money from the investors and put it an offshore account. I told her about the trust accounts I inherited from my mom. Duncan couldn't touch any of that."

They reached the courtroom and took their seats.

"Made it back in time," Matt told them.

Lillian looked up to see Duncan brought in. He wore county orange which made his skin look sallow. A pair of cuffs kept his hands behind him. The Assistant DA read the charges and requested that bail be denied. Lillian saw Jennings sitting at the prosecutor's table, her expression unreadable.

When Duncan's attorney stood and came forward, Lillian did a double take. The man in the expensive-looking gray suit reflected Rachel's short description. His thick mane of curly black hair was immediately recognizable.

"You know him?" Rachel whispered.

"Randolph McPherson," Lillian said softly. One of Houston's toughest and most feared criminal lawyers. His reputation earned him top fees, but since Duncan's accounts were frozen, who was paying McPherson's fee?

McPherson stated his argument for bail and the judge used her gavel and set bail at five hundred thousand. A wide grin spread across Duncan's face and his head swiveled toward the third row.

Lillian followed his line of sight and inhaled sharply.

Rachel saw her at the same time. "Elaine?" she said aloud.

Duncan's fiancé smiled back at him as she rose with her purse clenched in her hand.

Lillian stood and followed Elaine out. Rachel came with her.

Rachel reached Elaine first. "What are you doing?"

Elaine gave her a frosty glare. "Mind your own business." She turned to Lillian. "Stay out of this, Lillian. Duncan wants nothing more to do with you or his daughter. He's had enough lies and false allegations."

"You're still going to marry him?" Lillian said.

"Our wedding is going ahead as planned," Elaine confirmed.

"Are you as crazy as he is?" Rachel said, visibly shaking. "He's a crook and a murderer."

"Enough," Elaine said coldly. "Get out of my way."

Lillian pulled Rachel back, and noticed Matt coming up behind them. Rachel shook her off.

Matt stared past at them at Elaine's retreating back. "Did I hear right? She's going to marry him?" He turned to Rachel, his expression sympathetic. "Some women are drawn to criminal types. Never figured Elaine to be one of them."

They watched Elaine step inside the cashier's office.

"Can we stop her?" Rachel said.

"We warned her," Lillian said. "That's all we do."

"I can use a drink," Matt said, looking at Lillian. "Anyone else?"

"I'll pass on the drink," Lillian said, "but food sounds good. The Bull Room is close by if you and Rachel want to join me."

Rachel looked too numb to respond, but Matt agreed.

As they passed the courtroom, Lillian spotted Jennings. Court had been adjourned, and the investigator was collecting her papers and stuffing them into her briefcase. Duncan had already been taken away.

"Take Rachel and go ahead. I'll meet you over there," she told Matt, and turned into the courtroom.

She reached Jennings as the investigator started for the door. "Have a minute?" She didn't wait for an answer. "I didn't hear everything. Were there conditions to Duncan's release?"

Jennings didn't smile, but she wasn't aloof either. "Ankle bracelet."

"Does he have to stay in Houston?"

"He'll be staying with Elaine Westerfelt at her ranch. They're planning their wedding."

"The judge agreed to this?" Lillian wondered how Jennings could look so calm.

"He set the conditions."

"When is his trial?" When Jennings gave her the date, Lillian snorted. "That's six months from now."

"Right. I'm heading back to Austin, so if you'll excuse me, I want to get on the road."

Lillian moved aside to let her by. Before Jennings reached the door, Lillian caught up with her again. "Have you found the offshore account where he put the money?"

Jennings stared at her. "Why do you ask?"

Lillian shrugged. "Curious, that's all."

"Leave it alone, Miss Wallace. Have a nice day."

The bluntness of her answer stunned Lillian. What was wrong with a yes or no answer? Why was it a secret?

Lillian couldn't get the mystery out of her head as she walked the block and a half to the restaurant. Evidently the offshore account was still hidden and inaccessible to the investors who wanted their money back. Only Duncan knew how to get to the money, and he would bide his time if he was patient enough. But Duncan didn't seem to her to be the patient kind.

The Bull Room was a quiet refuge coming in from the noisy downtown street. For a moment she stood to let her eyes adjust to the change from bright sunlight. The walls inside were paneled with dark walnut that highlighted the black and white photos on the wall. A bar traveled the length of the room on her left. The booths and tables were mostly empty this time of day. She spotted Matt and Rachel in the back booth. A waitress delivered water and bread baskets and took Lillian's order as soon as she slid next to Matt on the curved leather seat.

"We were talking about Duncan," Matt informed her.

Rachel's frustration had switched to anger. "He gets

away with murder, and now he's going to walk. You'll see. He'll find a way."

"There's the offshore account," Lillian said. "You know anything about that?"

"You think he'd tell me?" Rachel said. "I'm the last person he'd want near that money."

Matt took a long swallow from his Shiner Bock. "What does Elaine get out of her arrangement with Duncan?"

Lillian tore a slice of bread from the loaf. "Maybe she wants to share the ill-gotten proceeds with him."

Matt looked askance. "You think she knew all along what he was doing with the investors' money?"

Lillian shrugged. "If she didn't, she knows now."

"That's why she marrying the asshole?" Rachel said, looking troubled.

"It's one answer." Lillian didn't like it any more than Rachel, but what else explained the high-priced lawyer, bail money and updated marriage plans?

Their sandwiches and drinks arrived and Matt waited to speak until after the waitress left. "I didn't know Elaine well, but the way she came across today surprised me. Seemed out of character."

"How do we know anyone?" Lillian contemplated her sandwich as if the answers were between the slices of bread.

"I'm going to visit them," Rachel announced. "They can't refuse to see me. I'll offer a deal to Elaine and see if she'll take it."

"What kind of a deal?" Lillian frowned.

"She must have drawn up a pre-nup to keep Duncan from grabbing her company. I'll offer to buy enough shares to take over control."

"Do you have that much left?" Matt asked.

"Don't make assumptions about my finances. You got

your share." She slumped in her chair. "She probably won't take my deal anyway if Duncan is around."

Lillian's phone beeped. She picked it up and read the text. She pushed away her plate with the half-finished pastrami sandwich and took several gulps of iced tea. "I have to get back to the office. You two finish your lunch." She withdrew two twenties from her purse and slapped them on the table. She gave Rachel one last look before leaving. "Be careful. Elaine's a grown woman. She won't take kindly to interference."

Matt got to his feet. "Thanks for all you've done."

She gave him a regretful smile. "I haven't done anything. Hope your wells come in as expected and there're no more fires."

She didn't expect to see either of them again. Nevertheless, she found herself speculating over the bond between Matt and Rachel and the connection with Victoria. Lillian didn't imagine the resemblance between the two, and wondered if Duncan noticed as well. Did seeing Matt make Duncan flash back on Victoria and Matt's engagement during college? Could Rachel be the reason Duncan tried to ruin Matt?

Don't waste time on lives you're not being paid to investigate. The reminder usually didn't stop her, but by this time she had arrived at her office and her thoughts went in a different direction. Kurt had accepted a new case and she was about to meet the client.

ℂℂℂ

Three weeks went by while Lillian caught up on the new case and put aside her thoughts of Duncan and Elaine. One Friday afternoon Val appeared in her office. She hadn't heard the door to her inner office open. Molly had refrained from announcing him. When she looked up, his body leaned against the frame, his black cowboy hat tipped forward shadowing his face. He was dressed in his customary black jeans and the turtleneck that rippled down his upper body and arms. A black leather jacket hung over his arm. Several days of beard shadowed his face. "Molly said you needed a lunch break," he said.

"I will kill Molly."

"I added the lunch part." He grinned. "We could talk, but I could really use a bite to eat. What about you?"

"I am working," she said in a clipped tone.

He sauntered into her office, his gaze steady on her. "You have something against lunch?"

She softened. Why did she find it so hard to turn him down? The last time she saw him he had signed the statement for Luke. Since then she put that sexy body out of her mind.

"I guess I could take a short break," she conceded.

Lillian closed her laptop and took her purse from the bottom drawer. He waited by her desk until she stood. She brushed against him and caught a whiff of an expensive men's cologne over the scent of leather and soap.

"You have a place in mind?" she asked.

"I passed a deli at the corner."

"I know the place. Food's good."

They made small talk about the change of weather while they walked. After they arrived and ordered their sandwiches at the counter, they got their fountain drinks and claimed a table in the back.

She rested her elbows on the table. "Okay, what do you want?"

"I'm worried about Elaine. Have you heard from her?"

"No. Why would I?"

"She's marrying Duncan."

"I know about her plans. I was at the bail hearing. Where were you?"

"Out of the country or I'd have stopped her."

She laughed at this. "How would you have done that?"

He shrugged. "Whisked her away if I could."

"Go visit." She folded her arms across her chest. "Nobody's can force you to stay away."

"You get a wedding invitation?"

She sipped her Coke. "No. Don't expect one. The date's set?"

"Next Sunday. Rachel wants me to take her."

"That soon." She set down her glass with a thud. "What did you tell her?"

"I said I would, if you come with us."

"You didn't."

"Elaine needs you." Val slid his hand along the table toward her. "She likes you, you know."

She glanced at his hand. "That's not how she acted at the courthouse."

"She probably was pretending in front of Duncan." He looked earnest when he spoke, especially when making excuses for Elaine.

Elaine wasn't anywhere near Duncan. "Ridiculous. When did you talk to her?"

"This morning on the phone."

"How did she sound?"

"Strained. Trying hard to sound normal."

How did he know that? "I don't get her. She got him out of jail, paid for a top notch attorney, and bonded him out. To what end? Duncan should be bending over backward and licking her boots if that would make her happy."

Their sandwiches arrived. When their server left, Val said, "He has no intention of spending time in jail. He'll figure a way to get the money or have Elaine get it so they can leave the country."

"Wow. You're talking about the offshore account, aren't you?"

He met her eyes. "That's his ticket to freedom."

"You really think Elaine is planning to leave with him?" She picked up half of her sandwich and bit into it.

Val looked troubled and searched for words. "I honestly don't know what her plan is. If I knew the woman better, I might have a clearer read on what to expect. That's why I want you to come with us."

"I don't know what I can do. I've only talked to her a few times. She seems like a smart woman. She must be. She runs a successful oil and gas business."

Val nodded. "At first I thought Duncan was after her company. She tried to talk him into signing a pre-nup. Of course, he resisted her attempts. But getting control of her company won't do him any good in prison. I'm sure the investors he bilked will sue him for any assets he has left, including the money in that offshore account."

Lillian put a piece of leftover crust on her plate and picked up the remaining half of her sandwich. "So what you're saying is, everyone's after the money he stole, including Elaine."

"No, not Elaine." He frowned. "At least I hope not."

She sighed in exasperation. "Explain to me then, what her motive was for bailing him out. She didn't seem crazy in love, or otherwise, when I met her. I don't care how persuasive the man can be. To me, he's just out for himself and to hell with whoever stands in his way. What does Elaine hope to gain, if it isn't the money he's hiding?"

"Okay, that thought's occurred to me, distasteful as it is. I just don't want to believe she would go that far. If I confront her, she'll deny everything. If I make a suggestion then I'm poking my nose in her business."

"So why do you want me with you? I'm not her close

friend. Not a friend at all, really. I tried to talk her out of marrying the man. So did Rachel. She'll see me as an interfering busybody."

"On the other hand," Val said. "It's been three weeks and the two of them have been cooped up together in that house with a trial looming. Then there's that stash of cash that only Duncan can access if he wasn't being watched. A ticket to freedom." His intense gaze held her.

"They're sitting over a keg of dynamite ready to blow," she supplied.

"That's right. And we're invited to a sham wedding. Elaine needs a woman to be there with her. Someone she feels she can trust. Rachel is too young and volatile with mother issues. You are her equal. She needs *you*."

"You've made your point," Lillian said.

"Then you agree?"

With some misgivings, she nodded. She pointed to his untouched plate. "Are you going to eat that, or what?"

He glanced down as if remembering his food. He grinned and picked up his sandwich. "All your fault.

They were silent while he tackled his pastrami sandwich and chips, and she finished what was left of her ham and cheese.

She got up and took their empty glasses to refill them. When she sat back down, she watched him. "Duncan can't go anywhere with that ankle bracelet he's wearing. If he removes it, the sheriff's office will be alerted."

He looked up. "He knows. I'm sure he's got a solution for that, too."

They finished their meal and Val walked her to the front of her office. "I'll pick you up at your apartment Sunday morning. Seven too early?"

"Yes, it's my day to sleep in. Better make it eight instead," she said. "How do you know my address?"

He grinned. "I hope you're going to give it to me."

She pulled out a business card and a pen. After she wrote down her home address, she tucked it under the collar of his turtleneck. "Don't get lost." She started to turn toward the revolving door, but stopped. "Bring coffee. I take mine with cream."

Inside the lobby, she watched him amble out of sight. She was actually looking forward to the trip. But first she would make a phone call to the DPS office and Investigator Jennings.

CHAPTER 34

Lillian chose an emerald green pants suit that showed off her burgundy hair, worn loose around her shoulders. She pulled on black high-heeled boots. A business look, nothing fancy, but acceptable for this wedding. Her phone rang at the same time as her doorbell. She hesitated, tempted to let the call go to voice mail. A glance at the name of the caller changed her mind. Investigator Christine Jennings. She answered. Three minutes later she hurried to answer the door.

Dressed in black jeans and a black shirt under a black leather vest, Val looked presentable for a funeral, not a wedding. She met his admiring stare and looked past him to his Toyota 4Runner. "Where's Rachel?"

"She took the Harley."

"Didn't want to ride with us?" she said.

"Too impatient." He walked her to his car. "Seen Matt lately?"

"No, why?" She opened the passenger's door and sat on the seat facing out with her feet on the curb, waiting for his answer.

He paused with his hand on top of the door. "I just thought—Never mind. I heard investors were interested in his project again."

"Good. He deserves it." She swung her feet to the

floorboard and pulled the door shut. While she adjusted the seat, he came around the front and slid behind the wheel.

He started the engine. "If Matt's well flows the way he swears it will, Rachel might get a good return on her investment in Black Gold. She's smart. Takes after her father."

"Get real. How can you compare her to a sneaky, underhanded sociopath like Duncan?"

"I wasn't." He kept his eyes on the road, but his chin quivered, hiding a smile.

"You're joking. You're saying she's not Duncan's daughter?" Was she finally getting an answer to the question that came up every time she saw Rachel with either of the two men her mother had an affair with?

When he didn't answer, she turned away and read license plates as they passed. She wasn't going to play his game this time.

He finally broke the silence. "You know Victoria was seeing three men when she got pregnant. She was engaged to Matt when she met Duncan. Her father thought the ambitious football hero was a perfect match. He regretted that decision. Still does."

"You were the third man," she said.

He nodded. "Instead of sticking around to see how it played out, I joined the navy."

"Duncan really could be Rachel's father," she said.

"He's never had any children before or since."

"Doesn't matter. He could have used protection."

His next words startled her. "What I'm leading up to is this. I want to do a DNA test with Rachel and me."

Lillian didn't know what to say. "Why are you telling me this?"

"I had to tell someone." He glanced at her. "Thought you'd know an independent lab."

She thought of the possible implications to the parties involved. "I might. But understand, Rachel will have to agree to being tested."

"I'm aware. I've given this a lot of thought."

"Why? Think about it, Val. What are you doing to Rachel by suggesting such an action?"

"I believe she would want to know the results."

She turned back to the window. The Houston landscape showed car dealerships, used and new furniture warehouses, chain stores, and fast food signs. After a while, the freeway narrowed and ran through small towns that took up only a few blocks before disappearing behind them. Cattle, sheep and horse ranches ate up the land and she felt her eyes grow heavy. She leaned back and gave in to darkness. Before she drifted off, she thought about what Val proposed. He wouldn't have brought up the suggestion if he and Victoria hadn't had sex. Did he know Victoria was pregnant when he left to join the navy? Maybe back then he didn't want to be a father. Besides Val, Matt seemed the likeliest candidate for fatherhood, other than Duncan. Would Matt want to take the same test?

Lillian awoke with a start. The car sat still. She felt the late morning sun through the windows.

"We're here, sleepyhead," Val said. "Ready?"

Straightening, she recognized the front of Elaine's house. To her right she saw Rachel's Harley. Val got out of the car first and Lillian joined him on the wraparound porch. She recognized the two chairs where she had sat with Elaine and drank tea.

No one appeared even after Val repeatedly pushed the bell and banged on the red door. From a nearby window she heard loud, angry voices, too muffled to understand. Lillian reached for the doorknob. The door was unlocked.

They entered the living room to a standoff between

Duncan Rosendekker and Rachel. Duncan looked fit and showed off muscles Lillian hadn't noticed before. Working out? Preparing for prison? Or for some unknown locale?

He wore a yellow Polo shirt with Bermuda shorts that drew attention to his black ankle bracelet. The object of Duncan's rage, Rachel, huddled behind a large stuffed chair and held up what looked like a kitchen knife. Lillian glanced around for Elaine and spotted her in the doorway between the living room and hallway. Her face and posture mirrored her anger and frustration, but she seemed powerless to move.

"Make him stay away from me," Rachel said in a high pitched voice. Lillian wasn't sure if her words were directed to Elaine or if she even noticed her and Val.

Val came up behind Duncan, who turned with a snarl. "Who the fuck let you people in?"

"What's going on?" Lillian demanded, ignoring his words.

Duncan turned to Lillian while pointing to Rachel. "What's going on is this traitor, my one and only child, waltzed in here to turn my fiancé against me."

Rachel raised up slightly, cheeks ablaze. "Traitor? That's you. I'm only now finding out what a crook you are. Dummy me, I thought you were just a murderer."

Elaine finally moved from where she had been standing and rushed to Lillian and Val. "I'm so sorry. They've been at each other since Rachel arrived. I'm so glad you came."

"What brought this on?" Val asked Elaine, ignoring Duncan's muttered curses.

"He thinks she gave him up to the cops," Elaine said.

"I know she did." Duncan glared at his daughter. "Confess, you lying snitch."

Rachel pushed against the back of the chair. "Fuck

you. I never went to the cops. I didn't even know about your secret offshore account."

"This the way you talk to your father?" He turned to his small audience as if she had proved his point. He turned back to Rachel. "Your mother told you, didn't she?"

Rachel brandished the knife in a shaky hand. "She didn't tell me anything. Were you worried about that? Is that why you killed her? Fuck. I don't want to be your daughter. You're ugly and I hate you." Rachel dropped the knife and slumped behind the chair.

Lillian rushed past Duncan and kneeled beside Rachel. "Let's go to the kitchen." She picked up the knife and helped Rachel to her feet

Duncan's voice rose. "Sorry little sneak, creeping around where you don't belong."

Rachel turned and looked back at him. "Yeah, I'm sorry. Sorry for Elaine that she wants to marry a sonofabitch like you. Sorry for my life."

She pushed away from Lillian and bolted to the kitchen.

Lillian followed. She settled Rachel in a chair at the table and brought her a glass of water. "Deep breaths," she instructed. "Don't worry about him. When you're ready, tell me what happened."

Rachel drank half the water and wiped her face. "They didn't answer the door so I let myself in. Elaine never locks the door. I waited forever. I checked upstairs. That's when I heard them arguing."

"Arguing about what?" Lillian asked.

Rachel glanced at the kitchen door. She lowered her voice to a whisper. "Money. Elaine was asking about the offshore account and when he could get the money. She mentioned Belize, I think. Duncan wouldn't tell her anything. I could have told her he wouldn't. He writes nothing down. He keeps numbers in his head." She grasped Lillian's hand. "Do you think Elaine agreed to marry him so she could trick him out of his stash?"

Lillian was about to refute Rachel's words, but then she remembered the phone call she got that morning. *Oh, God, Elaine. You should have waited for Jennings.* "Rachel, you should leave right now. Maybe a stop at the sheriff's office wouldn't be a bad idea. Tell him you're worried about Elaine."

A look of uncertainty crossed Rachel's face. "Are you sure?"

"Yes. Forget whatever you brought with you. Just leave." Lillian stood. "While you're doing that, I need to check something out."

When she came out of the kitchen she collided with Elaine.

Elaine looked furtively behind her before speaking. "Thank you for talking to Rachel. She shouldn't aggravate him that way."

Lillian didn't bother to argue. "Where's Duncan now?"

"Val took him outside. He's acting more and more paranoid."

"Rachel heard you two arguing about money."

Elaine gave her a sharp look. "Rachel knows nothing. She needs to go now."

Lillian kept her voice to a whisper. "That's what I told her. Elaine, I know what you're doing and it's dangerous."

Elaine frowned and backed away. "I don't know what you're talking about."

"Sure you do. Jennings called me this morning. You can't be too obvious about the money. Duncan will see right through you."

Elaine swallowed. "I've been pretending to go along

with him. He thinks we're going away together after he gets the money."

"And the wedding?"

"He says if we're married, I can't testify against him."

"Sure you can. You just can't be forced to."

Duncan's booming voice interrupted them. "What's all the whispering about? Is this a conspiracy?"

Elaine forced a laugh and turned to him. "We were discussing a surprise for our wedding."

"Where's Rachel?"

At that moment, they heard the motorcycle roar into action. Elaine forced a smile. "She decided to leave. She didn't want to upset you anymore."

"That's too bad," Duncan said, his voice calm. "What's a wedding without my daughter to walk down the aisle with me?"

"But you ordered her to leave, sweetheart."

"I changed my mind. She's a nosy, interfering little bitch, like the two of you, and I need to keep an eye on her."

Lillian felt a twist in her gut. Elaine didn't seem to realize how bad the situation had become.

The front door crashed open, and Rachel stumbled into the living room. Oil and dirt were smeared across her legs, arms and clothes. She took two steps toward Duncan and screamed, "What did you do to my bike? You cut the oil line, didn't you? The oil spilled out over everything."

"Where's the bike now?" Lillian said.

"Lying on the side of the road," Rachel said, tears streaking down her cheeks.

"You should have stayed home," Duncan said with an unnatural calmness. "But since you sneaked upstairs to listen at our door, you heard things you shouldn't have. Now I got to get rid of you, too."

Elaine's eyes widened with fear and contempt. "You bastard." She pushed at him and turned to run, but Duncan grabbed her and yanked her to his side. She cried out and tried to wrench free.

Duncan punched her in the face. She let out a scream and sagged. He shook her like a rag doll. "Just like Victoria. She thought I was a fool, too. She thought I wouldn't catch on to her tricks. She was going to the cops, too."

Elaine shook her head, blinking tears of desperation as she struggled to gain her footing. Her face flamed red from his fist. "I wasn't. I wouldn't." She pushed against him, but he held her tight.

"I read your phone messages," he snarled. "Not as smart as Victoria, but still a snitch and a rat. I trusted you, bitch. You think by bringing your interfering friends, you'd be safe? I'll take you all down."

"Leave her alone!" Rachel screamed. She jumped on Duncan's back, tearing and scratching him.

While Duncan shook off Rachel while holding onto Elaine, Lillian backed away, thinking feverishly, *where was Val?* Why hadn't he returned with Duncan? Certain he was still out back, hurt or possibly dying, she bolted for the back door.

Duncan grabbed her as she reached the door. He kicked it closed and swung her around. Before she could fight him off, he wrenched her arm around her back. Her chest smashed against his. Pain shot through her shoulder. She cried out, unable to move. He brought his mouth close to her ear. "Don't bother looking for your friend. He's out of commission."

She strained her head to the left, searching for Elaine and Rachel. Duncan had knocked them both down before he went after Lillian.

"Get up! Find Val!" she screamed.

Duncan banged his head against Lillian's so hard the

pain dazed her momentarily. "Shut up. Val can't help you. He's done for." He stepped back toward a small desk by the wall, dragging her with him.

"What did you do to him, you bastard?" She tried to twist away, but he jerked her arm farther up until she cried out again. He kept her clamped against him, emitting a soft grunt each time she tried to break free.

One thought sustained her. *Val couldn't be dead. No, please, no!* Out of her peripheral vision, she caught Rachel getting to her feet, eyeing the door. *Go! Run!*

She struggled harder, this time to keep him from looking for Rachel or Elaine. Each time she moved, he yanked her arm up. Any higher, he would dislocate her shoulder, if he hadn't already. The pain knifed through her even as she fought against weakening.

Duncan's other hand let go of her for a few precious seconds. Feeling the pressure ease slightly, she tried to kick him, but a second later she was staring at the semi-automatic now pointed at her head. The gun must have been in the desk. What the hell was he thinking? Just having a gun in his possession meant forfeit of his bond. He had to escape now, but first he'd have to kill them all. A wave of panic shuddered through her as another thought occurred to her. Had he used that gun on Val? She hadn't heard any shots fired. But he could have bludgeoned him to death.

A sudden movement to her left distracted her. Duncan turned his head in the same direction. Rachel was on her feet and sprinting erratically for the front door.

Duncan turned the gun toward Rachel. When he did, the hand that held Lillian's arm loosened. She pulled it free at the same time she slammed her body against Duncan's. The shot went wild. Without hesitating, she stomped the stiletto heel of her boot on the instep of his sandaled foot. He screamed. Rachel fled out the door.

Lillian didn't stop moving either. She ignored the searing pain in her shoulder and clasped her hands together. She brought the heel of her hands down on Duncan's wrist with all the strength she could muster. The Glock fell out of his hand and fired when it hit the floor. The bullet slammed into the far wall. Lillian kicked the weapon out of the way and twisted to gain enough momentum and strength to drive her elbow into his solar plexus. She followed up with a chop across his throat. He landed heavily on the carpet. Lillian rubbed her shoulder. Free of the pressure, the pain subsided slightly.

"Find something to tie him up with," she ordered Elaine, who had been watching, frozen against the opposite wall. Lillian's sharp demand acted like a puppet's string jerking Elaine upright. She rushed to the kitchen and returned with a roll of duct tape and a sharp steak knife. Lillian wrapped Duncan's wrists and started on his ankles, careful not to disturb the government bracelet.

"I think I have some rope in the garage," Elaine said. She left and quickly returned. Working as one, they bound Duncan's wrists and ankles together with the rope. Elaine unrolled more duct tape and covered his mouth. After that, all he could do was moan. Elaine sat heavily on the carpet next to him, breathing hard.

"How did you learn to do that?" she asked Lillian, pointing to Duncan.

"Police and martial arts training." She scrambled to her feet. "Call nine-one-one. Have them bring an ambulance, too. Pray Val's alive." She raced outside, shouting Val's name.

"Over here," Rachel called from the rear fence.

A gash at the back of Val's head was bleeding profusely. Lillian knelt beside him. His eyes fluttered open, and he tried to focus on Lillian. He struggled to sit up.

"Careful," Lillian said. "Lie still."

"Duncan?" he mouthed.

"Bound and gagged," she said.

Rachel knelt on the other side of Val. "I watched her through the window, Val. She's amazing."

"Sorry you had to go through that," Lillian said to her. "Hard, because he's your father."

"That's what people keep reminding me." Rachel grimaced.

Val moaned and lifted his head.

"Stay still," Lillian ordered again. She turned her attention back to Rachel. "You were plenty brave yourself back there. You could have run and instead you found this guy. I'm proud of you."

Rachel glanced down at Val. "When you yelled his name, I remembered he'd gone outside with Duncan and never came back in. I couldn't leave without looking for him."

Val struggled to prop himself up on his elbows. "Help me up, you two."

"Stay quiet until the ambulance gets here," Lillian protested. "You've got a concussion, at the least."

He locked his gaze on her. "I'm okay. I've been through worse. Help me into the house."

Lillian exchanged glances with Rachel. An unspoken agreement passed between them. They managed to get him on his feet. Twice they had to hold him up when he seemed about to pass out. Once inside, he paused to watch Duncan's squirming body on the floor before stumbling into the kitchen where he sank into a wooden chair.

Elaine was already waiting for them with clean towels to apply to his head. "You're a lucky man. Duncan wanted us to think you were dead."

"He probably hoped I was," Val said.

Elaine stepped away. "You have two beautiful women

looking after you and more help is on the way. So if you don't need me, I have a phone call to make. I'll be upstairs."

Lillian was hoping to talk to her before the sheriff arrived, but it was already too late. Sirens wailed as both the ambulance and the sheriff's cars sped to the house. Lillian showed the paramedics into the kitchen to examine Val.

Rachel stayed by his side, and didn't flinch when the medics removed the towels from his head. "Can I ride with him to the hospital?"

"I'll take you," Lillian said quickly.

"No hospital," Val objected, but his voice wavered.

Lillian gave him a stern look. "You don't have a choice. Hand over your keys."

Val started to object again, but Rachel dug her hand into his pocket and came up with his key ring. She ignored his sputtering attempts to stop her, and tossed the keys to Lillian.

"We'll see you there," Rachel told him.

The paramedics loaded Val, still protesting, on a gurney and rolled him outside where the ambulance waited. The constable summoned Lillian to the other room to give him her statement. She noticed handcuffs had replaced the rope on Duncan's wrists, and shackles kept him from running. He alternated between moaning and cursing. Lillian ignored him. She gave a quick blow by blow to the constable, knowing they'd would want a more detailed account of the events later.

CSU arrived. Elaine's house was now a crime scene.

Lillian made her way upstairs where Elaine packed a bag.

"I could be on that jet to Belize right now," Elaine said in a forlorn voice. "I was willing to give up my business, this house, my life for that man."

"Cut the bullshit, Elaine. You weren't going anywhere with Duncan."

CHAPTER 35

Elaine's eyes cleared and she straightened her shoulders to meet Lillian's gaze. "What are you saying?"

"I told you I talked to Jennings this morning. You've been working with her and Criminal Intelligence, along with the Texas Rangers, this whole time."

Elaine snickered. "Duncan thought I was a ditz. He was sure he could con me into anything."

"Did Duncan share the account numbers with you?"

Elaine shook her head.

"Jennings needs those accounts in order to prosecute," Lillian said. "There has to be a paper trail."

Elaine gave her a smug look. "Duncan's not as smart as he thinks he is. Let's take a drive."

"Where?"

"Hank Jamison's ranch."

"Luke's father?" Lillian said, puzzled.

"More important, he was Rosendekker Exploration's landman."

"I know that. He was Duncan's most trusted employee."

"He was Duncan's *closest* employee," Elaine corrected. "But that wasn't always true. Hank worked with Victoria's father for many years before Duncan bought Farley Kittering's business. Some would say that Duncan stole it. Whatever Hank felt about Duncan personally he kept to himself and accepted the job. He knew more about the business than Duncan ever would. The newly merged company would have failed several times over if it wasn't for Hank."

"I wondered why Hank stayed with him," Lillian said.

Elaine shrugged. "I think old man Kittering asked Hank to watch out for his daughter and the best way to do that was to work with her new husband."

Following her logic, Lillian said, "Then when Victoria died, Hank decided enough was enough."

"More than that. Hank hated what Duncan did to Kittering, just never showed it all those years. Victoria's death was a terrible blow. When Jennings approached him and offered him a deal to get the information she needed to put Duncan away, he jumped at it. Payback time."

"But until she locates the offshore account, Jennings will have trouble proving her case. Does Hank have the numbers?"

"We're going to find out," Elaine said.

"Is Jennings meeting us there?"

"I told her the two of us could get the job done."

Lillian shook her head in amazement. "I don't get you at all. Were you a spy in another life?"

Elaine grinned. "Something like that. Come on, we need to go. Duncan's on his way to jail, and no one's going to bail him out this time."

Downstairs, Lillian found an impatient Rachel and handed her Val's car keys. "I have to go somewhere with Elaine. Take Val's car to the hospital. I'll meet you there as soon as I can."

Rachel nodded and took off out the door.

Lillian jumped in Elaine's waiting BMW. She tried

not to think of Rachel behind the wheel of Val's car as they sped down the road. Instead she asked the question that had been bothering her since Elaine's confession. "Did you think by screwing Duncan, he was going to whisper the account number in your ear? Is that why you spent three weeks holed up with him after you got him out of jail?"

Elaine gaped at her in mock astonishment. "Of course. It's worked before." She laughed, holding up one hand in surrender. "I'm kidding. I had to give Hank time to do whatever he had to do to find the money."

Lillian tried to relax. Impossible with Elaine driving with a lead foot on the gas. A rock station played Ozzy Osbourne's *Crazy Train*. Elaine sang along with the windows rolled down and the wind blowing. Lillian's own thoughts became incoherent. Elaine wasn't interested in talking, and Lillian gave up trying to create a report of the day's events in her head.

They arrived at Hank's ranch home a little past three. Elaine turned off the radio and rolled the BMW up the driveway, stopping halfway to watch Hank and Luke. Father and son were in the middle of a basketball game using a basketball hoop in front of the garage.

The game looked competitive and serious. While they watched, Luke sank several balls in a row and seemed the clear winner. With a laugh, Hank shook Luke's hand. They both looked toward the BMW as their visitors were getting out of the car. Luke jogged over to them.

He stopped in front of Lillian and grinned. "When are we going to dinner again?"

Lillian laughed good-naturedly. "That was fun. Next time you come to Houston, give me a call." He impressed her. No longer was he the scared, uncertain young man she'd last seen in Houston, Luke looked comfortable in his skin and matured noticeably.

"I will," he promised. He turned to Elaine. "Guess the wedding's off."

"Most definitely," she agreed.

Hank joined them and put his hand on Luke's shoulder. "You ladies flirting with my son?" He looked proudly at Luke.

"He's a handsome young man," Lillian said. "I know you're glad he's home again."

"You bet," Hank said. He turned to Luke, "Keep practicing. I got some business with these ladies then I'll be back."

"Don't forget Mom's meeting us for dinner later."

"I haven't forgotten." Hank motioned to the women. "Come on in the house and I'll get us something to drink. Lemonade all right with you? Or would you prefer the hard stuff?"

"Lemonade's fine," Lillian said.

Hank took them to the den where it was darker and cooler. They sat on brown leather chairs facing a fireplace without the fire.

"Guess you're retired now," Lillian said.

Hank looked askance. "Not at all. I have years left in me."

"You're looking for another landman job?"

"Guess you haven't heard." He grinned. "Elaine offered me a partnership in her company. She's moving into more environmentally safe alternatives."

Lillian forced herself not to look at Elaine. "No, I hadn't heard." She tried to keep the annoyance out of her voice.

"He hadn't agreed to my offer yet," Elaine protested, giving him a pleading look.

"I'm agreeing now," Hank said, offering his hand to Elaine, which she shook.

"Congratulations," Lillian said in a dry tone. "Let's get back to why we're here."

"Yes, let's." Elaine kept her gaze on him. "You have something for us?"

Instead of answering, he smiled.

Lillian took that as a yes. "Wonderful. Why haven't you turned it over to Jennings?"

"I didn't have it until this morning."

Lillian exchanged looks with Elaine. "You better explain."

Hank glanced at the closed door before answering. "Duncan hired one of his guys to watch his ranch, including his home office. The guy followed me home after I completed a search of the place. Gave me a bad time about being on the property even though I hadn't found anything."

"You were trespassing," Elaine said.

"No, I wasn't. Duncan's attorney gave me the authority to check on the office and his home while Duncan was in lock up. Duncan must have forgot. Anyway, I looked into this guy's background, found out he was wanted on an arson case. After I questioned him, he admitted Duncan paid him to watch his place, but he screwed up. Seems he has a drinking problem. Didn't see me until I was leaving the ranch. He got real upset. Scared Duncan was going to find out. He said if I promised not to tell Duncan I searched his place, he would tell me what he had on Duncan. It seems Duncan never paid him like he promised and that pissed him off. So I promised, and he said Duncan had hired him to set the fire at Matt's well site."

Lillian sat back, remembering how Matt was so sure that Duncan was responsible for the fire, but had no proof. "So Duncan's in trouble because he didn't pay his arsonist." She laughed. "Stupid criminals."

"Right." Hank chuckled.

"So Duncan didn't have the paperwork," Elaine said. "Who did?"

"That was the next question I had." Hank pulled a cigar out of his shirt pocket and wet it with his mouth. "So now, I got to thinking about the way Duncan's mind works. And it all came back to Victoria. Why did he have to kill her? The answer, in light of what we now know, is obvious. She found out he was stealing the investors' money and planned to expose him."

Here, finally, was the motive Rachel was looking to prove murder. Lillian frowned. "Victoria wouldn't have come out and accused him. That would be like waiving a red flag at a bull."

"Under certain circumstances, she might have," Hank said. "When she got angry, that woman could not hold her tongue."

"But she wasn't stupid, Hank," Elaine said.

"No, she wasn't," Hank agreed. "I don't know what she did or said that made Duncan suspicious, but he decided he had to shut her up."

"She found the paperwork," Elaine said.

"And hid it somewhere in case something happened to her." Lillian met Hank's eyes. "Only no one found her evidence, and her death was ruled accidental."

Hank nodded. "A win for Duncan. He would never be charged with murder and he had a gold mine sitting in an offshore account. He must have spent many nights dreaming of freedom and a life of luxury."

"So what did Victoria do with the evidence?" Lillian said.

Hank smiled again. "Put them in the only place where she knew he wouldn't look. In a portable safe that she gave to her father. Unfortunately, Farley suffered a stroke shortly after Victoria was killed. He remembered nothing about the safe."

"How did you know where to look?" Elaine asked.

"I remembered only a few times she visited her father during her marriage. Duncan forbid her to have any contact with him after the takeover of Farley's company. The two men hated each other. Victoria went anyway, but faced all kinds of hell for it. Eventually she stopped going. The last trip she made was during a time Duncan was out of town and weeks before her death. She had a box with her. I didn't think too much about it at the time. Duncan never knew about the visit. Last week, I got to thinking about that trip. It came to me that I needed to pay Farley a visit."

He rolled the cigar in his hands and smiled as if recalling a pleasant memory. "He's almost fully recovered from his stroke. Sharp as a tack. But he still didn't remember that box. I told him my suspicions and he helped me search. We found it on a shelf mixed in with old junk Farley kept in the storeroom. The transactions, wire information, all of it there."

"Jennings must have been thrilled when you told her," Lillian said, casting a glance at Elaine.

Hank winked at them. "She's at her office, waiting for you."

Ten minutes later, Lillian carried the box to Elaine's car and they waved goodbye to Hank and Luke. She looked at her watch. "We better hurry before Jennings closes her office."

"She won't go anywhere," Elaine said. "She'll be waiting outside the office door. These offshore account numbers are all the evidence she needs to put Duncan away for good."

❦

Lillian entered Carrabba's Italian Grill with an eagerness she hadn't felt in a long time. The hostess greeted her with a friendly smile.

"I'm meeting a couple of friends," Lillian said, peering around the hostess until she spotted her party. "There. I see them."

It had been two weeks since Elaine had dropped Lillian off at Scott & White Hospital in Temple. Val had been treated and released with the order from the doctor that he seek further treatment when he arrived home in Houston. Rachel waited with him in the ER, watching him like he was a valuable piece of art.

Lillian hadn't liked the way he looked. His skin showed a grayish tint and his strained expression might have been due to a severe headache. "My guess is that you are defying the doctor's first recommendation to keep you overnight."

"I'm ready to get the hell out of Dodge." He jerked his thumb at Rachel. "She wouldn't let me drive. Good thing you got here before I overrode her objections."

"And leave me stranded here without a ride? Shame on you." Lillian shook her head at him. "I'm driving. If you get sick, it's your car."

"He wouldn't let them give him a brain scan either," Rachel complained.

"I told this young woman I've been through worse," he said to Lillian. "If three stints in Afghanistan didn't kill me, a pop on the head from that asshole sure wouldn't do me in."

Lillian didn't say anything. She was just so relieved to see him on his feet, even when he was giving her the evil eye.

In a surprisingly gentle tone, he added, "I wouldn't have left you without a car, even if it meant renting one."

"Gee, thanks," she said. At least he sounded better than he looked.

The drive home seemed to take forever. Rachel wouldn't let Val drop off to sleep and they argued the whole distance. Lillian wasn't sure if the caution had been necessary, but she didn't argue with Rachel.

Now, as she approached their table, she noted how well Val looked. Like his old self, which wasn't bad at all, she thought. Sitting on the other side of Rachel was Matt. They hadn't seen her yet. Lillian slowed, watching the three of them chatting together, almost feeling like an interloper. They looked happy. She couldn't help wondering again if two of them were related by birth. She hadn't heard any more from Val about setting up a DNA test.

Rachel stood and waved to her. Their excitement was contagious. There were hugs all around when she got to their table.

"Looking good," Lillian told Val, as she sat opposite Rachel. "Better than you did at the hospital."

"Told you," he said in an offhand way. "It was nothing."

"Don't let him kid you," Rachel said, slapping Val lightly on the shoulder. "He won't tell you about the headaches and nausea he experienced."

"That's over with. I'm good." Val picked up his water glass and drank.

"Concussions aren't something to play around with," Matt added. "Especially for a man who's going to be working with me."

This was news Lillian hadn't expected. She wasn't sure what line of work kept Val traveling on short notice or driving expensive cars. Had never asked him. Assumed he still contracted work with the military.

"I needed a legit job," Val explained, grinning. "Finding new prospects and investors is something I've done before. I'm told I can be persuasive, in a good way." There was merriment in his eyes. Was he playing with her?

Rachel spoke up. "I'll be working with them, too. Matt and Greg are training me to be a geo-tech."

The three went silent, and Lillian sensed a change had occurred that she somehow had missed. They were holding something back and that secret wanted to bust free. She felt a low humming like a violin string stretched so tight it could break with one word.

Rachel broke the silence. Her eyes danced. "We invited you here to celebrate with us."

"I'm flattered. Celebrate what?"

Rachel glanced at Val and Matt before she answered. "Duncan has been convicted. He'll spend his life in prison."

Lillian had already heard the news, but she nodded. "That's good."

"What's really good, really great is—" Rachel, with tears shining in her eyes, suppressed a tight laugh. "He finally confessed to killing my mother. Justice served."

Before Lillian found words to express a relevant response, Rachel flung herself in Matt's arms and burst into sobs. Matt held her, and Val reached over to rub her neck and shoulders.

Lillian realized her only reason for being with them now was to observe, record, and witness. She was looking at a family. It no longer mattered—if it ever did—whether or not they were blood related. Rachel belonged to Matt and Val, and they belonged with her. If Lillian believed in ghosts, she was certain Victoria would be hovering over them right now, and smiling.

THE END

About the Author

Laura Elvebak sometimes feels she has led several lives, but throughout the years, her passion for reading and writing has never faltered. Before the twenty-something years, she worked for lawyers and oil and gas executives. She held a variety of occupations, including working as waitress and even as a go-go dancer in the late sixties in Philadelphia. Born in North Dakota and raised in Los Angeles and San Francisco, she settled in Houston after living in parts of New York, New Jersey, Pennsylvania, and Florida. She is happily unmarried after six attempts with men who would make fascinating characters in books but didn't succeed as husband material. She presently lives with her grown son, her dog Sherlock, and twelve cats.

Elvebak studied writing at UCLA, USC, Rice University, and Beyond Baroque in Venice, California. After taking a directing class in Houston, she co-wrote, directed, and acted in a one-act play. She optioned three screenplays to a local production company and co-wrote a script for the 48 Hour Film Project. She is a member of MWA, Sisters-In-Crime, The International Thriller Writers, and The Final Twist Writers and has a presence on Facebook, Twitter, LinkedIn, Good Reads, and Amazon Author Central.